JONATHON ISLAND ✦ SEASON 1

MEET ME AT THE GRAND

LINDSAY HARREL

sunrise PUBLISHING

Meet Me at The Grand
Jonathon Island, Book 1
Published by Sunrise Publishing
Copyright © 2025 Sunrise Media Group LLC
Print ISBN: 978-1-963372-79-3

This book is a work of fiction. Names, characters, places, and incidents are either products of the author's imagination or used fictitiously. Any similarity to actual people, organizations, and/or events is purely coincidental.

Scriptures taken from the Holy Bible, New International Version®, NIV®. Copyright © 1973, 1978, 1984, 2011 by Biblica, Inc.™ Used by permission of Zondervan. All rights reserved worldwide. www.zondervan.com The "NIV" and "New International Version" are trademarks registered in the United States Patent and Trademark Office by Biblica, Inc.™

For more information about Lindsay Harrel, please access the author's website at the following address: www.lindsayharrel.com.

Published in the United States of America.
Cover Design: Sunrise Media Group, LLC

A Note to Our Readers

Here at Sunrise, we hope you enjoy every story we publish. However, we are aware that some subjects may be more sensitive to you than others and want you to have all the information you need to select stories that will protect your mental and emotional health.

In that vein, the content in this story touches on the following subjects:

- Death of a parent (past)
- Mentions of alcohol abuse (past)
- Mention of an extramarital affair (past)

God bless!

To Susie.

Thank you for the vision, guidance, mentorship, and friendship. It means the world that you invited me into this great adventure to work alongside you and learn from you. Love and all the hugs . . . and to all the beautiful stories to come.

"... With man this is impossible,
but with God all things are possible."

Matthew 19:26b

Jonathon Island

Meet Me on Jonathon Island (prequel novella)
Meet Me at the Grand
Meet Me on Lilac Lane
Meet Me at the Fudge Shop
Meet Me on Blueberry Hill
Meet Me at Sunset Cove
Meet Me at the Christmas Cottage

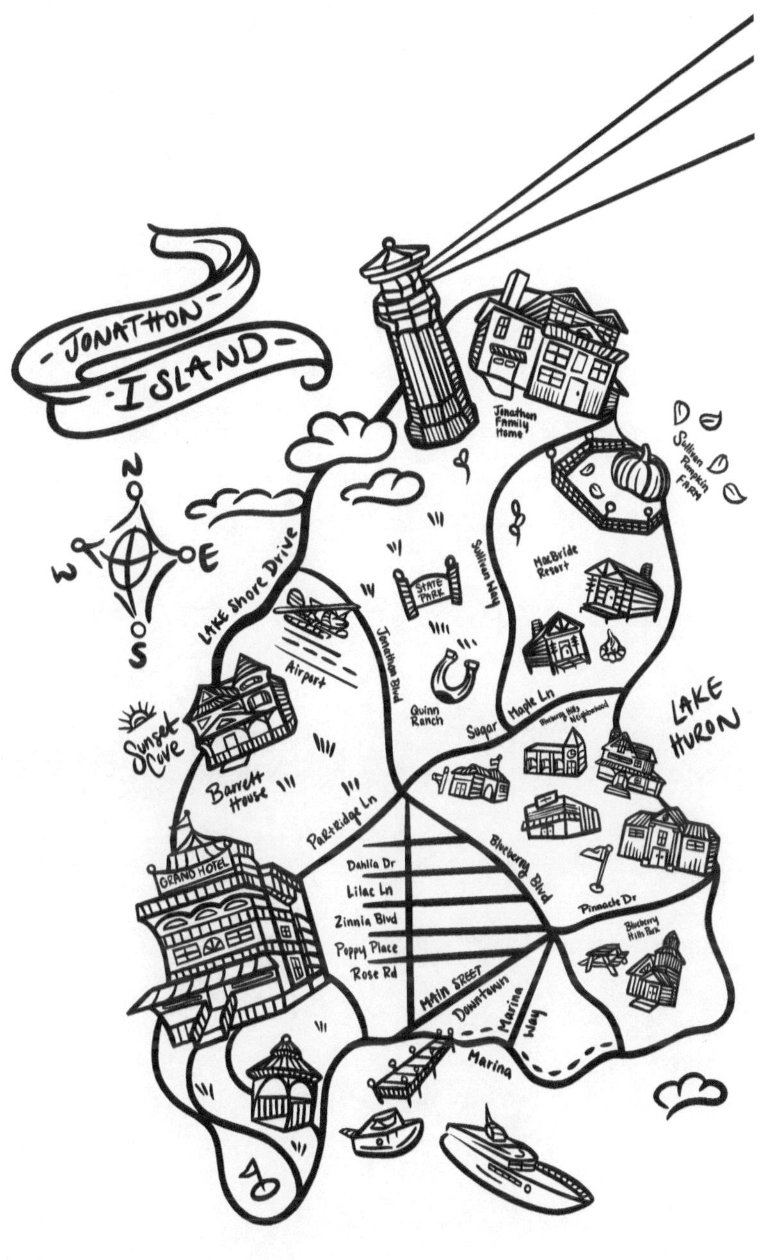

JONATHON ISLAND
N E S W
Jonathon Family Home
Sullivan Pumpkin Farm
Lake Shore Drive
Sullivan Way
MacBride Resort
Airport
State Park
Jonathon Blvd
Quinn Ranch
Sugar Maple Ln
Blueberry Hills Neighborhood
LAKE HURON
Sunset Cove
Barrett House
Partridge Ln
Dahlia Dr
Lilac Ln
Zinnia Blvd
Poppy Place
Rose Rd
GRAND HOTEL
Blueberry Blvd
Pinnacle Dr
Blueberry Hills Park
Main Street
Downtown
Marina Way
Marina

One

FOR THE LOVE OF ALL THAT WAS HOLY– where had she placed those boots?

Dani Sullivan switched her cell to speakerphone mode and placed it on the edge of her bed before dropping to her knees to inspect underneath the full-sized mattress. The hardwood floors bit into her knees. "So, Florida's good then?"

"More than good." Her dad's baritone filtered through her phone, the sound only slightly muffled by the fact her head was now underneath her bed, her eyes scanning around the wrapping paper and boxes of old junk she'd shoved there when she'd moved into the apartment above the now defunct Island Pizzeria five years ago. "Seventy degrees and sunny. Unlike somewhere else I know."

She popped her head up. "Aw, come on. Our winter has been positively toasty this year, and the spring's starting off the same. It's only March seventh, and next week it's supposed to reach forty-five. Can you believe that? I mean, the ferry's already running regularly and everything."

"Not that anyone is ever on it. Unless they're leaving."

Dani held back a sigh. This again? "Dad, you know I love talking to you, but why do we have to have this conversation every time you call?"

"We don't. I—"

"Hang on a sec, okay? I've gotta find my shoes so I'm not late to Myrtle's retirement party." Ducking back under her bed, she did another quick scan in case she'd missed the boots the first time. Wait, was that them? Lying flat on her shoulder, she stretched her arm toward the lump in the shadows.

It meowed indignantly. A flash of orange bolted past her, squeezing through the crack in Dani's bedroom door and out into the tiny living room, most likely to wreak havoc on her cat palace with her claws.

"Sorry, Roma," Dani called after her.

"Who are you talking to?"

Standing, Dani dusted off her hands before grabbing the phone. "The cat."

Dad chuckled, whistled. "We need to get you off that island, girl. Get you around some people."

She forced a laugh—it wasn't like it was the first time Dad had said it. And it wasn't any funnier now than it had been then. More like a slice to her heart. "Dad, there are plenty of people here."

"Not many from what I've heard. Didn't the Hayworths finally jump ship?"

"They retired. Wanted to move closer to their daughter in Dallas."

"Mmm hmm."

"They *did*." Dani stalked into her living room. Good thing this wasn't a video call or Dad would surely berate her for how she'd left her Eiffel Tower throw blanket tossed askew over her tiny green couch, or the way her plump London Bridge- and Colosseum-printed pillows dotted the floor beside the couch.

How she'd left on her forty-inch television all day despite the terrible waste of electricity that was.

Her beloved Travel Channel flickered back at Dani from its mount on a turquoise rummage-sale TV stand. She reached for the remote to turn the TV off. But no, the pictures of the gorgeous Italian countryside brightened her space, and she didn't want them to disappear.

"And I *also* heard the Johnsons abandoned the bookstore and their home. They've owned that place for fifty years, Dani. Fifty. Years. And now they're gone."

Pivoting from the television, Dani stuck her phone on the kitchen counter next to the tiny box she'd wrapped for Myrtle in purple paper—her former boss's favorite color.

"The Johnsons just . . . decided they wanted a new adventure." Well, that and the bank had been about to foreclose on their home. Uncle Seb had offered an extension on the bookstore lease payment, but Bob and Lucinda had seen the writing on the wall.

And they weren't the only ones.

"New adventure, my right eye." Dad snorted. "And what about Henrietta? Gave up the bakery, I heard. Oh, and the Quinns left for a year-long RV trip, didn't they? They'll probably find somewhere else they love and let the horse property go to rot."

"Henrietta is well past retirement age, and managing the place without Hank was too hard." Hands on her hips, Dani walked the room. If she were a shoe, where would she hide? She'd already searched the closet, underneath the couch, over in the corner behind the couch. And with a four-hundred-square-foot apartment, there weren't that many places *to* hide. "And the Quinns didn't let anything go to rot—they left a nephew behind to tend the place."

"That may be, but it seems to me that Jonathon Island is past its glory days. I just don't want you wasting away along with it."

"I got a promotion, remember?" Myrtle's leaving meant Dani was moving up in the world. A chance to make a difference . . . somehow. "And yeah, people have left the island over the years, but that's normal. People move. People leave. But they can come back, if the enticement is big enough."

Oh, how she hoped that was true. Otherwise . . .

Opening the tiny hall closet—where she'd originally begun her boot search—Dani kicked at the dust bunnies that attacked her foot. If the boots weren't in here, she was calling it. Staying in, curled up on the couch watching the Travel Channel with the leftover soup she'd heated on the stove yesterday.

That didn't sound half bad, really.

Oh, but wait. There. In the corner of the closet. Her

white coat had somehow fallen from its hanger to the ground.

"That's a big 'if,'" Dad said. Something like paper shuffled in the background. Was he at his home or still at the office? Knowing Daniel Sullivan, Dani wouldn't be surprised if it was the latter—despite the fact it was past seven on a Friday night. "I know you think things will change now that you're the tourism director, but it's time to face facts, kiddo. It's too big a job for any one person. And it's too late. Too much damage has already been done."

"Thanks, Debbie Downer." Coughing, she bent down to pick up the jacket. And underneath—yes! Her missing black, mid-calf boots. She stood and shook out her jacket before rehanging it. "The proper response is 'Congratulations, Dani! You're going to be the best director of tourism since sliced bread.'" She held a tease in her voice, trying to keep out the hurt.

"Come on, Dani. You know I didn't mean to say . . ." She could practically hear his frown, picture his handsome face, tan from one too many golfing games on the Florida course at the hotel he owned in Palm Coast.

"That you don't believe in me?" Dani headed for the couch, boots in one hand, phone in the other. As she sank into the couch's familiar comfort, she breathed past the heaviness in her chest and placed the phone next to the old family photo she kept there to remind herself of what used to be.

Of the things her dreams were made of.

A smiling Dad, his arm wrapped around Mom, who looked at him—not the camera—with pure love in her eyes. They were surrounded by seven kids, a range of ages and dispositions.

James, the oldest, so serious even at eighteen, looking straight at the camera, no smile but a hitch upward on one side of his mouth. A seventeen-year-old Ashley, every bit the actress she still was today, flashing a brilliant smile and pretending not to be annoyed by the antics of Tyler and Zachary, whose eyes lit with mischief while they poked Ashley's ribs from either side of her. Then there were the twins, Kate and Oliver, fifteen at the time, their arms slung around each other's shoulders. Loyal to each other, to the end.

And finally, an eight-year-old Dani—the caboose kiddo—standing a bit off to the side, her eyes turned not to the camera but toward her family. Taking them all in. Smiling. In awe, even at a young age, that this wonderful thing was hers. That she belonged to it. Safe and confident in the love her family had for one another.

If that little girl had only known how her life would change in six years.

"Dani, you know it isn't *you* that I don't believe in." Dad cleared his throat, paused. Strange. He wasn't one to get overly emotional unless he'd been drinking, and he hadn't had a drop of liquor since that day ten years ago when he'd accidentally burned their family legacy to the ground. "Besides, sliced bread is overrated."

"Dad." Dani rolled her eyes, at once fighting a laugh and wanting to shake the truth into her father. Why couldn't he see her side of things? How much this meant to her? "I know things have been rough here since the pandemic, but I've got the chance to turn things around. I have all kinds of ideas for driving up tourism—"

"Honey, *what* tourism? The Jonathon Island we knew is dead, and it isn't coming back."

Her boots thudded to the ground, and her head sank into her hands. His words pierced and burned, and suddenly the heated apartment felt like ice.

She'd been praying for weeks, months—okay, *years*—for a solution. And at any moment, one could be just around the bend. She simply had to keep the faith.

Or maybe God had abandoned Jonathon Island just like he'd abandoned the Sullivans fourteen years ago.

Not that she could exactly blame God for her mother's actions. Or her father's. But couldn't He have stopped all of her brothers and sisters from leaving? Not even her Uncle Bryan, Aunt Mary, and three Sullivan cousins had stuck around. Pieces of her heart had been taken, scattered on the wind in every direction.

"I just want you to have a life that isn't attached to a dead, stinking carcass," Dad continued, pausing. "Which is why I wish you'd consider coming to work for me in Florida."

"Really, Dad? A dead, stinking carcass? Lovely metaphor." Dani shoved one foot into a boot, then the other. "I appreciate the job offer. I really do. Working at your new hotel with you and James would be wonderful. But this island is home. And it isn't dead. It's just . . . hibernating. Now that I'm the tourism director, I'll have a little more say in ways to fix the tourism problem."

"Some broken things just can't be fixed, Dani."

Inhaling sharply, Dani closed her eyes against the tremor in Dad's words. "I don't believe that." She couldn't.

Meow.

Dani's eyes opened to find her tabby sitting at her feet, looking at her like she expected something of Dani. *Get in line, cat.*

Dani bent down and hauled Roma into her lap, petting her against the cat's protest, which she wailed right into the phone on the side table.

"All right, well, I'm burning daylight here, so I'd best let you go. Think about my offer, Dani. I love you."

"I love you too, Dad." So much.

The phone screen went dark and Dani just sat there, staring at the television and petting the cat. She was *late* late to the retirement party now, but nothing in her wanted to face the crowd of Jonathon Island regulars. Not Martha Kelley, who had already told Dani she wanted to speak on Monday—Dani's first official day on the job—about ways the Tourism Bureau could support local small businesses like hers.

Not Mac, who was still looking to offload the now de-funct "adventure resort" his family owned on the north-east side of the island. He had hopes of selling it to the town for a pretty penny. If only he was privy to the town's painfully low coffers, maybe he'd sing a different tune.

And she definitely didn't want to face Myrtle herself, who—despite her old-fashioned ways—had taught Dani everything she knew about hospitality and tourism. Who had taken Dani under her wing when she was just a hurting teenager. Myrtle, who was herself moving away to be closer to her kids.

Sure, it was only an hour from their little island on the upper Michigan peninsula, but it might as well have been a whole country with how isolated they were. The only ways in or out were by ferry or prop plane.

Roma settled on Dani's lap, her claws digging into her jeans ever so slightly. Dani gently unhooked them and then stroked between the animal's eyes. Her purr warmed Dani through as visions of Italy flashed across the TV.

Dani's shoulders sank into the back side of the couch just as they always did when she did her "travel-watching therapy," as her cousin Mia liked to call it—a funny thing for someone who had never *actually* traveled anywhere exotic.

She was already late. Maybe just a few minutes more of this would help her power through the party.

Reaching for the remote, Dani turned up the volume. While the camera swept across different angles of a small Italian village nestled among trees, open areas of green, and the Maiella and Gran Sasso mountains, a narrator described the village—and the problems Italy had experienced post-pandemic.

"Like many European countries, the lockdown was difficult, especially on urban centers where residents could not easily get out of their homes and enjoy fresh air. Relationships suffered from lack of physical gatherings, something we all took for granted before that."

Thank goodness that hadn't been Dani's experience. Sure, there were some who had stayed locked in their homes on the island, but for the most part, they'd been like many small communities, still going about their business and seeing each other once they felt it was safe. Of course, the island had closed for tourism for a full year, and many had left during that time because they simply couldn't afford to stay.

The narrator continued, his words highlighted by shots of deserted cobblestone streets. "However, something the pandemic *did* do was show the world at large that remote work was possible. And those who worked from home began to see more work-life balance—and to crave even more. At the same time, many smaller communities were in need of a fresh influx of residents to revitalize them."

Seemed Jonathon Island and the small Italian villages had something in common.

"So experts decided to do something radical." The narrator paused for dramatic effect. "They sold small village homes for one euro—the equivalent of $1.16 at the time."

Dani's hand stilled. Roma meowed in protest, head butting her fingers. But Dani couldn't do anything but sit forward and listen. The cat leaped to the ground, and Dani clutched the couch cushion beneath her.

"This scenario was a win-win for both the village and those looking for a more peaceful existence. It made such a move affordable to the outside world, and it brought in much-needed money to small, struggling communities whose tourism had lagged or dwindled completely thanks to the pandemic."

"This is it." The answer she'd been praying for—she

could feel it in her bones. Maybe God hadn't abandoned Jonathon Island after all.

And maybe He hadn't abandoned the Sullivans either.

Liam Stone usually celebrated the end of a business trip with an ice-cold root beer—a call back to the days of his youth.

But tonight's drink would, apparently, have to wait.

"You need me to do what?" He unbuttoned his gray suit jacket and swiveled on the stool at his favorite pub at Orlando International Airport, where the crew knew him by name. Just outside the bar, the masses bustled past, headed to their destinations all over the world. Flicking back his wrist, he stared at the face of his Breitling Aviator 8. "I'm supposed to be boarding a flight home in thirty minutes. And why are you working so late, anyway?"

"I'm so sorry, shoogs," Marianne drawled through his AirPods. The administrative assistant at Stone Development may have lived in Los Angeles for thirty-six years, but she'd never forgotten her Texas roots. "I know you've been on the Pascal Hotel job site for two months, but there's just nobody else to cover the McAllister. Allan feels terrible, but his mother's fall is hardly his fault, and he's the only one who can take care of her post-surgery. He can't possibly spend the next three weeks in New York. And everyone else is committed to new jobs at the moment. Plus, you're already on the East Coast."

"Yeah, no, of course. I understand." Liam rubbed the

corner of his right eye, which itched with a lack of sleep. "Whatever the company needs."

"And that's why I'm working late—because this company means a lot to me too. As do you and your father." She paused. "He isn't any happier about this than you are, you know. He'd planned a whole welcome-back dinner for you at the penthouse."

"And by that you mean that *you* planned a welcome-back dinner." Liam couldn't help but laugh at the thought of his sixty-four-year-old dad planning anything domestic. Not that he wouldn't want to—it just wasn't on his radar.

"Yes, well, he approved it. And paid for it."

"I believe it. Dad's nothing if not generous." He loosened the knot on his favorite blue tie. "Speaking of the old man, how is he?"

"As stuck in his workaholic tendencies as ever. Y'all are just two peas in a pod in that regard. Oh, and he's been taking his medicine just like you instructed. Though I must say, he was a wee bit on the stubborn side at my constant nagging."

"And by that you mean he huffed at you and called you a nuisance?"

"How'd you know?" She laughed. "But it's nothing I can't handle."

"Aw, Mare, you're too good to us. I know it's not really in your job description to take care of him like that. To take care of us." Then again, Marianne had been like a second mother to Liam since his had passed when he was ten, and a good friend to Dad too. Liam slid off the stool, tossed a twenty on the counter, and grabbed the handle of his suitcase. "Now, when's my next flight?"

"Same time as your previous flight. I've already sent you the details via email, along with your hotel check-in information and the details on the McAllister project and what'll be expected of you the next few weeks. Do you need me to call the airline about transferring your luggage?"

Liam already had his phone out, scanning his email for the flight number. "Nah, I've got everything in my carry-on. You know I'm an expert at packing light by now."

"Don't I know it. All right, now, skedaddle. And let us know you got in okay."

"I'm not texting you so late at night. I'll be fine. Thanks for everything. And tell Dad I said not to worry." Dad had enough on his plate—helming a multi-million-dollar corporation with fifteen full-time employees and thousands of contractors around the country was enough to make anyone stressed. But a diabetic who already struggled to take care of himself?

Yeah, that was a recipe for disaster.

But Liam had a plan to help alleviate some of that stress—if Dad would approve it.

Checking out the Departures screen in the airport concourse, Liam groaned. Of course his new gate would be at the opposite end. He'd have to hoof it.

Twenty minutes later, a bit sweaty and in desperate need of some hydration, Liam was boarding his new plane to a new city instead of home.

Although, did something really count as home if a guy was elsewhere more often than there?

Liam waited his turn in line, scanned the boarding pass on his phone, smiled at the gate attendants, and waited again in the jetway, the white noise of the plane's engine cocooning him in the space, muffling out the conversations of the people around him excited to travel to their next destination.

Sliding off his suit coat, Liam tucked it over one arm and finally made his way to his business class seat at the front of the plane. Most of the seats were already filled with an assortment of guests who were drinking champagne and cocktails, dressed up in designer suits just like him.

After removing his laptop and phone, Liam placed his suitcase in the overhead compartment and settled into his aisle seat beside an older Asian gentleman typing away on his own computer.

A flight attendant who looked around his thirty-two years approached, her sleek brown hair pulled back in a low ponytail. "Good evening, Mr. Stone. We are so glad you could join us. Is there anything I can get you to make your flight more comfortable?"

"Some coffee would be great." He glanced at the name tag pinned to her blue uniform shirt. "Thanks so much, Pamela."

She lifted her eyebrows knowingly, a smile in her eyes. "Coffee, huh? Guessing this will be a working flight for you?"

He chuckled back at her. "You got it." Liam slid out the

tray table in front of him and placed his laptop on it. "I'll need you to keep me well supplied."

She winked at him. "I'm on it." Then she turned and made her way to the service galley, disappearing behind a red curtain.

Liam allowed his shoulders to sink back against the seat. This airline wasn't his favorite, but it definitely beat the one he'd flown to Seattle six months ago. And the one to Dallas a few months before that. Must have been what was available last minute, though. Oh, well. He'd have to make the best of it since he was due to meet Phil McAllister, CEO of the McAllister Hotel, tomorrow morning at ten.

Yawning, Liam pulled up Marianne's email and began to scan the basic details of the project. Stone Development specialized in designing, building, and revitalizing high-end, boutique hotels, and this project wasn't much different from the rest. Shouldn't take too long to get up to speed.

His phone rang, and Liam snatched it up. What was Travis doing calling him on a Friday night? "I'm surprised Monica let you call this late."

"She's out with her friends. I'm on diaper duty."

"Wow. That's the life."

"It's something, all right. I love my son, but this guy produces more poop than can possibly be healthy."

Liam pictured his gym rat friend trying to change a diaper—and just couldn't. He laughed. "That's disgusting." The captain said something over the loudspeaker. "Hey, I won't be able to talk long. My flight's about to take off.

I'm assuming you didn't call me to talk about your kid's pooping habits."

The man across the aisle from Liam turned his head slightly toward him, his lip curling in disgust. Liam offered an apologetic shrug.

"Ha, no. I wanted to tell you that I finally heard back from one of the locations we were scouting. They weren't planning to sell, but they're willing to entertain an offer. So I set up a meeting with the realtor tomorrow—"

"Dude, I can't." Liam groaned. "Allan's mom broke her hip, so I'm on my way to New York to take over his project. Won't be home for three weeks."

"Seriously? Bro, you were just gone for two months. That's insane."

"You don't think I know that?"

"Aren't you tired of living out of a suitcase? That's the whole reason we're pitching this project, right?" Travis paused. "You're still in this with me, aren't you? Because even though we've both worked at Stone for ten years, I don't think a pitch coming from *me* will mean much to your dad. But from the Golden Boy . . ."

"Shut up." Liam shook his head. "And yeah, of course I'm still in this. We'll just have to postpone a bit. Or you go to the sites, take lots of photos, or maybe even video chat me in. We're going to find a way to make this project work."

"All right, cool. Because Monica is really excited about the prospect of me staying in town full time. Can you imagine? No more travel for weeks on end."

"I really *can't* imagine it." But Liam wanted to. He

needed to. Dad would never consider retiring unless Liam was in California more often. But most of their home-based projects went to their senior site managers and those with families. "But I get it. This life definitely isn't for everybody."

"Admit it—even you're tired of all the travel. Sure, at first, jet-setting around the world was fun and exciting. But once you have something to come home to, it's just not the same."

Something to come home to. Now wouldn't that be something?

A deep ache wound through Liam and squeezed.

"Mr. Stone?"

He glanced up to find Pamela there with a white cup of coffee, steam rising from the top. "Oh, hi. Thanks." He moved his laptop aside, making room for it.

"I'm so sorry it took so long, but I wanted to brew you a fresh cup." She placed it in the empty spot, along with a napkin. "Only the best for our most distinguished guests." With another smile, she moved to the next aisle to help another guest.

"Who was that?" Travis asked.

"What? Oh, just the flight attendant."

"Is she hot?"

Liam rolled his eyes. "Does it matter?"

"You should get her number."

"You know I don't date when I'm working." Raising his coffee to his lips, he took a sip of the brew, the warmth trailing down his throat and whooshing energy into his veins.

"You're always working."

"Yeah, well." He took another sip. Ah. "Maybe once we get this proposal off the ground and I'm in California full time, I can actually settle down. Become boring like you."

Travis snorted. "Monica and I are anything but boring. Just the other night, we—"

"Dude, I really don't want to know."

Travis's maniacal laughter nearly drowned out whatever the captain was saying now.

"Shoot, man, I think I have to hang up in a sec."

"All right, well, I'm going to move forward with the Bertram viewing tomorrow then."

"Good. If it's as good in person as on paper, I think it would go to the top of our list of potential properties. As far as the rest of the proposal goes, you might have to keep working on anything we need to be on site for, and I'll keep working on the rest in the evenings." Liam finished off his coffee. "We'll get this thing done, and hopefully it'll be ready to present at the end of the month when I'm back."

Like a magician, Pamela appeared again ready to collect his trash. He smiled his thanks, and she beamed back at him. Then, pulling his laptop off the tray, he tucked it away before putting the tray back into position for takeoff.

"You think your old man is really going to go for this?" Travis asked. "It's not what we usually do."

It was true. They'd never purchased their own hotel to revitalize. But Liam's projections didn't lie. If this thing succeeded, it could set Stone Development up for the future. Dad's retirement could become a reality—if Liam could convince Dad to actually give up the reins. "He'll see the potential."

"I hope so, man. Monica and I are really counting on it. But I know how reticent Chaz is to take risks."

"I can convince him. You do your part, and I'll do mine."

"Deal. Have a good flight."

"Will do." Liam hung up with Travis, buckled up, and prayed he wasn't in over his head on this thing.

Because the idea of finally making a life in California full time—for Dad's sake, if not for his own—was almost more than he dared hope for.

Two

HOW COULD ANYONE WHO HAD LIVED here any length of time not want to stay forever?

Dani bustled against the wind down Main Street, Myrtle's gift in her large brown purse that had seen better days. She was utterly alone. Everyone was either tucked away in their homes or celebrating at Martha's on Main, one of the only eating establishments still open on the island.

The flicker of light from the wrought-iron streetlamps lent an ethereal glow to the dusty windows of deserted buildings. Dani's breath hovered in the air as she hurried down the deserted street, past quaint shops with white-washed walls, green accented beams, and striped awnings. Some okay. Some tattered and in desperate need of re-placement.

If she weren't a local—if she hadn't read every sign taped to the abandoned shops, thanking customers for their loyalty over the years—she wouldn't know which were closed permanently and which were just waiting for Memorial Day, when the island officially opened for the season.

Unfortunately, there were only a handful in that category anymore. But maybe things could be different. If her plan had any merit, anyway.

Dani picked up her speed. The road curved, opening up to a brilliant view of the harbor abutting Lake Huron in the distance—and the hulking shell of her family legacy. The Grand Sullivan Hotel, burned half to the ground. An ache that never ceased pulsed deep in Dani's chest, but she pushed it aside.

Hope. There was always hope. Especially now.

She passed Good Day Coffee and Kelley's Bar & Grill, both of which had their signs turned to Closed, and finally set eyes on the lit interior of Martha's on the left—nearly the last building on Main, save the public library. When she pulled open the door, a chorus of hellos rang out, and Dani was met with the mingled smells of cooked meat, wine, and chocolate. Even as she tugged off her coat and hung it on the overstuffed rack just beneath the sign that read "Check your guns, politics, and religion at the door," the warmth of the place, of the people, enveloped her.

Now to find Uncle Seb.

"There you are." Mia Jonathon Franklin appeared at her side and pulled Dani into a hug. "I was starting to think you weren't going to show." Her petite younger cousin tucked a piece of her curly brown hair behind her ear, eyebrows raised expectantly.

"Sorry. I got busy talking with my dad—"

"Ah, say no more." Mia turned to the wooden bar and snatched a glass of dark fizzling pop, shoving it into Dani's hands.

Dani laughed. "He's not that bad." She set her gift and purse on one of the green-topped wooden stools and took a sip of the drink. Ah, Dr Pepper. Mia knew her well. Then again, despite their four-year age difference, they'd been close ever since Mia's family had moved full time to the island when they were both kids.

"Uncle Daniel isn't *bad*. He's just . . . persistent." Mia waggled her eyebrows as she took a sip from her straw.

It was nice that she still referred to Dani's dad as her uncle, even though he hadn't legally been that for a long time. It was Dani's mom, Becky, who was Mia's aunt by blood.

But Mia was kind like that. Always attuned to everyone else's feelings. And she knew Dani's deepest wish. Might be the only one who wouldn't laugh at how utterly ridiculous such a hope really was.

"He is that." Dani shook her head, her eyes scanning the room. Dark hardwood booths lined one side of the restaurant, and the square tables and chairs that sat in between the booths and the bar had been cleared out to make standing room for the party goers. "I don't see my favorite little cousins. Are you kidless tonight?" She took another draw from the Dr Pepper, and the bite of the carbonation burned her throat going down.

"I am. Mom offered to watch them for me." Mia blinked and smiled, but there was something falsely bright in the action. And who could blame her? At twenty-four, she'd experienced more tragedy than anyone should have to in a lifetime.

"Well, that's great."

Mia shrugged a delicate shoulder. "I think she wants me to get back out there, you know?"

Snagging her cousin's hand, Dani squeezed. "There would be nothing wrong with that. If it's what you want."

Closing her eyes momentarily, Mia sighed. "All I *want* is to be snuggled up in bed with my babies right now."

Aw, Mia. "Nothing wrong with that either. We all miss Troy, and I can't fathom how hard the last two years have been for you all." Especially Finn and Maggie, the latter of whom had never even met her daddy. "But I'm proud of you for coming out tonight regardless of how you feel."

A whoop rose from the corner booth right next to the kitchen door that swung open as Jordi Chamberlain brought out a platter of appetizers that looked like Martha's famous sliders. Dani's stomach rumbled at the thought, but her eyes caught on a seventy-something man dancing a jig beside the booth. His arms were raised in victory while the other older men sitting with him—big-as-a-bear Stuart "Mac" MacBride, retired pastor Augo Kennedy with his familiar flat cap, and the very bald, very curmudgeonly Frank Kelley—grumbled good-naturedly, a card game spread in front of them.

"Looks like Lyle won gin rummy again," Mia said, this time a true smile creeping onto her face.

"He always does. I'm surprised the others keep playing with him."

"It's a matter of pride at this point. Eventually one of them has to win." Mia cocked her head, eyes glittering. "Dad almost had him once, but old Lyle still won in the end."

Ooo, the perfect segue. "Speaking of Uncle Seb, where is he?"

As mayor of Jonathon Island—which was originally founded by Mom and Seb's great-great-great-times-a-hundred grandfather, Jacob Jonathon—Seb might be talking with anyone, really. But he wasn't there, by the small group of gossiping church ladies, or there, by the large window overlooking Main where two of the troublemaking Barrett brothers flirted with a waitress. Or there, where guest of honor Myrtle was surrounded by a few of her dearest friends, not looking a day over her seventy-one years and, in fact, looking much younger thanks to her spiked white hair and purple cat-eye glasses.

No Uncle Seb to be found. Dani tapped her boots against the tiled floor.

"Mom said he was coming," Mia said. "Probably got tied up in some meeting or other. Why?"

"I really need to talk to him about something important." And yes, it could technically wait until Monday, but the idea was threatening to burst out of Dani at any moment. She had to know if she was grasping at straws or if this was something actually viable.

"Sounds intriguing. Oh, look. Speak of the devil."

A bell jingled overhead, and Uncle Seb's tall frame filled the doorway. Though more salt than pepper, his hair was thick and full, and his shoulders were strong enough to carry the needs of the town. He was a natural leader, with his jovial wave around the room and loud, booming voice as he called out congrats to Myrtle. Then his eyes focused on Dani and Mia, and he walked toward them, leaning in for a tentative hug with his daughter.

She patted his back, a bit awkward and stiff. "Hey, Dad."

He returned the pat and released her, then turned to Dani. There was no hesitation when he pulled her into his arms. "Danielle! So good to see you." His Old Spice cologne tickled her nose as he smashed her against the buttons running down his collared shirt.

"You too." Thank goodness for Uncle Seb, Aunt Elise, and her cousins. They made sure she was never alone, having her over for dinner at least once a week. Likely they felt obligated, since they were her only family left on the island.

Maybe not forever, though. Not if her plan worked.

"All right, you two have fun now. I need to make the rounds."

Dani almost missed Mia's subtle eye roll, but she turned quickly back to her uncle. "Actually, do you have a second to talk?"

"Sure, sure. Let's catch up, Monday, eh? I can't wait to see you settle into your new office. Did I tell you I'm having a new desk delivered? That old one Myrtle used is falling to pieces." He patted Dani on the shoulder and started to move on.

"Dad." The sharp word ejected from Mia's throat so quickly, it threatened to shatter glass.

Dani blinked at her, and Uncle Seb spun slowly, one eyebrow lifted.

"Yes, Mia?"

"Dani has something important she wants to talk to you about. Now."

Dani waved her hand in protest. "Oh, it's fine. He's right. This is a party. We can wait until Mon—"

"No." Mia jutted her chin. "If you say it's important, Dad should be able to take the time for that. After all, isn't family the *most* important thing, Dad?"

His jaw tightened as he blinked at his daughter, and he turned once again to Dani, forcing a smile. "Of course. Why don't you snag that booth under the window, and I'll be right over."

"Sure. Thank you. It won't take long, I promise."

"Anything for my lovely niece."

Once Seb slipped away, Dani shot Mia a look. "It's refreshing to see the fire in you again."

"Nothing like Dad to bring it out in me." Her cousin shrugged and slipped onto the stool, soda in hand, as she moved her attention to the TV hanging in the corner above the bar.

"That's true. You good here for a bit?"

"Of course. I'm always good." Mia smiled, but it didn't reach her eyes.

Dani gave her a quick shoulder squeeze. "All right, I'll loop back around with you later."

Mia waved her off, so Dani grabbed Myrtle's gift and found her old boss, handing over the present and a quick hug before snagging the booth Seb had pointed out. She yanked her phone from her purse and started an internet search for more information on the small Italian village covered by the Travel Channel broadcast.

She was fully engrossed when two plates of food clattered in front of her, making her jump. Her head darted up to find Uncle Seb removing his jacket and laying it over the back of the booth before sliding into the seat across from her.

He motioned toward the plates, which were piled with mini meatloaves, chips and artichoke dip, Martha's famous chili fries, and chicken wings. "Thought you might be as hungry as me."

Dani set her phone back into her purse and picked up a wing. "No vegetables being offered, huh?"

Uncle Seb let loose his hearty chuckle. "Come on, Danielle. It's a party! No need to get all healthy on me."

"I wonder what Aunt Elise would think of that." Taking a silverware set from the cheery yellow bucket at the end of the table, she removed a fork.

Uncle Seb did the same, cutting a tiny meatloaf in half. "I'm swearing you to secrecy."

"Duly noted." She winked at him before clearing her throat and sitting up straighter. She set her fork tines-down on her plate. "I'm sorry to interrupt your party. This will be quick, I promise."

"You're never an interruption. I enjoy spending time with my niece." He took a bite of the meatloaf, studying her thoughtfully while he chewed. "You know who else would enjoy spending time with you?"

"She knows where I live." Dani didn't mean for it to

sound so immature, but really. The woman who had thrown a grenade into their family fourteen years ago had no right to complain to her older brother about the fact she never saw her children.

Not that Dani's secret wish didn't involve Mom. It did—especially the deepest part of it. The part that was less likely to happen than the Leaning Tower of Pisa to suddenly straighten.

She sighed. "I hate that look of disappointment you're giving me, Uncle Seb. And the bitter taste in my mouth when I think about Mom, about those years I was forced to live with her and Ryan. About the fire. All of it."

"I know, sweetie."

"Can we please just leave it in the past?" Her eyes wandered away from Seb and over to Jack, the scruffy terrier that belonged to the whole town and that was just now trotting from booth to booth seeking scraps of food. Martha often tried to keep him locked up when it was her turn to take him in, but maybe she was simply too busy bustling around that she hadn't noticed his boldness tonight.

Oh, to be a dog whose biggest problem was choosing whether to first scarf down the sausage or hamburger he was currently being offered by one of Patrick Kelley's boys.

"Dani . . ."

Dani rubbed her right temple and refocused on Uncle Seb. "I'm just saying, I haven't gone anywhere. Mom's the one who left."

"You know that people here don't look at her the same way anymore. She feels judged everywhere she goes."

"Yeah, well, for good reason." Dani's lips tightened. This

conversation was going off the rails. "As much as I respect you and your position, Uncle Seb, that's not what I wanted to talk with you about today."

He pursed his lips but silently took a chip and dug it into the artichoke dip. "All right. What's up?"

Dani's heartbeat accelerated. Which was dumb. This was her uncle. But right now, he was the head of town, the main holder of real estate on the island. If he didn't think this idea had potential, nobody else would listen. "So as you know, I'm taking over for Myrtle as the director of tourism."

Uncle Seb's mouth twitched beneath his mustache, but thankfully he didn't say that she was stating the obvious. After all, he and the town council had appointed her. "Go on."

"I've found myself thinking over the last week or two about how Jonathon Island used to be so much more than this. I know we've had a rough few years, but I believe we can recover." She paused to make sure Uncle Seb was tracking. His nod was a good sign. "We just need to do something radical to make it happen."

"I've long agreed with that sentiment. Do you have something particular in mind?"

She smiled. "I do." Dani launched into an explanation of Italy, of what they had done to relaunch their economy. "And we have all of those empty houses just behind Main Street. All of those empty storefronts just waiting for new business owners—business owners who would surely be enticed by essentially free housing, as well as extremely affordable rent for the first year or two."

"I suppose that's where I would come in?" Uncle Seb flashed her a wry smile.

"Exactly. I know renting the storefronts for super cheap wouldn't be ideal, but it's better than them sitting empty, right?"

"Indeed." Uncle Seb nodded, slow, steady—just like him. But he didn't say anything else. Just sat there, blinking at her.

Dani's heart pitched to and fro, her muscles tightening and coiling until she could hear the pounding of her own pulse in her ears. "So, what do you think?"

"I think it's brilliant, Dani. Simply brilliant."

She was just about to leap to her feet and join Lyle—who, incidentally, was doing yet another jig across the diner—when Uncle Seb spoke again and deflated all hopes.

"But . . ."

Her shoulders tucked down. "But what?"

"It won't work."

"Oh. Um, okay." Had her dream of her family all being together again clouded her judgment? "Could you tell me why?"

"I should rephrase. It won't work on its own."

"What does that mean?"

"The pandemic isn't what killed our economy. It was only the final nail in the coffin, so to speak." At Dani's wrinkled nose, he continued, pinning her with a sympathetic look. "The decline of Jonathon Island began ten years ago when the Grand Sullivan Hotel burned partially to the ground."

Oh. *Oh.*

"Now that you say it, I think I kind of knew that." She'd been able to sense a shift back then, but she'd been so caught up in her own pain—her own sense of betrayal, of loneliness, of fear, of guilt—that she hadn't stopped to consider the larger impact. Even now, though, the details were fuzzy. "Can you clarify how that played a role?"

"A large part of the hotel that burned was housing for seasonal staff. Once we had no place to house the hundreds of workers who came in just for the season, businesses couldn't get as much help as they needed, which meant they couldn't stay open as many hours. It was a snowball effect." He shook his head. "I suppose for now we could take a handful of the empty homes and use them for seasonal staff, but unless we rebuild the Grand, we have no long-term solution."

A buzz started low in Dani's stomach. Rebuild the Grand? That was more than she could have hoped for. If anything could get her family back to the island, it was that. Especially James. "Great. Let's do it then."

Uncle Seb laughed, but there was no humor in it. "Don't you think I've tried over the years? There's one problem with that—your father."

"Right. How could I have forgotten?" It was the whole reason the divorce and the four years between her fourteenth and eighteenth birthdays had been so terrible—the fight over the Grand Hotel, which had been built on Jonathon land but with Sullivan money. Uncle Seb and Mom still owned the land, but Dad still owned the heap of ashes formerly known as the Grand. And he had refused to sell it to the town ever since.

"What if I asked him?" Yes. Maybe. "What if I got him to sell it?"

Uncle Seb's eyes lit, and he leaned forward—so far that his shirt nearly touched the food on his plate. "If you could do that, then I'd say you're a miracle worker."

Dani bit her lip. "But then who would develop it? The town hardly has the resources to invest in something like that."

"I still have connections in New York."

"Of course you do." Despite now living on the island full time, he still kept one hand in the dealings at the New York-based law firm where he was partner and where her older cousin Bash worked.

"If you can get your dad to sell, then I'm confident I can find a developer willing to work with us on this."

"Really?"

"Yes, really." Her uncle reached across the table, took her hand, squeezed it. "And you, my sweet niece, may just yet save us all."

Ah, home sweet home.

Or close enough, anyway.

Liam stepped inside the twentieth-story office of Stone Development, wheeling his suitcase behind him. The familiar smell of peppermint—thanks to the diffuser on Marianne's desk—swept over him, catching each one of his tired nerves and stretching them until they relaxed.

His suitcase wheels got stuck momentarily on the lip of the plush, blue rug that Marianne insisted made the office feel cozy and "not so sterile."

And they all knew Marianne was the real boss around here.

Speaking of the angel herself, she glanced up from her large white wooden desk and grinned. "Liam! You're back." The administrative assistant stood and rounded the desk quicker than he'd thought was possible, given she'd just received a new knee three months ago.

Liam offered a warm smile and pulled the woman into his arms. The top of her gray-streaked curls just barely hit the center of his chest. "I'm back." Hopefully for a while this time—if his pitch with Dad went well. He released her. "What did I miss?"

"Oh, nothing much." She leaned in and lowered her voice. "Just a whole soap opera."

He rubbed his hands together. "Do tell." Honestly, he wasn't one for office gossip, but Marianne delighted in knowing everything about everyone.

As Liam rested his tired body against the desk, Marianne quickly filled him in on how Dominic and Toni had finally gone on a date. Everyone had apparently seen that one coming from a mile away. Liam hadn't. And how Layla was pregnant and would be going out on maternity leave in about six months. And how Rob and Duke had nearly come to fisticuffs—Marianne's words—in the break room over a project they both wanted.

Liam smiled and nodded the whole time, until Marianne suddenly giggled. "Oh dear, I fear I'm boring you, sugar." Leaning back against the desk, she bumped the large photo frame next to her computer, which held a photo collage of her three kids, seven grandkids, and her late husband Jerry.

"What? Never." He tried to hide the yawn behind his hand but knew the secretary had caught him. "Sorry. Had a really early flight from New York."

"I thought as much, seeing as how you brought your suitcase with you to the office on this fine Monday morning. But honey, why didn't you just go home and rest? You've been working nonstop on those two job sites for the last three months, and you logged time every weekend to boot. You're at least owed a nap." Marianne adjusted the sparkly white frames of her glasses and glanced down the hallway toward his dad's office. "I know for a fact the boss wouldn't mind."

"Yeah, I know." But did the hotel penthouse he shared with Dad whenever he happened to be back in Los Angeles really amount to a home? Besides, he had a presentation to prepare for. Liam shifted from one foot to the other. "I need to talk with him about something anyway."

The phone on Marianne's desk rang, and she settled into her chair. "All right, get on then." Picking up the receiver, she said, "Stone Development, this is Marianne. How may I direct your call?" Though focused on her computer screen, she waved her hand at him.

Dragging his suitcase behind him, Liam resumed his walk down the hallway. Before he got to the big corner office, he removed his keys from his pocket, slipped inside his own office, and set his suitcase against the wall. It was hard to say which felt more like home—this place or the penthouse. Or rather, which felt less like home.

Because nothing compared to the home he'd once known. The one lit with warmth by his mother.

But if he could pitch the proposal successfully, maybe he could at least try to build something like he'd once had. And if he made it easier for Dad to retire in the meantime . . . perfection.

Shaking his head, Liam flipped on the light and moved to the desk, whipping his laptop from the briefcase hanging from his shoulder and setting it down, plugging it in. Turning it on.

A layer of dust coated the desk, the external keyboard, the mouse, and his pen holder—the only things on his desk. And the whole office smelled like an attic that had been shut up for years.

A knock sounded on his door, and he glanced up to find Travis, who looked like he belonged more in workout gear than a navy three-piece suit, with muscles bulging all directions. Liam liked to hit the gym and stay fit, but Travis was on a whole other level.

"Dude, you look like garbage."

Liam glanced down at his suit, which was only slightly rumpled from his flight. He brushed a piece of lint off his pants. "You're so good for my ego."

Travis ran a hand through his styled hair. "Isn't it already battered after playing my wingman for so many years before I found Monica? I mean, being out on the town night after night, right next to God's gift to women . . ."

Liam grinned and walked toward his friend to give him

a fist bump. "With a head as big as yours, I'm not sure how you and Monica fit into the same apartment."

"Sounds like jealousy talking." Laughing, Travis leaned against the doorway, hands slung in his pockets. "How was New York?"

"Let's just say Phil McAllister had opinions. Lots of them."

"Ouch. It was that kind of project, huh?"

"Yep."

Travis hummed then knocked his knuckles against the door. "So. You ready for this?"

"Was just about to head down the hall to enact step one."

"More like step one hundred."

"True." They'd been talking about this project for the last six months. Preparing. Scouting. Strategizing. But now that they'd settled on the perfect property—the Bertram, as it turned out—it all came down to convincing Dad to go for the project. Invest the funds. Let two of his head site managers take the lead and run with it.

"No worries," Liam said. "I've got this."

"Good. You know I'm on standby if you need me. And I've got the conference room booked for tomorrow just in case he actually says yes to hearing us out." Travis jutted his chin toward the hallway. "You wanna do a dry run after you talk with him?"

"Definitely."

"Sweet. I'll be ready." Travis nodded before heading out.

All right. Showtime.

Liam stretched his neck back and forth and trudged

down the hall toward Dad's office. When he arrived, he found Dad with his office phone in hand, the cord stretched across his desk to where his father leaned back in his bulky chair.

He always sounded larger than life on the phone, in total command.

But one look at Dad, his body heavier than three months ago, his hairline receding just a little bit more, his beard maybe just a smidge whiter than before, and Liam's whole body tensed.

This was his only family—all he had left. And since Dad wouldn't take care of himself, it was up to Liam. It was what Mom had wanted. Her last request.

And Liam wouldn't let her down. Not this time.

Dad's eyes lifted and connected with Liam, and a huge grin stretched across his tan, weathered face. He waved his son inside and continued speaking into the phone. "No, no, Douglas, you have my word—and you know my word is my bond. We will definitely meet the deadline." He paused, nodded. "Yep, you've got it. All right, I'll have Marianne contact you with the details."

One step into the office and Liam felt the difference between Dad's office and his own. It smelled of the familiar Styrofoam carton of Don Juan's salsa in Dad's trash. It was open, and air moved from the vent in the corner. A path was worn into the carpet from the desk to the window where Dad did his best pacing.

Yes, for better or worse, this office was lived in. And someday, hopefully soon, it would be Liam's. Or partially his, because even a partial retirement would do wonders for Dad's health.

Dad hung up and leaped to his feet with more enthusiasm than Liam thought possible. "Liam, my boy!"

"Hey, Dad."

Dad wrapped him in a bear hug—one that just five years ago would have been much fiercer and stronger, but still had all the depth of feeling Liam had come to know from Chaz Stone. After another good thump on his back, Dad let go and stepped back. "Not that I'm not glad to see you, but why are you here? You should have taken today off. I would have seen you at home tonight." He leaned back against his desk.

"That's what Marianne said too."

Pressing his pointer finger against the side of his nose, Dad nodded. "Wise woman."

"I hear that wise woman had to force feed you your pills while I was gone."

"I changed my mind. That woman is a doggone nuisance." Dad's grumble was soft and laced with all the love he had for his old friend, who had been with the company from the beginning, thirty-five years ago.

Liam settled into the plush crimson chair facing Dad's desk. It was one that his father called "half comfortable"— enough to make visitors feel welcome, but not so relaxing they wanted to stay all day. He crossed his arms. "Who was that on the phone?"

"Bah, just Douglas Kutcher out in Minneapolis. He's a bit concerned that his renovation won't get accomplished on time, but I assured him we have it well in hand."

"Is that the job Jimmy had to leave early?" His wife had gone into labor just last week.

"That'd be the one."

Hmm. "Trav or I can head on out there if you need someone to assure Mr. Kutcher we've got things handled." He took a breath. Here was his opening. "Though before we do, we've got a project we want to pitch you."

"Atta boy. Always on the lookout for the next client."

"Actually, this project would be kind of different. But still a fabulous opportunity."

Dad cocked his head, frowned. "*Different* seems to be going around."

"What do you mean?"

"Well. I've got a new iron in the fire. I was waiting until you were back to discuss it with you." Dad walked to the large window overlooking downtown Los Angeles. The skyline was mostly other tall buildings, but slices of blue sky slipped through in a few places. "But tell me about this project of yours first."

Liam stood, joined him. "I don't want to give it all away, but basically we've found a property right here in L.A. that is ripe for renovation. It's a great location, has great bones, and we've already drawn up plans that would make it the perfect modern retreat for the luxury traveler."

"Sounds great." Dad elbowed him, smiling. "So where does the difference come in?"

"We'd be the owners."

"Ah."

So much meaning in one little muttering. "I know that means more risk, but it also means more reward. And the price is right. The owner is willing to sell, but only to us. Because of our reputation." Liam stood straighter. "Just say you'll take the meeting, and Trav and I can show you exactly what you'd stand to gain."

Dad stroked his chin, his eyes still locked on the plain brick of the building across the alleyway. "Tell you what. You indulge my request, and I'll indulge yours."

Liam turned to Dad, eyebrows raised. "What request?"

"The new project I mentioned. It's a bit of a unique situation and mostly a favor for an old friend."

"What friend?"

"Seb Jonathon. Remember him?" Dad caught his eye, his brow furrowed. "He was my college roommate at NYU."

"Yeah, of course. We visited his family a few times in New York when I was younger."

"Right. And I don't know if you remember *this*, but he took off work for two weeks and flew out here to help with the funeral and other arrangements after . . ."

Yeah. He remembered that too. Liam cleared his throat. "So what's the project?"

"Renovating a hotel on Jonathon Island. That's where Seb and his family live now. Upper Michigan peninsula. Small town. Not really our normal place. And the deal's different too."

"In what way?"

"Well, look. No other developer would touch this, but we owe the Jonathons a lot. Seb, he held us together when your mother . . ." Dad swallowed, looked away again. Stuck his hands inside the pockets of his wrinkled gray pants.

"Thing is, we will take on the initial expense of rebuilding the hotel. Then, along with the town, which now owns the hotel, we'll sell it and split the profits. Hopefully, we'll recoup whatever we spent on the restoration."

"Hopefully?" Liam paused. "Dad, I respect that Seb did a lot for us when Mom died. But how can he ask you to risk our company's reputation and financial security? We have to provide for fifteen employees."

"Now, I'm not entering into this deal lightly. I've thought about all of that, and I think there's great potential there."

"Why do they even need us to do this? Can't they just hire us like any other client?"

"The town has had a big economic setback after the pandemic. The hope is that rebuilding this hotel will bring tourism back." Dad rocked on his toes, blew out a breath. "But of course, nothing's guaranteed."

"In other words, we might completely lose our shirt with this thing."

"It's a minor possibility."

"Dad—"

"I've already made up my mind, Liam. We're doing this. If we don't have loyalty, we've got nothing in this life."

"Yeah, Dad, I know you're loyal, and you've created a good business by remaining that way. But you're so close to retirement. What happens if this deal goes south and it somehow bankrupts the company?" Liam started to pace, then stopped, looking Dad dead in the eye. "I know you. You'd rather take care of your employees than yourself if that ever happened. And you've already shown that you will work yourself ragged to the detriment of your own health."

Dad frowned. "That was one time, Liam."

"Yeah, well, one time was enough." And next time? Dad might not be so lucky.

His dad placed a hand on Liam's shoulder. "Son, I know there's a lot at stake, which is why I need you to be the one to go. It'll mean more to Seb if a Stone goes."

"I'm not changing your mind on this, am I?"

"I don't know if you realize this or not, but your old man is stubborn."

Liam huffed out a laugh. "Think I caught that." He lightly punched his dad in the upper arm. "All right, Dad. I'll go. But it sounds like this is a multi-month project. And I can't stay that long. Not if I'm going to head the California hotel project here with Travis." He lifted his eyebrows in challenge.

His dad chuckled. "Methinks the stubborn apple doesn't fall too far from the tree. Yes, fine. You go, get the project started, draw up the plans, and stay until they're approved. Once demo starts, we'll get Rob out there. Hopefully we'll be in, be out, and make a tidy profit in the end. And I'll feel good about repaying an old debt."

Liam's heart rate started to slow. Okay, fine. He could do this and probably be back by the weekend. With a few late nights, he could draw up the most modern and luxurious of hotel plans in his sleep.

Especially with the right inducement. "So you're willing to consider our proposal when I get back?"

"Absolutely."

All right then. "When do I leave?"

"That's the thing. I need you on a plane bound for Jonathon Island tomorrow."

"Good thing I'm already packed."

Three

HE WASN'T IN KANSAS—OR RATHER, Los Angeles—anymore.

Liam stared from the window at the approaching island beneath the "air taxi," which was no more than a tiny puddle jumper that looked like it had seen better days—with a pilot to match. For some reason, the shape of the island reminded him of those beehive hairdos women had worn in the 1950s, though one that slightly listed to the right.

Dad had told him the hotel, along with the rest of downtown, was located on the southern tip of the island, and as they flew overhead, Liam saw a large harbor with boats dotting the white surf where the island met the surrounding Lake Huron.

The pictures he'd looked at on his phone had shown a quaint town, something almost out of another world—a town time forgot. According to his very quick online search, they didn't even use motor vehicles, just bicycles and horse buggies to get around.

Hopefully they at least had Wi-Fi.

"Don't get many visitors in these parts at this time of year." The pilot's voice came through Liam's headset, crackly and tinny. Then, the guy—Pete—twisted slightly in his seat to look back at Liam. "Will you be here long?"

Hopefully not. The sooner he worked out the details of the hotel renovation with the town, the sooner Liam could get Rob out here—and get back to his own plans. "You know, Pete, I'm not quite sure."

"Must be from the city, I'll betcha." Pete, who had the bushiest, wiriest eyebrows Liam had ever seen, looked Liam up and down.

"Los Angeles." Liam smiled. "How could you tell?"

That made Pete snort and turn back around in his seat. "Don't see too many suits is all. Most folks round here are all about functionality and comfort." That was definitely true of Pete, who was dressed in jeans and a flannel shirt with a puffy navy-blue vest and a weathered ball cap on his head. "And California?" He whistled. "Wouldn't be surprised if you freeze while you're here. Unless you were smart enough to bring a coat."

"I packed one in my bag, but read you guys are having a warm snap, so I doubt I'll have to dig it out."

"A warm snap here is probably colder than the coldest day in your parts."

"Thanks for the tip, but I'm sure I'll be okay." He'd worked at plenty of job sites around the world, after all. Sure, the only time he'd landed in the Midwest had been

July and August, but how cold could it really be if the ferry was already running?

Speaking of the ferry, it was going to be one of Liam's main challenges—specifically, getting building supplies from Port Joseph on the Upper Peninsula to the island. It could possibly cause some delays. But Liam was willing to figure it out for his dad's sake.

For the sake of his future.

And really, it would most likely be Rob's problem, since Liam would be long gone by the time it came to renovate.

"Who did you say you were visiting while you're here?" Pete's tone lilted up at the end, laced with curiosity and something else. Suspicion, maybe?

"I didn't." Because from what Dad had said, Seb wanted secrecy, at least at first. "I've got a meeting with someone, though, and—"

"Ah. Attorney-client privilege. I get it."

Liam wanted to laugh at the assumption, though he supposed to Pete he might look like an attorney in his favorite blue, two-piece, micro-pattern wool Armani suit and brown leather penny loafers. "Thanks for understanding, buddy. Hey, would you mind letting me get a good look at the island on our flight? It's my first time here."

"Sure." Pete lowered the nose of the old bucket of bolts, and they got a bit closer to the island. "Hang on."

Bracing himself, Liam peered through the filmy plane window. He still couldn't make out many details of the downtown area, though most of the buildings seemed to be located on one main street.

To the east of downtown, there was an expanse of

green—most likely a park of some sort—and more of-ficial-looking white buildings were north of that. Maybe a school too. Huge clumps of trees coming back to life after winter filled in any empty spaces. Liam's very limited research—conducted on his two flights here—had shown that Jonathon Island had once been a popular, bustling tourist destination for hiking, horseback riding, and bik-ing, so there were probably trails hidden under the trees' branches.

Pete swung the plane westward, and they zoomed back over the downtown. Neighborhoods spread out from the main town into the island like veins and arteries branch-ing off a heart, and Liam squinted in the direction of the hotel, which, according to the map on his phone, was west of the downtown. But then Pete turned north, and Liam couldn't make out the hotel's details. No matter. He and Seb would be getting a personalized tour by the director of tourism once Seb picked him up from the airport.

Pete took them northwestward, skimming along the western coast, where a slew of large homes were clustered together. A paved roadway hugged the curves of the bluffs and vistas that likely created stunning views at sunset.

As they made their way toward the northern tip of the island, he glimpsed a lighthouse and a stately home sitting alone on several acres. "Who lives there?"

"That would be the Jonathon family, of Jonathon Is-land fame. They've been here for more than two hundred years, and Seb Jonathon owns almost all of the real estate downtown."

"Wow, I had no idea." Though he should have figured

that, given Seb shared a name with the island, he would be an important man here. "Does that cause a lot of friction, one person owning so much?"

"I think you'll find people here are much kinder than you might be used to." Pete paused. "We look out for our own."

Then the plane dipped, and Liam gripped his seat. *Note to self: don't make the pilot mad.* "I didn't mean any disrespect." Liam's heart rate slowed as the plane leveled out and Pete circled the northeastern shore, where a red barn sat on a stretch of farmland. "I didn't know Jonathon Island had farms."

"We don't anymore. That's the old Sullivan pumpkin farm. Abandoned years ago."

Shame. Even from up here, it looked like a beautiful property.

A little farther south, they flew over a large section of land partially cleared of trees, with one large building and lots of smaller cabin-looking structures surrounding it. "That looks interesting down there. What is it?"

"The old MacBride adventure camp. An outdoors resort of sorts. It's defunct now, but back in the day they offered some truly fabulous stuff for the outdoorsy among us. Used to give the Grand Hotel a run for its money— luxury versus adventure. Sad what happened to both of them."

"And what was that?" He hadn't been able to find any pictures of the Grand in recent years, save one small article in the local paper from a decade ago with a grainy photo of a gazebo and an article about a "small fire" that had taken out "a portion of rooms" at the Grand.

When he'd agreed to this, he hadn't known he'd be dealing with a partial reconstruction. Then again, it would allow for a fabulous new wing with luxurious amenities—and that was Liam's specialty.

Pete fell quiet. "We're almost there. Make sure you're buckled for landing."

Guess he was done talking. "Will do. Thanks, Pete."

Below, the trees suddenly opened up to reveal a runway that had to be half the size or less than normal, but Pete had no problem bringing it down. The plane clattered to a halt. As far as Liam could see, they were the only people here, though several small aircrafts lined the runway, which lead to a small municipal building that couldn't have been more than a few thousand square feet. It probably had the world's smallest waiting room.

When Pete gave the all clear, Liam pulled off his headset and climbed out of the puddle jumper. Ah, steady ground. Despite the sunny sky, wind whipped at Liam's suit coat, and okay, yeah, maybe Pete had a point about the cold.

Pete wheeled Liam's carry-on-size suitcase around and handed it off to him. "Guessing you're staying at the Island House Inn?" He stuck his hands in the pockets of the jacket he'd pulled on over his vest.

"Yeah, how did you know?" Another blast of wind came out of nowhere, and Liam glanced toward the building, which he bet was much warmer than here. But the windows were dark.

"It's the only place open this time of year." Pete lifted his hat and scratched his nearly bald head underneath before replacing the cap. "The owner, Caleb, now there's a nice guy. Loyal and as small-town as it gets. But he's off island at the moment."

"Wait. There's only one hotel for the whole island?" No wonder they needed the Grand rebuilt.

"A few summer-only residents rent their places out to tourists, but we really don't get many of those anymore in the off season."

"Ah."

"All right, well, I'm out of here. The missus has a pot of soup on for dinner. Need a lift to the hotel?"

Liam popped up the handle of his suitcase, turning his back to the wind. "Thank you, but I've got one." Dad had told him Seb would be grabbing him from the airport—though the prospect of biking all the way to downtown sounded downright terrible.

Maybe he should have rethought the suit and loafers after all.

"Looks like they're coming now." Pilot Pete pointed toward the main road.

Liam turned to find a brown, double-bench golf cart headed their way. "I thought motorized vehicles weren't allowed here." That's what the internet had said, anyway.

"Just golf carts and snowmobiles, and only in the off season. And of course emergency vehicles. Sometimes construction vehicles, but only for a very limited time and with a permit."

Liam breathed a sigh of relief over that one. At least the

hotel renovation wouldn't have to revert back to the Dark Ages when they'd had to use pulleys and ramps.

"Otherwise, it's bikes and buggies for us," Pete continued. "Though we've only got a handful of horses on the island anymore, and they're up on the Quinn property, so walking and biking are the only real options. Get used to using those things called legs."

Liam laughed. "Thanks, Pete. I will." He extended his hand.

Pete took his offering and shook. "Buckle up, Fancy Pants. Looks like Dani's grabbing you today." Then, whistling, he walked away toward another cart sitting near the building.

Danny? Maybe Seb had sent the director of tourism in his stead. The guy who, apparently, would be giving Liam a more in-depth tour of the island and hotel, and with whom Liam would be working to get the plans approved by the town council.

Turning, Liam lifted a hand in greeting as the golf cart, which was decked out with winter tires of all things, pulled to a halt beside him. A woman—not a man—climbed from behind the wheel.

A beautiful woman, tall and willowy, despite her white coat, jeans, and brown duck boots. Her long blonde hair hung nearly to her waist, and her big green eyes—framed over high cheekbones, a pert nose, and pretty lips turned downward—studied him. "Are you Mr. Stone?"

"Liam, please. Mr. Stone is my dad." Liam stepped forward and shook her hand, which was much warmer than his, thanks to her lightweight yellow gloves. "And you are?"

"Dani Sullivan."

"The director of tourism?"

"Were you expecting someone else? A man, perhaps?"

"What?" Liam coughed, caught off guard. "Not at all." Then he flashed her a smile. "With all the great things Seb told my dad about you, I thought you must be older."

She looked him up and down. "I could say the same about you. This is a pretty big project. I guess I expected your father to come."

"He's needed back at the office. But don't worry, Ms. Sullivan. He sent the best." Then he winked at her.

She frowned, clearly not impressed. "I hope that's the case. There's a lot riding on this."

That's what every hotel owner thought—and Liam had proven his worth to them all. "I know I've got a baby face." Liam patted his cheeks. "But trust me. I've worked on hundreds of hotels, and every single one of my clients has been thrilled with the results. In fact, even though I just learned of this project yesterday, I've spent the last twenty-four hours drawing up some preliminary plans for the Grand."

Dani blinked at him. "Maybe you should actually see the hotel first. And the town. They kind of go hand in hand."

"Of course, of course. Don't worry. Really. I've got this."

She smiled, but it didn't appear to reach her eyes. "All right, then. Well, we need to scoot if you want to see the hotel before sunset." Dani thumbed over her shoulder toward the golf cart. "You can throw your suitcase in back."

"Great." Liam stuck the suitcase on the back bench and climbed in beside Dani. "Will Seb be joining us?"

"He planned on it, but something came up. He's a busy man."

Now that, he understood. "Of course." He hung on to the grab bar while Dani pealed out like it was a NASCAR race. Then she came to a sudden halt. Started again. Mumbled something under her breath as she stared at the controls.

"Everything okay?"

She grunted. "This is Uncle Seb's. I just don't drive that often."

Uncle Seb, huh? Interesting. "We could always walk. It's only, what, a mile or so?"

"In those shoes?" She eyed his loafers, her lips twitching. "It's paved, but early spring in the Midwest means more mud than usual as things are drying up. Though we've had warmer temps than normal this year, there have still been a few storms. Just had one a few days ago." She got the golf cart going again. "The point is, I wouldn't want you ruining your fancy shoes." Then she gave him some serious side-eye. "And sorry in advance, but you might be kind of cold on the drive if you aren't used to this climate."

"Oh, I'm aware." Liam laughed. "Pete already razzed me about my choice of clothing and lack of a coat."

"Yes, well, the weather here can change on a dime in the spring, so I hope you packed something a bit warmer just in case." Dani adjusted her rearview mirror, though why she felt the need was beyond Liam. They were literally the only "vehicle" on the road, which was now quickly moving from open airfield to forested land.

"Don't worry about me, Ms. Sullivan," Liam teased. "I'm used to being in a variety of climates. Just call me Mr. Flexible. And this suit coat provides more warmth than you'd think."

"Hmm." Dani's hands tightened on the steering wheel. "Guess we'll see."

The cart bumped a bit as it descended down the hill. Sunlight glinted through the canopies of the tall oaks and firs, spotlighting the ground. The lush smell of wet earth mingled with that of cedar bark, and over the hum of the golf cart, birds chanted a merry tune.

It almost made Liam forget how cold he was. Would it be too obvious if he sat on his hands? "So Sullivan, huh? I think I saw your pumpkin farm during my flyover."

A flicker of a frown, gone so quickly he maybe had imagined it. "Yes, it used to be run by my uncle and aunt."

"Pete said it was no longer open?"

Dani's fists rotated on the wheel. "Unfortunately."

Hmm. Not overly chatty, this one. Or maybe he'd hit upon a sore subject.

A cyclist worked his way up the hill, a toolbox affixed to the back of his bike. "Hey, Dani," he called as he pulled to a stop.

"Hi, Cody!" Dani idled beside him. "You headed to fix the toilet at the airport office?"

"How'd you know?"

"Doris was complaining about it at church on Sunday."

Cody, who looked five to ten years younger than Liam, laughed good-naturedly, adjusting the strap on his helmet. "She hounded me about it, and my schedule finally freed up. That storm took down a few trees, and I was needed to help haul them off." Looking past Dani, he nodded at Liam. "Hey, there."

"What's up, man."

Then back to Dani. "Who's this?"

"A guest of Uncle Seb's. I'll see you later."

"Have a good one." Cody waved again and took off, powering his way up the hill.

"Friend of yours, I take it?" Liam asked as Dani continued down the hill, halting at an all-way stop before continuing straight. "Or do you just know everyone here?"

"Yes and yes." Dani lifted an eyebrow his way. "It's a small town."

"Right." Liam laughed again, despite the breeze scraping across his cheeks. "Just how small is small?"

"Small enough."

Just below the tree line, Liam could make out flat gray- and blue-shingled roofs. From what he could tell, they were coming in the back way, making a straight shot across the middle of the island toward the southern tip, where the downtown area was located. And it appeared they were coming down through a neighborhood of older-looking homes.

"Have you ever been to Jonathon Island before?"

"First time."

"Then prepare to be mesmerized."

And that's when the trees fell away and the road opened up to the heart of the island.

Liam sucked in a breath. Compared with the bustling metropolis of Los Angeles, it was a blip, but the history showcased in the residences on the path toward the downtown business area was enough to make his heart stutter.

Several Victorian homes sat on large plots of land facing each other, competing for grandeur despite their weather-worn paint. Enormous porches wrapped around the fronts and sides, hugging the homes, which boasted sweeping, multi-gabled roofs.

Closer to the edge of town, a hulking Greek Revival-era home with a crooked bed-and-breakfast sign looked abandoned, its full-height white portico cracked but still proud, its gable arched and towering over the Queen Anne-style cottage just beside it. Ivy wound up the side of the cottage, thick and resilient despite the low temperatures.

"This is Jonathon Boulevard, one of the first residential streets built by our town. With seven historic homes and one bed-and-breakfast, it's a hallmark street."

"Who owns these houses?"

"Many of them are second homes that used to be owned by Chicago and Minneapolis residents who would vacation here for the summer."

"Used to?"

"Yes." Dani turned left down a residential street called Lilac Lane. "I'll take you the long way around so you can see more of downtown before the main event. The homes here aren't as stately, but they house a lot of the downtown workers. Fishermen, restaurant and shop owners, that kind of thing."

The difference in size was stark, with most of these homes being small craftsman bungalows that couldn't have more than two or three bedrooms. Many of the windows were dark, though others had signs of life—flower boxes beneath the windows, bicycles and kids' toys strewn in the yards, a fresh coat of paint on the front door.

Liam crossed his arms. "They remind me a little of the homes down by the beach back home."

"How so?"

"Small, functional. And with a kind of island charm that comes from being near a body of water."

"Hmm. I like to think Jonathon Island is unique, but I guess I can see that."

"I sense a pride when you talk about it. You lived here long?"

"My whole life. And I'm never leaving."

The surety in her voice zinged through Liam and left him feeling hollow. Strange.

A few seconds later, they were turning right onto Blueberry Boulevard and hooking another right onto Main Street, just where it ended at the opening to the park he'd seen during the flyover. It looked much bigger from down here.

Multi-story white-and-gray storefronts with pops of color on their tattered awnings lined either side of the wide road. As they bumped over the cobblestones, still the only golf cart in sight, Liam couldn't look away from the faded signs in darkened window shops, the sidewalks with weathered benches, the crumbling columns and banisters on the pop-out storefront porches. The street was dotted with old-timey-looking lampposts that boasted tear-drop globes with what appeared to be hand-blown crackled glass. Many of the shops were multi-storied, which would have provided extra apartments for residents—once upon a time.

And Liam could see it, in his mind's eye . . . what once was.

A fresh coat of paint, repairs to the cracks, flowers by the benches, and shops reopened—plus the charm it clearly had in spades—and this town could be brought back to life.

Not by him, of course. He was here to draw up sufficient restoration plans for the hotel, and the hotel alone. A hotel that needed the Stone touch. That needed to be grander than grand.

Even so, his fingers itched to sketch out his vision for a restored downtown Jonathon Island.

"Well?" Dani's voice brought Liam back to himself. "What do you think?"

"It's like another world."

Here and there were signs of life. A woman and her little boy stepped out of the tiny market—Doug's—with a paper sack. The boy flashed a gap-toothed grin at Liam, and Liam waved.

Liam squinted down the side streets as they passed the Tourism Bureau and a coffee shop. "Can you get fudge in there? I heard your island was famous for it."

"No, they only offer coffee and some pastries. And yeah,

we were famous for it, once upon a time. There's an old fudge shop at the end of Main Street on the right side—we'll pass it on our way to the hotel. It used to be run by the Hart family, who also had a fishing company down by the marina. Then there was another up just behind that, on Jonathon Boulevard, started by the Kelley family. They own all of the other restaurants in town, and let's just say thus began the great Fudge Wars of Jonathon Island."

Liam chuckled. "A real-life feud? Like the Hatfields and McCoys?"

"Kind of. If you take away the guns and killing. But they definitely don't like each other."

"Why not?"

"Loaded question. Homer and Melinda Hart came over from the mainland and started their shop in 1951. Their second oldest son William became friends with Barry Kelley in the sixties. Barry even worked in the Harts' shop for a few summers alongside William. But then, in 1970, when both of the men were in their mid-twenties, Barry Kelley started Kelley's Classic Fudge, mostly at the behest of his dad and the family patriarch, Casey Kelley. Rumor has it that the fudges tasted very . . . familiar, if you catch my drift."

"Yikes." So much drama in one little town. "Do you think Barry stole the recipe?"

Dani shrugged. "No idea. I personally think the whole feud is based on the fact the Harts felt like the Kelleys already had a corner on the food market and didn't need to encroach on the thing they'd been doing for nearly twenty years at that point."

"I guess I can understand that. Though as a business-person, I also understand how a little competition can be a good thing." Liam studied the buildings as they passed more. "Now, though, it doesn't look like a lot of restaurants are open. Are the Kelleys still around?"

"Oh yes, and all three open restaurants belong to them. Kelley's Bar & Grill, Good Day Coffee, both of which we just passed, and Martha's on Main. It's coming up here on the left." She pointed at the second-to-last building on the southern side of the road. Bikes lined the front of the white building with clapboard siding. Black stately awnings stretched over the black front door and panel of large windows flanking the front. White scripted font on the main window boldly declared the diner's name, as did a round sign extended high over the door from a white, wooden post. People stood just outside the door in their jackets, leaning against the building and chatting as if they were waiting for a table.

"Looks busy."

"Try her chicken salad and you'll see why. It's island famous."

"I'll do that. Maybe we can grab a bite after you show me the hotel." Speaking of, they must be getting close.

She glanced over at him, her lips pursed. "Maybe. But I've got a lot of work to do after our meeting."

They rounded the corner, and Liam got his first glimpse of the most beautiful—and maybe the most tragic—thing he'd ever seen.

His jaw dropped. "Is that . . . ?"

"Yeah." Dani parked the golf cart and sat there a moment before exhaling a deep breath. "Welcome to the Grand Sullivan Hotel."

"This isn't a hotel." He climbed from the golf cart and stared at the pile of debris and charred wood in front of him. He knew this place had been a lovely four-story resort at one time, set on three acres with a fabulous view of the lake plus its very own golf course. He knew that, and yet, that knowledge did not compute with what he was seeing. "This is an ash heap. A scar."

And there was no way this project was going to take three months. Try three years.

Did Dad know about this? Seb wasn't one to lie, was he? Had he lured Dad—Liam—out here under false pretenses?

"Excuse me. I need to make a phone call."

Liam Stone was in way over his head.

Dani had known it from the first moment she'd seen him standing there in his fancy suit and charming dimples. She didn't care how experienced he claimed to be or how handsome he was with that heart-shaped face, that clean-shaven jaw, and those deep chocolate eyes.

He was way too young to handle this massive of an undertaking.

Maybe he realized it too, given the fact he'd just spent fifteen minutes on the phone with his dad, arguing in hushed tones before marching back, that fake smile in place as he rubbed his hands together and said, "Let's get this show on the road."

Unfortunately, whatever her objections, Liam Stone was all she had. No other developers had agreed to Uncle Seb's terms.

Which meant it was up to Dani to make sure he understood her vision for the project—and just how much was at stake.

Now his appraising eyes were back on the hotel, taking it all in. Four stories high and built of strong, white Michigan pine, the Grand Sullivan Hotel stood sentinel on a grassy bluff overlooking the harbor. Its slim lines and curved roof, the veranda that ran along the third story, the white columns lining what had once been a six-hundred-foot summer porch—they all served as reminders of what the hotel had represented, both to Dani and the community at large.

But where once there had been symmetry on either side of the hotel, now one half was charred or missing, merely ruins thanks to the decade-old fire.

"You said this was the Sullivan hotel . . . as in Dani Sullivan?"

Liam's question jarred Dani from her thoughts. "Yes."

His frown was enough, and he didn't have to even say it—this was another failed family property. Though the reasons for her Uncle Bryan, Aunt Mary, and three cousins abandoning their farm were a lot less complicated than the situation with the hotel.

He scratched the back of his head. "And you're Seb's niece?"

"I am. On my mom's side. She's a Jonathon. My dad's

a Sullivan." She pointed to the hotel. "And this ash heap, as you called it, is my family's legacy."

Liam winced. "Look, I'm sorry about that. I was just taken aback. The only recent article I could find about the hotel claimed there was a small fire, but not . . . this." His hand swept toward the structure, which had once been so magnificent, but now bore the marks of greatness on one side alone.

"The fire was an embarrassment to the community, as was the fact we had to cancel so many reservations and could no longer house seasonal employees or most of the tourists who wanted to visit." Dani started walking the perimeter. "We didn't exactly want to advertise that fact to the world at large. The people who needed to know, knew."

Liam quickly caught up with her. "I'm assuming that includes you. You know what happened here, right?"

"I know enough." The memories were an ice pick to her heart. "But that's in the past. I'm more interested in what we can do to rebuild. To bring this place back to its former glory so that all of Jonathon Island can be restored."

And so her family would have a path to come home.

"I like that. I'm all about creating a better future."

She frowned. "The past is still important. I didn't mean that. Just . . ."

"I understand." He smiled at Dani again with those dimples of his. Did that really work on others? This guy sure was slick.

"Basically, there was a fire ten years ago. As you can see, it burned down or damaged half of the main building. The half without visible outer damage still has some water damage on the inside due to the sprinklers. Thankfully, the ballroom and gazebo were spared because they're separate from the guest room areas. But essentially, this renovation would be a nearly complete reworking of the hotel at large."

"Good to know. Will you show me around? I'd love to see the extent of the damage to get a feel for the scope of the project." He paused. "To be honest, it's much larger than what I expected."

"I gathered." She cocked her head. "Does that mean you'll be calling in the big guns to help?"

He blinked. "No. I can handle it. It's just a shift in expectations is all."

"You sure?"

"Absolutely."

Hmm. They'd see about that. "Come on."

They started ambling around the structure, and Dani went into tour guide mode, something she'd been doing since she was first hired at the Tourism Bureau in high school. In the island's heyday, Dani had given six or seven walking tours a day during the season and at least one a day during the off season. Now, she gave exactly zero in the off season and maybe one per week during the season.

"The hotel was first built in the 1890s. It was a huge boon to tourism from the first season it was open. People loved coming to Jonathon Island to experience rest and rejuvenation. And for the locals, the hotel's long summer porch became a principal gathering area. Islanders used to come here and walk the porch with their romantic partners, and it was dubbed the Flirtation Walk. The elderly used to use it as a way to get exercise and have somewhere to go—kind of like how city dwellers will walk shopping malls nowadays."

She spent the next several minutes spouting various facts about the hotel, including all the big-name guests they'd hosted (like Mark Twain), renovations and additions that had happened over the years (the West Wing had been added quickly after the initial opening thanks to an increased demand for room availability), and how the hotel had celebrated 125 years with a smashing party attended by former Michigan governors just a few years before it had burned.

"And your family owned the hotel that entire time?" Liam pushed a hand through his tapered brown hair, which was as neat and tidy as the two-piece suit beneath the black overcoat he'd casually grabbed from his suitcase after the phone call with his dad.

"Yes. The Jonathons have always owned the land, and the Sullivans paid rent on it."

"And what happened when your parents got married?"

Oy. That was the problem, wasn't it? "They decided to make the arrangement permanent in solidarity. To keep it all in the family. Which meant that as long as my dad wanted to pay rent on the land, the Jonathon side had to let him. And once the hotel burned, they couldn't do anything else with it. The rent they'd locked in had been low. So poor Uncle Seb lost his shirt on that land every month because my father refused to give the Jonathons the satisfaction of clearing his hotel off the land and selling or renting it to another buyer." She paused. "Basically, it's complicated."

"I'll say." He kept walking before stopping in front of the colonnades lining the porch up ahead. "It's really remarkable. I'm a big fan of the Colonial Revival style." Liam placed his hand reverently on the outer wall, his face lifted upward. "It's just so graceful."

A thrill ran up her spine. Someone else understood her enthusiasm. "I couldn't agree more. Are you into architecture? Not that I'm more than a hobbyist myself."

"Studied it for my undergrad, actually."

"But you didn't pursue it?"

"Not solely as an architect, but I do use it in my work now." He shrugged. "Dad wanted me to come work for him, and I couldn't say no. Family's gotta stick together, right?"

"Right." Though as much as she believed the words, not everyone in her own family did. In fact, she might be the only one.

That's why she *had* to get this project right.

"I've watched countless documentaries on the Travel Channel about the architecture in Europe, how much history there is to be seen. So much still preserved. The United States' history pales in comparison."

"Yeah, it really does. You definitely have to see the cathedrals especially. St. Paul's in London is exquisite. Have you ever been?"

"Haven't really had much of a chance to travel. But I want to. Someday."

Liam studied her for a moment. "I hope you get to do

just that. The world is a wonderful place." Then his gaze shifted back to the hotel. "But so is your little town. I can see why you like it here. And this hotel, it's got real potential. You can tell it used to be really grand."

"I'm glad you recognize that." And hopefully, he recognized how important it was to preserve that history for generations to come. She pivoted away from the hotel and pointed in the distance. "That way is a golf course, which actually is in decent shape. And out there is the island's famous gazebo. You see it?"

He stepped closer to her, and hints of his expensive-smelling cologne drifted toward her. Then he squinted. "Oh, yeah. I feel like I saw pictures of it during my brief research. Wasn't it built as part of a movie set?"

"It was! *Still the One*. Fabulous movie if you haven't seen it. About a small town, just like this one, and an Army Ranger and wedding planner slash single mom who used to be childhood friends, and now . . ." She laughed. "Anyway, that gazebo is my favorite place on the whole island. And there used to be picnics on the lawn held out there for hotel guests every weekend evening under the stars." She sighed. "They were magical."

Liam hummed. "I can definitely see that being a big attraction back in the day."

"Really?" Her heart squeezed. Maybe Liam was catching her vision after all.

"For sure." Liam pivoted and pointed to the hotel's front porch. "Think it's safe to walk on?"

She nodded. "Uncle Seb had someone out to evaluate it once we knew we were going to pursue the redevelopment project. There's tape around the sections that are unsafe. We can walk about halfway down the porch before we reach that point."

They took the steps together, and even though the porch granted a very similar view as the spot where they'd just been standing, there was still something magical about it to Dani. "This is my second favorite place on the island." So many memories revolved around this porch.

Watching fireworks with her family.

Painting terrible artwork on easels with Mom and a group of guests.

Taking in the sunset with her older brother James before he left for college. Him telling her that he'd always come back, for this, because the hotel was the greatest spot in the world—and his family, the safest landing place.

Of course, that had been *before*.

"Wow." Liam leaned against a column, hands in his pockets as he stared out at the boats bobbing in the harbor. "I could totally picture eating a lazy Sunday brunch out here with that view."

"Pretty spectacular, right? And look up." She pointed at the porch ceiling, which was painted a turquoise color—her favorite part of the whole thing. "That color was chosen to keep the birds from nesting on the porch roof. But to me, it's always been like a secret, something you only know when you take the time to step out and look up. And there's something special about the hidden things. The special things. Being in on the secret when not everyone is."

Liam angled his neck upward and whistled. "That's really something, huh?"

"Yep." The sun had started its descent toward the horizon, and the moon was already trying to grasp for dominance as the sky darkened. With the encroaching darkness came a chill that settled deep in Dani's bones. She tried to shake it off, but maybe it went deeper than the physical. "I'll show you the inside when you're ready. But now that you've seen the outside, what are you thinking in terms of scope? Can you do this?"

"I get the feeling *you* don't believe I can do this."

"What? No." Yes, exactly that. But she couldn't scare off the only person willing to help. "I just wondered if seeing the place had you reconsidering at all."

"No." He pursed his lips. "But what kind of timeline are you thinking?"

"I'd love to finish by Christmas."

"Of *this* year?"

"Yes."

"I'm going to be straight with you. Even Christmas of *next* year would be aggressive. A project of this magnitude will take three years—maybe two—at a minimum."

"That won't work."

"I can't make it go much faster than that. Maybe we could speed it up a bit, but you're asking for eight months. Less, since we still need to get the town council on board with our plans, find contractors, and get the site manager updated on all the details."

"Wait. Aren't you going to be the site manager?"

He looked out across the lake. "That's normally how it

works, but I've got another project I'm due back in L.A. for."

"When?"

"A few weeks? I don't know. The point is, you'll have to get the idea of this Christmas out of your head, or I'm afraid Stone Development can't help you."

"So you're just going to back out?"

Liam leaned closer. He studied her through eyes now hooded by the darkness. "Look, Dani, I'm good, but I'm not a miracle worker. This place, it's got potential. I can picture it. My fingers are itching to go sketch up some fabulous new plans right now. But what you're asking is impossible."

"Fine. It'll take longer than I'd like. I can deal with that. But are you sure you're up to the task?" How could he be? Maybe she was asking too much.

But she had to try.

"I've already got ideas brewing up here." Liam swirled his hand around his head. "So yes, I'm up to the task. Trust me, okay?"

Ha. Like trusting him was so easy. But at this point, it looked like she didn't have a choice.

Four

SOMETIMES, AFTER A RESTLESS NIGHT of tossing and obsessive worrying, there was only one solution.

Okay, two solutions: one of Jill's chocolate croissants and a cup of Joe.

The warmth of Good Day Coffee's interior enveloped Dani as she stepped through its doors and out of the April air. It was early still, but she didn't have to be at work across the street at the Tourism Bureau for another fifteen minutes or so when Seb was meeting her for a debriefing of last night's tour of the Grand with Liam.

Maybe her uncle could ease some of her fears about Liam's ability to handle this. After all, he knew the Stones best.

Jill Kelley, a fifty-something woman with a shock of bright-red hair and an apron thrown over her thin figure, waved to Dani even as she rang up Henrietta Hudson at the cash register. The whir of the coffee grinders drowned out some of the chatter of residents scattered throughout the airy space, which consisted of simple black iron chairs and light wooden tabletops, pastel teal accents and knickknacks on the wall, and a pastry display case that stood in front of a wall lined with bright white subway tiles. Behind Jill, one of the local teens made coffees and fetched pastries from the case where cheesecakes, cookies, muffins, and scones held center stage alongside adorable tiny chalkboards with descriptions of each.

Henrietta turned, a pastry bag tucked under her arm, and the wrinkles around her eyes grew even more pronounced when she smiled at Dani. "Hello, dear. You look tired. I hear there's a good reason for that, though, hmm?"

The gossip mill had clearly gotten an early start today. Dani smiled. "Yes, I'm tired, but nothing a good coffee can't fix."

"Who was that man with you last night? Looked downright important, he did, with his fancy suit. I saw you drive past Martha's diner with him in tow."

"Oh, he's just . . . a friend." Dani grimaced, realizing how *that* sounded. No better way to get the island gossips going than to imply there was more between her and Liam than there was. "A friend of Seb's, that is. I was just giving him a quick tour."

"What's he doing here at this time of year, though?"

"You'd have to ask Seb."

"Hmm, all right, dear. Have a good morning."

"You too." Dani winked at the older woman as she hobbled past, clearly favoring one hip more than the other. Then she stepped up to the counter.

Pushing a piece of hair behind her ear, Jill tilted her head. "The usual?"

"Yes, please. With an extra shot of espresso. And some extra caramel too, if you don't mind."

"You got it." After turning to her helper—her eighteen-year-old niece, Olive—and giving her Dani's order, Jill rang up her total. "So you're really not going to tell us who the new guy in town is?" Jill swiped Dani's card without looking at Dani at all.

But no matter how nonchalant she might try to seem, everyone knew that the Kelleys—who owned all three of the eating establishments currently operating on the island—were the central hub of the gossip mill.

Dani had to hold back an eye roll. "Nothing to tell." Yet.

"I heard he's handsome." Tapping the credit card on the edge of the register, Jill peeked up at Dani while the receipt printed out. Then she tore it off and held both it and the card out to Dani.

"Really? I didn't notice." Okay, technically not the truth. He was objectively handsome. But he was a city boy. Besides that, he was only here for a week, maybe two, if that. And Dani knew better than to entertain thoughts about an outsider.

"Gonna be close-lipped about it, I see." Grabbing a pair of tongs, Jill slipped behind the pastry case and pulled out a chocolate croissant, which she slid into a teal bag. "Go ahead. Keep your secrets. The truth will come out . . . eventually."

Now Dani really did let loose the eye roll as she took her pastry from Jill and her coffee from where Olive had placed it on the counter. "Have a good day, Jill."

"I'll find out, you know!" the woman shouted from behind her.

Dani's only response was to hold her drink in the air on her way out the door, as if to toast Jill's efforts. Sometimes, living in a small town could be suffocating. Those were the times Dani dreamed of traveling abroad. But as her eyes scanned the adorable downtown—in one direction, Doug's grocery store, Blueberry Hill Park, the old church, the Island House Inn where Liam was staying, and the historic Fort Jonathon down by the water; in the other, Martha's on Main, the old fudge shop, Kelley's Bar & Grill, and the public library—she couldn't help but wonder how she would ever leave.

It's why she hadn't really and truly considered Dad's offer to move to Florida and work for him. If she did that, then it would be the end of an era. The Sullivans had lived here for two hundred years.

What would it mean for her family legacy—for her *family*—if she left too?

She crossed the street and approached the door to the Tourism Bureau, holding her pastry bag by the teeth as she fished her keys from her purse with her right hand. She inserted the key into the lock.

"Need some help?"

She glanced up to find Uncle Seb strolling toward her, a silver coffee tumbler of his own in hand. Aunt Elise must have made him one to go. Pushing the door open, she dropped her keys back into her purse and snatched the bag from her mouth. "Got it!"

He chuckled. "I don't doubt it."

"Sorry, am I late?" Dani stepped inside the one-story building that was over a hundred years old. Getting to work here had always been a highlight of Dani's life. She loved everything about it, from the way it smelled like old books—thankfully minus the mold that often accompanied the scent because Uncle Seb was religious about checking his properties for the stuff—to the walls papered with a vintage anchor print.

"No, I'm a few minutes early." Seb flipped on the lights, which flickered before roaring to life. "Anxious to hear how everything went last night. I'm sorry again for not being there. My virtual meeting went long."

"I understand." Dani set her coffee and croissant on the large wooden desk at the entry, where brochures were arranged in an oak case that desperately needed updating, then headed to the thermostat to turn on the heat. "To tell the truth, after my tour with Liam, I was anxious to meet with you too."

"Uh oh. That doesn't sound good."

The heat kicked on, and Dani turned to pick up her coffee and croissant again. "I just want to get your perspective on a few things, is all. Come on back." She waved him through the lobby and down the tiny hallway.

They passed the one modern thing in this place—a conference room with a twelve-person table, sound equipment, and a projector. Since it was the only place equipped for business meetings on the whole island, the office was often in use by those who belonged to the local busines-sowners association, as well as the town council when they were in closed-door meetings—and they were about to have plenty of those, what with the revitalization project now under way.

Just down the hall from the conference room, Dani opened the door to her small office crammed with book-cases, two chairs, and the old secretary desk—with its scroll-back top and scarred but well-loved writing sur-face—that Uncle Seb wanted to replace.

Seb's eyebrows rose as he studied the piles of paper, open and tabbed books, and pens scattered along her desk-top. "You've been busy, I see."

Dani slid into her chair behind the desk. "For the last few weeks, I've spent my time researching other places that have done something similar to what we're planning here. You know, selling housing for cheap in exchange for businesses coming to town. And I've been brainstorming ways to entice business owners to settle here and creating a timeline for all of the special tourism events we can hold even while the hotel is being rebuilt. What?"

Uncle Seb was leaning back in his own chair across from her, arms folded and looking amused. "Nothing. I just shouldn't be surprised you're taking this so seriously."

"Of course I'm taking it seriously. This is our big chance." Dani finally took a swig of her coffee. *Ah, hot, hot, hot.* She lowered it. "But none of it will matter if Liam Stone isn't able to do this right."

"Oh? Are you concerned?"

"Did you know he was the one being sent? I guess I

thought his father would be coming, but Liam seemed to imply he's too busy."

"Yes, Chaz told me he'd be sending his son. But from what I know of Liam, he's a diligent and intelligent young man."

"I don't doubt his intelligence." Dani huffed, remembering the astute questions Liam had asked as she'd shown him the hotel last night. "But, well, he didn't seem to realize the full magnitude of the project when he arrived. Almost like he was surprised there was so much to restore and rebuild."

"That would be my doing, I'm afraid." Seb drummed his fingers along the silver body of his tumbler. "After getting so many rejections from other builders, I decided to simply ask Chaz Stone to send me his best guy and just to trust me to work out the details with him. And I promised it would be mutually beneficial. If they help us do this, they'll get a tidy profit at the end of all this."

"But why didn't you go straight to them if they're the best?" At Seb's silence, she leaned forward. "They *are* the best, right?"

"They are the best at what they do, yes."

"And what's that?"

"They usually work on high-end hotels. Luxury stuff. Very modern remodels and new builds."

The coffee felt heavy in Dani's gut. "Okay, but they know that's not what we want them to do here, right? That we are trying to bring the hotel back to life as it once was? Because my worry was more about whether Liam could handle this, being so young and all. But now you have me worried that he is even going to be able to produce a satisfactory product."

"I did explain to Chaz that we want to maintain the historical integrity of the hotel, and he assured me they always keep that in mind when drawing up their plans. But . . ."

"But what?"

"But it's going to be up to you to make sure that Liam understands that too."

"Why me? I know I'm working with him closely on this, but it's your land." She held up a hand. "That's not to say I'm not happy to take the lead on this. But I guess I assumed we would all three be working together."

"I've got to do my best to remain impartial, since the town council has expressed concern that I will try to sway the project in a way that best benefits me financially."

The town council consisted of four people: the pastor's wife Tara Chamberlain, local bar and grill owner Patrick Kelley, president of the Historical Society Janine Dirks, and restaurant owner Martha Kelley. It wasn't hard to guess who Seb meant. "So Martha made a fuss?"

Seb tapped his finger twice against his nose and pointed at Dani. "Bingo. Which means I can consult here and there a bit, but the bulk of the work will have to be between you and Liam. That being said, I'm a bit worried about how this is all going to play out."

"Why? I thought you said Liam was up to the task."

"His father seems to think so, and I want to believe that, but there's just so much riding on this project. If the plans aren't approved by the council, then the hotel rebuild won't happen. And then the revitalization project as a whole will fail too. They don't know it yet, but the entire town is counting on us."

"Liam promised he's got it under control."

"And you believe him?"

The package of the pastry bag rustled as Dani reached for it and hauled out the croissant. "I don't know him well enough to believe him."

"Then get to know him better. Communicate our vision for the hotel. Unless you've done that already?" Seb's voice turned hopeful.

Had she? "I mean, I told him tales of the old days, the history of the place. And he seemed intrigued. He even said a few things that made me think he appreciated the old things. He's kind of an architecture nerd, and . . ." Frowning, she shoved the croissant back into the bag. Breakfast could wait. "I guess I just assumed he was on the same page with what the rebuild should entail."

"I wouldn't assume anything one way or another. I would talk to him immediately." Seb fixed his eyes on her, his gaze intent. "Then, once he's got his plans drawn up, if there's any way to get a peek at them before Liam presents them to the council, do it. It'll ease my mind, and yours too, I suspect."

"Right. Good idea. Don't worry, Uncle Seb. I know what's at stake here. I won't let you down." Dani glanced at the old ticking clock over the door, then stood. "Do you think it's too early to pay Mr. Stone a visit?"

Liam really wanted to like this town, but at every turn, he was reminded that Jonathon Island was stuck in the past and just plain worn out.

And, judging by the broken showerhead in his hand, the Island House Inn was no exception.

Really? Just what he needed.

Groaning, Liam placed the broken showerhead onto the white marble counter. Then he stepped from the white tiled bathroom into the small bedroom, with its white king bedspread and shabby beige carpet and light blue walls decorated with floral paintings. In the corner, under the curtained window, sat a little round table with wicker chairs that hadn't done his lower back any favors after spending hours up late working on the Grand remodel plans.

At least the place was clean and the bed somewhat comfortable. But it was no Vail or Napa resort, that was for sure.

He glanced at the retro wood clock on the bedside table. Eight-oh-two. Hopefully a handyman would be on call by now. Sitting down on the edge of the bed, Liam picked up the phone receiver and dialed. A middle-aged female greeted him. "Goooood morning, Mr. Stone! I hope you're enjoying your stay. This is Sarah. How can I help you?"

"Hey, Sarah. I hate to bother you so early, but the shower in my room wouldn't start, and when I jiggled the showerhead, well, it popped off. Any way we can get that fixed sooner rather than later?"

"No problem, Mr. Stone. I'll get our handyman on it at

once. He's already on the premises, and I'll divert him to your room right quick, for sure and certain. Alternatively, we could switch you to another room."

The peppy woman must have had her coffee, unlike Liam. "No, as long as the fix is quick, that should be fine. Thanks. I sure do appreciate it."

"Abso-too-da-lutely!"

Liam chuckled—small towns had all kinds of characters, didn't they?—and then quickly got dressed in his black suit. His cell phone rang on the small table just as he was deciding on what tie to wear—though maybe he could ditch one just for today?

He strode across the room and glanced at the caller ID. "Hey, Trav."

"So, how's Podunk, USA?" His friend's tease furled over the phone.

"About how you'd think." Liam opened the floral curtains and glanced out his window, which overlooked Blueberry Boulevard. That road intersected Main Street one direction, but in the other, it kept going south until it hit the curving waterfront. Even from here, Liam could see the sparkling water courtesy of the sun that had decided to make an appearance. The light filtered in through the large picture window and across the paper on which Liam had sketched some of his ideas last night. "I mean, it's a gorgeous setting, but dude, this backward town is stuck in the eighteen hundreds."

"Seriously?"

"Case in point: they don't allow motorized vehicles on the island at all."

"That *is* backward. But does it have any cute girls?"

"Not interested. I don't need another Tiffany."

"So that's a yes then."

He could practically hear the smile in Travis's voice.

"I've met exactly two women since arriving on the island—a waitress who could be my mother, and the director of tourism."

"And what's wrong with the latter? She's not cute enough?"

"Sure, maybe in a small-town kind of way." Liam touched the paper's curled edge, examined the bold strokes, the lines that he'd been so inspired to draw. "But she clearly thinks I'm an idiot, and I don't blame her. I showed up thinking this was going to be a three-month remodel, and it's a full-scale rebuild that's going to take two or three years."

"Yikes. Where did the disconnect come from?"

"See, that's what I wondered too, so I called my dad when I saw the place. He said Seb—the guy who hired us—told him it would be a 'big project,' but he didn't know exactly what that meant since that's such subjective language. I guess Seb told Dad that he needed us to assess it and help them establish a timeline for the renovation. I tried telling Dad it's too big of a project, too big of a risk, but he's determined to keep his word and move forward with it."

Travis whistled. "So what does this mean for you?"

"I'll be here at least until Monday, when the town council meets. If I can get them to approve the plans, I'll be able to brief Rob and skip out of here."

"And what of the Bertram project?"

"Dad reassured me last night that if I can do my best for his buddy, for this town, then he's still on board to listen to our pitch."

"That's awesome, dude. You know I'll be prepping while you're away. But how are you going to convince this woman that you're not an idiot? That might be harder than you think."

"Ha ha, thanks for that." Liam sat down in the wicker chair. "I guess all I can do is try to build trust with her. Tell her about the past projects I've done, how I've helped create spaces that other hotel owners can be proud of. And you know, I *do* think I can help her do the same. As soon as we were on the hotel property, I got all kinds of ideas about ways to keep some of the original design but update it with new innovations, a new look."

"And that's what she wants?"

"Isn't that what all hotel owners want? They're always looking to be a step ahead of the rest, to offer their guests modern amenities that will help them relax within seconds of arrival. This hotel already has a gorgeous location going for it. Now it just needs a breath of fresh life. I just have to convince her I'm the man to do that."

"With the way you wrangled Isaiah Beem's property into shape? And oh, how about how you and I transformed the Bentley property in Maine from a trash heap into a Top Ten Diamond Destination? Yeah, if anyone can do it, it's you."

"Thanks, man. Now I just gotta convince Dani of that."

"The sooner you do, the sooner you can get those plans

approved and get your sorry butt back here to work on our project."

Yep, and the sooner he could try to convince Dad to retire. "That's the plan." A knock sounded on the door. "Hey, gotta go. Keep me posted on any updates to our plan."

"Will do. And you keep me posted on any updates to your love life."

The guy wouldn't lay off. Liam groaned. "Goodbye, Travis."

Tossing the phone back onto the table, Liam stood and strode across the room, opening the door to find a well-built guy with brown hair, a friendly smile, and a tool belt buckled around his waist—the same guy who had chatted with Dani from his bike yesterday. "Oh, hey. Cody, right?"

"Yep, Cody Hart. I don't think I caught your name." Cody held out his hand, and Liam shook it.

"Liam Stone."

"Good to see you again. Sarah said something about a shower problem?"

"Yeah, the showerhead came off when the water wouldn't start, and I fiddled a little too hard with it." Liam went into the bathroom and emerged with the part. "I know embarrassingly little about home repair stuff." He'd never needed to, not since he and Dad had moved into the hotel penthouse of one of Dad's friends after Mom died. What had started as a temporary arrangement had stuck, and Dad had never bothered moving them.

Cody chuckled and rolled up the sleeves of his flannel shirt. "I can relate. I fell into this work a few years ago after . . ." His smile faltered for the barest of seconds but then was back. "Let's take a look." He headed for the bathroom and whistled. "Yeah, all right. This is fixable, but I'll need a few hours." Cody re-emerged. "I don't think the hotel is full by any means. In fact, you might be the only guest at the moment. Sarah could get you moved to another room."

"She said that, but I don't want to trouble the staff. A few hours, you said?"

"Two, maybe three tops."

"Perfect. I'll just get out of your way and go grab some breakfast. Where is there to eat around here?"

"Depends on what you're in the mood for." Cody scratched at the stubble on his tan skin. "I know Sarah's got some granola bars and fruit at the front desk for guests if you want something light. Then there's Martha's on Main, which is the closest thing to a sit-down restaurant we've got right now, or Good Day Coffee, which is more like breakfast sandwiches and pastries, that kind of thing. The bar and grill doesn't open till lunch, but it stays open till ten during the week and midnight on the weekends."

"Sweet. Thanks, man." Liam grabbed his hotel key card and wallet and threw on his overcoat before slipping out into the hallway, through the lobby—with a wave to Sarah—and out the front door of the inn.

The air was crisp and clean, such a change from the city, and other than the lake lapping the rocky shore and the clang of metal on masts from the marina beyond, it was quiet too.

Until a familiar voice spoke from the bottom of the steps. "Hey!"

His eyes moved and focused on Dani, who looked—okay, yeah—cute in a pale-blue beanie with a white pom, her blonde hair in two braids that fell down the front of her familiar white jacket. The fact she also wore a scowl somehow didn't detract from her cuteness.

"Have you already started on the plans for the hotel?" she asked.

Liam flashed her a smile. "Good morning to you too." He tilted his head and descended the front steps. "I thought we didn't have another meeting until tomorrow. To what do I owe the pleasure?"

"I just told you. I need to see those plans—the ones you said you started. Or whatever plans you've come up with between then and now." She crossed her arms over her chest.

"I thought you told me I couldn't use those plans since I hadn't yet seen the hotel or the town when I made them." Which ended up being a wise remark, since there was so much more to the project than he'd originally thought.

She stepped closer. "So you haven't done any work on it since then?"

"No, I have. I found our tour . . . inspiring." Being on that long porch, with that view, had him immediately picturing an add-on to the side with swim-out rooms on the first floor. And when Dani had shown him the interior, he'd imagined one large, fluid, open space instead of the ten-foot ceilings and small concierge desk shoved into the corner that currently existed. And the hotel rooms themselves—they simply had to have floor-to-ceiling windows that were sure to use the view to best advantage. "Trust me. You're going to love what I've come up with."

"Prove it." Her eyebrows drew together underneath the lip of her beanie. "Show them to me now."

"Call me superstitious, but I don't show anyone my designs until they're complete." He stepped onto the sidewalk and pointed toward town. Other than a few cyclists who rode by and waved at Dani, the street was deserted. "Hey, have you eaten? I was about to head into town and scrounge up some food."

"Well, no, not yet, but I really think—"

"Perfect. Let's go." He snagged her elbow and turned her down a small path that led to the marina and boardwalk, the latter of which ran from the place where Blueberry Boulevard ended at Fort Jonathon all the way along the southern tip of the island—past the harbor and the ferry landing, running just south of downtown until it ended where Main Street became Lake Shore Drive right in front of the Grand Sullivan. He'd explored just a bit last night in the dark, but it was much easier to get his bearings now.

"I feel like we got off on the wrong foot yesterday. Both of us had different expectations of the project and the person we would be meeting with, yeah?"

"I guess." Pausing at the edge of the harbor, she eyed him warily.

"Let's start over. I'm Liam Stone." He stuck out his hand, waiting patiently until she begrudgingly shook it. "I've got a bachelor's in architecture, an MBA, and I've worked at Stone Development for a decade. During my tenure there, I've helped bring almost one hundred properties up to date, have helped my team win two International Architecture Awards, and have worked hand in hand with hotel managers and owners to bring their visions to life."

"I'll admit—on paper, you sound impressive."

He leaned in. "Don't be too impressed. I didn't even shower this morning."

That got a lip quirk out of her, and her shoulders dropped just a bit from their anxious perch near her earlobes as she stared out across the marina. It wasn't overly large, with five or six floating wooden decks attached to a rocky quay just beside the boardwalk running along the water. Each deck hosted five to ten boats of varying sizes that bobbed in the lake. In the wind, colorful flags fluttered out from the boat masts, which cut confidently against the blue horizon. A lone brick building sat behind the marina. Maybe a yacht club of some sort. If so, maybe it had gone defunct too, because the boats here looked anything but fancy.

It was strange to be standing so close to what appeared to be the ocean but to smell no brine in the air.

"What about you?"

She turned, eyebrow quirked. "What about me?"

"Well, I introduced myself to you. It's your turn now."

"Not much to tell."

"Humor me."

"Fine. I've worked at the Tourism Bureau since high school and was recently promoted to the director position when my longtime boss retired. You already know that

I've lived here my whole life, but what you don't know is that Jonathon Island means everything to me. The people here, they're my family. And I want my family to be okay."

That was a strange way of putting things, but to each their own. "I love hearing your passion for this place. It'll serve you well in your position and on this project. We've got a chance to do something great here, don't you think?"

"Of course I think so. Do you?"

"I just said I did."

"But I'm the one with the most at stake."

Likely she didn't understand just how risky his dad's involvement was. "I take pride in my work. It means something to me too, okay?"

"Yeah? And why is that?"

"I believe that giving people the vacation of their lives can *change* lives. Rest, relaxation, yes, but also memories. Memories they can take with them back to their busyness, back to their brokenness at home. Memories to last when the hard times come."

There was a softening in her eyes, and that's when he knew—a trumped-up list of qualifications wasn't what would build trust with Dani Sullivan. But maybe something true, something personal, would. "When I was nine, my parents took me to this amazing resort in Arizona. It had a waterpark and Mom, Dad, and I spent hours and hours in the lazy river. We sipped on fun drinks with those umbrellas in them and got to watch the sun set from our amazing balconies right up against the mountains. It was just such a great time. And I held on to that memory in the years later, after she died."

"Oh." Dani looked away, pressing her lips together. "I'm sorry."

Liam stuck his hands in his pockets, swallowing past the unexpected thickness in his throat. "The point is, I care about each one of my projects, all right? We're going to tackle this together, and when I present the plans to the council on Monday, there's going to be a resounding victory."

"That sounds good. It's just…" Dani sighed. "You know what's at stake, right? We've got to get this right the first time. Because every season we don't have a hotel is a season our economy suffers. And we have a whole plan built around bringing this hotel back to life."

Wait, what? "This is the first I'm hearing about anything more than the hotel rebuild."

Dani shook her head. "This would have been so much easier if Seb had just gotten on the phone with you ahead of time. But he thought…"

"He thought what?"

A gull called somewhere in the distance.

"It doesn't matter. You don't need all the details. Suffice it to say that when the hotel burned, it started a snowball effect that led to a depressed, nearly non-existent economy. The hotel redevelopment is the first step in our plan."

"And what comes after that?"

"Does it matter? You won't be around anyway."

"True. But I'd still like to know."

Dani finally started walking along the path again, toward the town. "We have a whole plan to bring people back to the island by offering low-cost houses and storefront rent. But none of that matters if we don't restore the hotel to its former glory. It needs to be what it always was to this place—a symbol of Jonathon Island, of what life here is like. A bastion of history, of glory, of strength. Does that make sense?"

"Yeah, it does." But wow. No pressure or anything. It was one thing to renovate a hotel. Another completely to bring an island back to life.

But he was up to the challenge. Dad wouldn't have sent him if he wasn't.

"Liam . . ." Dani stopped walking and turned to face him. "This plan means everything to Jonathon Island. To me personally."

Liam studied her, pretty in a small-town sort of way—and that wasn't necessarily a bad thing. But it wasn't her petite figure or the clothes she wore that got his attention. It was those big blue eyes, the way they were open, vulnerable. Not fully trusting, not yet, but needing him. Needing this.

Because this project *was* more than work to her.

This was about her home. Her life.

He swallowed, nodded. "I won't let you down. I promise."

And that was one promise he intended to keep.

Five

A GIRL COULD ONLY BE PATIENT FOR so long.

And if Liam wouldn't give her a glimpse of his plans after three days of working on them, then Dani wasn't above trying to sneak a peek when he wasn't around. Because if he didn't get this right, the council would never approve the plans. Nothing would change on Jonathon Island.

And her family would never come home.

She stepped from her office and peered down the hallway toward the lobby. All was quiet—not surprising, given the fact it was a Saturday evening. The only one who would be here at this time was Liam, who had taken to holing himself up in the conference room to spread out his plans and work ever since their tentative truce on Wednesday morning. And she knew for a fact he wasn't here, because from her office window, she'd seen him head into Kelley's Bar & Grill next door about ten minutes ago.

The only sound was the weak buzzing of the fluorescent light panels above her. Now was her chance.

She winced as the wooden floorboards beneath her feet creaked. "Stop it, Dani. You're alone." Holding her head high, she hurried the short way down the hall and pushed into the conference room. Eyes quickly scanning the space, she could see Liam had made himself quite at home—empty takeout containers in the trash, an open can of Coke, his leather messenger bag briefcase strewn over one of the chairs.

And there, in the middle of the table, alongside a dozen or so drafting tools and pencils, sat several large pieces of tracing paper.

After another glance over her shoulder, Dani approached the papers, which were upside down. Almost like Liam knew she'd be coming. Like he knew Uncle Seb had texted her at least once a day asking if she'd gotten a peek yet.

Well, today was the day. Trusting someone she barely knew could only take her so far. There was too much riding on this project to not know if Liam was truly up to the task.

Fisting her fingers tight, she unfurled them and started to reach for the papers.

"Whatcha doing there?"

With a yelp, she jumped back and pressed her hand to her chest.

Liam stood in the doorway, a large pizza box in his hands, a frown on his lips.

"What? Nothing."

He placed the pizza box on the edge of the table and strode toward her. She barely had time to notice he'd discarded his suit jacket and tie, that his sleeves were rolled to his elbow, before he stopped right in front of her and placed his hand on top of the pile of papers. "Didn't look like nothing. It looked like you were trying to see my plans before they're ready." His eyes bore into hers, squinting, and wow, he was standing close.

She wanted to look away but held his gaze instead. "It's just . . ." Her tongue stuck to the roof of her mouth.

"I thought we agreed you were going to trust me, Dani." The words were softer than she'd expected, and her jaw loosened.

"More like you told me I should, but since then, you've given me nothing to go on." And maybe she just needed to ask again. "Are you sure you can't give me a small glimpse at what you're planning?"

"That's not how my process works."

"I get it. You prefer to work alone."

"It's not that." Liam took a step back, cleared his throat. "It's just that the creative juices can't flow when I've got too many voices in my head."

"But shouldn't the main voice in your head *be* that of your client? The whole point of this is to make the plans something the council will approve." She placed her hands on her hips. "And how are you supposed to know what they'll approve if you haven't listened to what they want?"

He blinked, then nodded. "You know what, you're right." Liam moved toward the end of the table and opened the pizza box, turning it so Dani could see the golden crust, bubbling cheese, and pepperonis inside. "Why don't you join me for dinner and tell me all about what to expect from the council? Let's hammer out some of the details so I can foresee any obstacles. Because it's important to me to get this approved too. Believe me, there's a lot at stake for both of us."

She narrowed her eyes, even as the aroma of garlic and onion filled the room. "What's at stake for you?"

"Simple." He picked up a slice of pie, nestled it onto a nearby napkin, and sat in one of the chairs, propping his feet up on another. "My dad is doing this project as a favor for Seb, and he's staking his reputation and a lot of his finances on this. It can't fail."

"Oh. I guess that makes sense."

"It does. And that means we both want the same thing." He gave the pizza box a little push toward her and picked up his slice, taking a bite, chewing, swallowing. "So what do I need to know about the council?"

Well, if she wasn't going to get a look at the plans, she supposed the next best thing was helping Liam create a foolproof strategy.

Sighing, Dani grabbed a piece of pizza and settled into the chair that was next to Liam's footrest. "Okay, well, obviously you know Uncle Seb. He's the mayor, but that doesn't really give him any more power than the rest of the council. For the purposes of this revitalization project, he's just another vote. He leads the meetings and sets the agendas, but he has to do his best to balance out the interests of everyone."

"He's probably very invested—being a Jonathon on Jonathon Island and all. How long has he been mayor?"

"He's in the first year of his second term. But even before he was elected, he was viewed as a leader around here—and not only because he owns a large majority of the land and shops on the island."

"So he's got even more of a stake to make all of this financially successful than I thought. Smart guy."

Dani raised a brow. "He *is* smart, which is why he's making this a town-wide effort and not just doing all of this privately with the property he already owns. Having the council involved will help the naysayers who claim he's got too much power, especially since this project has the potential to effect so much change on the island."

"Small towns are so fascinating." Grabbing a fresh napkin from his stack, Liam wiped his mouth. "So on the council, I notice we've got two Kelleys. I'm surprised they were both elected. People don't think that's a little unfair?"

"Probably only the Harts." Dani chuckled, but at Liam's raised eyebrows, she continued. "Remember the fudge wars I told you about? That was between those two families."

"Ah. And Cody's part of the Hart family, yes?"

"Yeah, although if you remember, some of the Harts were into fishing, not fudge. His dad used to own a commercial fishing boat, and Cody worked on it. There was a terrible accident a few years back. My cousin Mia's husband, Troy, and Troy's father, Steve, both died. Cody . . ."

Well, Liam didn't need to know *all* of the town's dirty laundry. Just what was relevant to the topic at hand. "Anyway, back to the Kelleys. Patrick and Martha—who are siblings-in-law, by the way because Martha is married to Patrick's brother, Frank—are some of the only local business owners left on the island after the economic downturn, and they've both lived here their whole lives, so it's only natural they both have a stake in the council. They can't really stand each other, though, so people definitely won't see them as being in cahoots. But it might cause trouble for you, because you'll have to sort of balance their interests. Though we only need a majority to get an approval."

"Good to know. Patrick seems cool, though I only talked with him briefly when I picked up the pizza tonight. I met Martha the other night when I ordered a sandwich to go. She was . . ."

"Pushy? Loud? Opinionated?"

Liam laughed. "Yes to all three. Told me that Seb had spoken highly of my skills, but she wasn't holding her breath that some city boy could understand the inner workings of a special small town like Jonathon Island. She didn't know I have a secret weapon—you." He glanced at Dani and winked.

"Oh." Dani's cheeks heated, though she didn't know why. She picked at one of the pepperonis on her otherwise untouched piece of pizza. "Well, like you said, we want the same thing here."

"Absolutely." Liam polished off the crust of his pizza and brushed off his hands. "Okay, so that's three of the council members. Anything I should know about Tara or Janine?"

Back on solid ground. Good. "Tara is kind of known as the island mom. She's this former dignified debutante from Boston and came here on vacation with her rich family. She met poor seminary student Arnie Chamberlain, and that was it. She moved here to start a new kind of life."

"That's such an interesting story." Liam removed his feet from the chair and sat fully upright. Leaned forward. "I wonder what would inspire someone to give up everything like that."

"Isn't it obvious?" But apparently, to Liam, it wasn't. "She fell in love."

His brow furrowed. "With the man or the place?"

"Both, of course. Eventually Arnie took over the pastorate here, and Tara stands by and supports all the ministries the church offers, especially the women's ministry and several charities here on the island for the less fortunate. She knows practically everyone and is kind of the representative for the 'every man'—or every woman, as it were."

"So, will she pose any problems?"

"I don't imagine so. I'm sure you'll charm her easily enough."

A grin stretched across Liam's face, and he placed his hands behind his head. "So, you think I'm charming then. I was beginning to wonder."

She couldn't help but laugh at the ridiculous look on his face. "I'm going to chuck this piece of pizza at your head if you don't quit."

"You're just so fun to tease."

Dani finally picked up her pizza and wagged it at him. "I'm serious. This is no laughing matter. Because by far your biggest obstacle is going to be Janine Dirks."

The smile left Liam's face—and rightly so. "In what way?"

"She's old school, completely against anything modern. Like me, she wants to maintain the historical integrity of things on the island." Dani blew on her pizza slice, though it was far from hot at this point. "But unlike me, the only reason she wants things to stay the same is because she hates what technology has done for the world. She'll probably request that we remove the air conditioning that was installed in 2007 and would even be crazy enough to ask that we revert back to kerosene lamps instead of electricity."

"You've got to be kidding me." Liam's eyes widened.

"Nope. In fact, when one of the underground power cables between here and Port Joseph was damaged—that's how we get electricity to the island, you know—she sent around a petition to have it retired instead of repaired, which would have reduced electricity to seventy-five percent of its current usage."

"But why would anyone want things to be so . . . backward?"

Dani shrugged and put her pizza back down. "She just firmly believes that we're better off staying in the past."

"Wow. I don't think there will be any pleasing her with my plans. Might as well write her off as a no and work on getting the other votes."

"Show me the plans and I can help see if you've kept things historically accurate enough for her."

"There it is again. You don't trust me." Leaning forward, Liam snagged Dani's hand. "I've got this, Dani. I've presented to heads of major corporations before. I know how to make a persuasive case." His palm was warm, and there was something comforting in it. And his eyes—they were earnest. Like he really believed what he was saying.

"I know you do. But this is my home, Liam. If we don't do this right . . ." She couldn't even fathom what came next. Because without this, there was no hope for more.

"We will." Liam squeezed before letting go of her hand. "Look, I know what it's like to feel like you're alone, carrying the weight of the world on your shoulders. But we're in this together, okay?"

She swallowed hard. "Okay."

"One question though."

"What's that?"

"You said that unlike you, Janine wants things to stay the same because she hates technology. I assume you mean that you want things to go back to how they were before. So why is that important to you?"

She sat back in her chair, turned her eyes to the white-washed ceiling. How could he even begin to understand? But he had shared something personal with her the other day. Maybe it wouldn't hurt to tell him why this meant so much to her. Or an inkling of the reason anyway.

"Because something about Jonathon Island calls to me—has always called to me. This is home. In addition to my uncle, aunt, and cousins, I've got a big immediate family—six siblings—and they've all left the island for one reason or another. But here . . . here is where we were a family, you know?"

"And you're not a family anymore?"

"It's not the same."

Liam waited a beat before responding. "That must be nice. To have a home."

Oh? She glanced at him again. "Isn't California home for you?"

"Sure, it's where my driver's license says I'm from." Liam tapped the tabletop with his knuckles. "But it's hard to really have a home when you're on the road constantly for work."

"I can't imagine that."

"It's part of the job. Though I'm trying to find a way to change things up a bit." Without explaining, he plowed on. "Does your family visit you often? It's probably hard to get them all in one place, huh?"

"That hasn't happened in years, unfortunately." Did she tell him the rest? She may have just met Liam a few days ago, but in this moment, he felt like somewhere safe to land. Like maybe he was trustworthy. At the very least, knowing why this mattered to her might persuade him to do his very best on the hotel plans—though from what he'd told her, he already felt that way. "That's why I feel this aching need, deep down, to preserve this place—our home—not just for my family but for future generations. Who knows? Maybe if things go back to the way they once were . . ."

"They'll have a reason to come back."

She gave the barest of nods. "I know it's probably a ridiculous dream, but I have to try."

"It's not ridiculous. And Dani?"

Her heart tapped double time at the earnestness in his voice. In his gaze. "Yeah?"

"Everything is going to work out."

Something in her chest loosened at those words. At the prospect that maybe she wasn't alone in this after all. That Liam had understood her ramblings and that they really were working toward the same goal. "Promise?"

"You have my word."

And if she couldn't get a peek at Liam's plans, then maybe his reassurance was good enough.

His head throbbed, his neck ached, and his fingers were sore, but the plans were done.

Liam sat back from his spot at the small table in his hotel room and heaved a sigh. Sunlight filtered in through the window onto the mylar drafting paper where he'd sketched the final lines.

After he'd caught Dani snooping around last night, he'd thought it safest to move here, but he really did miss the space afforded by the conference room table. No matter though.

After tomorrow morning's meeting, he'd be on the next ferry out of town and back to his posh L.A. office.

There was a knock on the door and Liam stood and stretched before making his way over. Who'd be visiting on Sunday afternoon?

But when he opened the door, he found Cody there, holding a wrench that he wiggled in the air. "You rang about a radiator?"

Liam snorted a laugh. "Oh, yeah. I forgot. It started clanging the other day, and I think I mentioned it to Sarah this morning on my way out to breakfast." He waved Cody in.

"Hope it didn't keep you from working." Cody caught a glimpse of Liam's plans and whistled. "Looks like it didn't. This for the hotel?"

Liam rushed to roll up the paper. "Thought that was supposed to be a secret."

Cody snorted. "A secret in Jonathon Island? Impossible." He kneeled by the radiator, which abutted the chair where Liam had been sitting. Holding his hand in front of it, he smiled. "Good, it's cool."

"Yeah, with the weather heating up this week, I haven't even needed my overcoat." Liam grabbed his laptop off his side table and settled on the bed, which squeaked when he sat.

Cody turned. "Has it been doing that all week?"

"What, squawking like a baby bird that needs its mom? Yeah. Why?"

"I'll look at that next. Probably just a bolt needs tightening."

"Can you fix the loose bathroom door handle while you're at it? Oh, and the closet keeps getting jammed." Liam chuckled as he opened the computer on his lap and booted it up. "They call this place charming, but I think that's just another word for old."

"Can't it be both?" Cody smiled and started examining the radiator with his tools. "Did you know this place started out as a family's beach home? Then it was bought by a retired military captain—he served on a boat on the Great Lakes, actually—and turned into a hotel way back when."

"Aw, so you're a history buff then?" Liam peered over the lid of his laptop as the guy wiggled the radiator.

"If you live on Jonathon Island long enough, everyone becomes a history buff."

"And how long have you lived here?"

Cody pulled a short silver tool from his belt pouch and placed it on the radiator valve, turning it. Air hissed from the contraption. "My whole life, same as Dani."

"Oh right. She mentioned that your family was in both the fudge and fishing trades. Those don't seem to go together."

"Mom was the fudge maker, but her arthritis has stopped her from doing that for a while now. My sister Lily took up the candy making, but she doesn't live here anymore." His new friend offered a sad smile. "And as for the fishing, well, Dad retired a few years ago. And I'm doing this now. A lot of people have had to make adjustments to their livelihood just to stay on the island."

"Really? Dani mentioned a downturn in the economy, but I didn't realize it was so widespread."

"Oh, yeah. Tons of shops had to close because the economy is so highly influenced by tourism. No tourism, no money coming in. That started with the closure of the Grand, but when the pandemic hit, this place became a shell of its former self. All it needs is a little fixing, a little paint—and a new hotel and crop of fresh residents, of course." Cody shifted to look at Liam. Air continued to leak from the radiator, but the pace had slowed. "If this plan of yours doesn't work, I'm afraid even more people will leave, and it'll become a complete ghost town."

The radiator clearly wasn't on, so why did it suddenly feel stifling hot in here? "Dani said something similar, but I guess I thought she had some other plans up her sleeve too. You know, things to re-attract the tourists, to boost tourism numbers."

"Can't have tourists if you have nowhere to house them. And this hotel only has about thirty-five rooms."

"Makes sense I guess." Heat crawled up Liam's neck. "I promised her I'd get this right."

"Dude, you look a little green around the gills. I didn't mean to freak you out. I'm sure those plans are great. Between your skills and how much Dani cares, you'll knock it out of the park." Cody turned the valve key back and studied the radiator again.

Liam closed his computer lid and pushed it from his lap onto the white comforter beside him. "She really does care, doesn't she? I've never met someone so passionate about their home before."

"That's Dani—always putting others before herself. She's got a really big heart."

At the words, Liam's gut pinched. He coughed. "You, uh, don't have a thing for her, do you?" Not that it mattered. Why would he care?

"What?" Cody threw back his head and laughed. "No,

man. She's like a sister to me." Then he cocked his head at Liam as he stood from his squat. "Why? Do *you* have a thing for her?"

Yeah, definitely it was burning up in here. "What, me? No. Not like that. I mean, she's cute and all, and super smart, and determined, and I . . ."

And he kind of wanted to knock Cody's huge smile off his face.

"Shut up, man. Dani's cool, but I'm not looking for anything right now. Besides, I've done the long-distance thing before, and it only ended with both of us being disappointed." Liam scooted to the edge of the bed and tugged his suit jacket off. Why had he even bothered to wear it today, given he'd mostly stayed inside? But there was something comfortable about it, something that made him feel more like himself.

More secure in his abilities.

"If that's all true, then why are you acting so flustered, huh?"

Liam stood and started to pace. "Maybe because the more I think about it, the more I hear about what this whole hotel restoration means to you all, the more I wonder if my plans are going to pass the council. If they're going to approve the plan. If my plans have what it takes to wow visitors so you all can breathe new life back into the island as a whole." Frowning, he stared at the threadbare carpet. "Because I'm starting to realize I can't separate the one from the other, can I?"

And that it was all up to him.

He was going to fail the town.

Fail her.

Just like . . .

"No. You can't. But Liam, have you done your best? Do you feel like the plans you've drawn up are the best way to help revitalize the town?"

"I do, yeah. And I've gone over them again and again, tweaking them till they're perfect." But there were so many unknown variables. Despite what Dani had told him, what did a city kid from the beach know about what these small-town Midwestern residents wanted or needed in a hotel?

But the meeting was at ten o'clock in the morning. It was too late to do anything but double down on the plans he already had. And honestly, he should be fine whatever the result. Because even if the council rejected his proposal, he could tell Dad he'd given it an honest shot, and he'd be home in time for supper either way. Ready to pitch the Bertram project and provide a path for Dad's eventual retirement.

So why did the idea of letting Dani down twist Liam's gut like it did?

Cody approached and placed a steadying hand on Liam's shoulder. "Then trust that what you've done will be enough. That things will work out just the way they're supposed to."

"Thanks, man. I appreciate the vote of confidence."

"It's about time this town came back to life, and I'm happy to be on the sidelines watching it happen."

"On the sidelines? What do you mean?" Liam pointed to Cody's tool belt and gave him a little friendly shove.

"From where I'm sitting, you're fixing up the place one broken radiator at a time."

"Ha. Not quite yet. I bled the pipes, but I think part of the problem may be that it's tilted. I'm going to snatch a piece of wood from my workshop. Be right back."

"No worries. I've got some emails to go through anyway."

At Cody's exit, Liam sat back on the bed and dove into his extremely full inbox, which he'd neglected since arriving on Jonathon Island.

But he couldn't focus on anything on the screen. His vision swam, and frowning, he closed the lid again and re-approached the plans on the table.

Just one more look wouldn't hurt.

Because whether for Dad, for Seb, for Jonathan Island, or for Dani herself, Liam would make these plans the best he could with any hours he had left.

He'd given his word, after all.

Six

JUST ONE MORE HOUR AND SHE'D KNOW
if all the faith she'd put in Liam was good—or not.

But she hadn't been able to sit around her apartment, or the Tourism Bureau, alone another minute.

Holding her goodies in one hand, Dani knocked on Mia's front door with the other. Squeals of laughter rang out from inside, and stomping feet carried closer and closer until the door flew open and four-year-old Finn peered up at Dani. "Hi, Dani! Mom's-letting-us-watch-*Paw-Patrol*-isn't-that-fun-Chase-is-my-favorite."

"Is that so?" Laughing, Dani ruffled Finn's blond curls and stepped inside the warmth of the tiny bungalow on Lilac Lane that Mia and Troy had purchased when Mia had been pregnant with Finn. "Are you supposed to be answering the door though?"

The TV blared from its spot over the fireplace.

"Not to strangers. But you aren't a stranger."

"Dan-Dan!" Sweet Maggie toddled over from the couch wearing nothing but a diaper and a pink T-shirt stained with applesauce. She gripped a doll in one hand.

"Hi, sweet girl." Closing the door behind her, Dani squatted and set the box of donuts she'd picked up from Jill on the living room floor. "Come here." She opened her arms for a hug, and Maggie came willingly, smelling of graham crackers and milk.

Despite the chaos of Mia's home—of little children in general—that hug went a long way to calming her anxiety.

"Where's your mama, huh?"

At that moment, Mia came through the arch that led to the dining room. "What's going on out here?" Her hair was tugged up in a messy bun, and she wore sweats and an oversized Hart Fishing Company T-shirt that had probably been Troy's. Her hand flew to her chest when she saw Dani. "Dani? Hey! What are you doing here?" Her cousin came forward for a hug, and Dani stood to receive it.

The *Paw Patrol* theme music came back on, and the kids rushed back to the couch.

"Sorry to just drop in." Dani bent to pick up the box of donuts. "But I come bearing sugary gifts."

"Just what my kids need." Mia rolled her eyes but snatched the box from Dani's hands and waved her toward the dining room, which led to the kitchen. "If their behavior is atrocious after their inevitable sugar crash, I'm bringing them back to hang out with you all day."

"Ooo, sorry, I've got a big meeting today."

"The hotel one?"

"So the whole island knows about it, huh?"

"Well, Mom told me, and Dad told her." Once inside the humble kitchen, Mia pulled a stack of paper plates from her cupboard. "But would you be surprised if the whole island *did* know about it by now?"

"Not really. Martha can't exactly keep her mouth shut."

"Understatement of the century." Opening the box, Mia slid out a chocolate Long John and split it in half. She divided them between two small plates. "You have a minute to stay and talk?"

"Yes, please. I need the distraction anyway. You got coffee? I would have brought some but didn't know if you'd already had a cup."

Mia chuckled and pointed at the microwave. "My mug has been in there about three times already this morning. I keep reheating it thinking I'm going to have a chance to drink it hot. I have been sorely mistaken."

Her cousin laughed, but being a single mom couldn't be easy. Thanks to Troy's life insurance, she only had to work part time at Martha's, but still. Finn and Maggie were so young, and still needy. "I need to babysit again soon. Give you a break from all the busyness."

"You're sweet, but I'm fine. Constance and Mom help out when I'm working. Besides, you're the busy one. I've hardly seen you since Mr. Handsome came to town." She waggled her eyebrows at Dani.

"I don't know to whom you are referring." Dani made her way to Mia's Keurig. She flipped it on to warm the water and opened her drawer to peruse the selection of K-cups.

"Mmm hmm." Mia grabbed the plates and headed for

the living room, tossing a "we're gonna talk about this when I get back" over her shoulder.

When the Keurig was ready, Dani inserted her chosen K-cup, placed a pink ceramic mug under the spout, and pressed down on the closing handle. The machine whirred, lulling her into a moment's peace as the delectable brew began to fill her cup.

"Smiling just at the thought of Mr. Stone, are we?"

Dani sighed. So much for peace. "At the thought of coffee and nothing more, I assure you."

Folding her arms over her chest, Mia leaned against the counter beside Dani. "Oh, come on, Dani. He's gorgeous, and the two of you have been working so closely together. What's he like?"

"Liam's nice enough. Charming, even." The coffee trickled to a stop, and Dani removed her mug, moving to the fridge to fish out a container of heavy cream. "And is he cute? Yeah, sure, but he's a big-city guy at heart. And even if he wasn't, he doesn't understand what it's like to live in a small town, to be part of a community like this. And we all know I belong here. This is my home."

"Methinks the lady doth protest too much," Mia said in a singsong tone.

"Whatever. Besides all of that—which are all valid points, thank you very much—he's leaving after we get the council's approval."

"Doesn't mean you can't have a bit of fun tonight before he leaves."

When Dani turned wide eyes on her, Mia laughed.

"Not *that* kind of fun. But it's okay to go on a date now and again and enjoy yourself."

"What's the point if I know it can't go anywhere?"

"You're such an old lady. Come on! I've only really seen you interact from afar, but there seemed to be a vibe between the two of you. Am I right?"

"It's not like I'd know it if there was. You know I'm horrible at dating."

"Correction. You don't even try at dating."

"I try. Sometimes."

"Mom!" Finn rushed into the kitchen, chocolate smeared on his cheeks. "Maggie bit me!" He pointed to his hand, where there was a glob of slobbery chocolate.

"Ugh." Mia snatched up a rag and wiped off Finn's cheeks and hand like it was an Olympic sport and she was the reigning champion. "Hang on, Dani. Mags!"

Mia and Finn rushed out.

While they were gone, Dani poured cream into her coffee and stuck the lid back on, shoving it back into the recesses of Mia's fridge. Then she reached for the sugar.

"Okay," Mia said as she slid back into the kitchen, "one blind date with some guy in Port Joseph two years ago does not count as dating. Especially when you bailed after like ten minutes."

"How do you do that?"

"Do what?"

"Go back to a conversation like it wasn't just interrupted."

"Practice, cuz. Lots and lots of practice." Mia flashed a wry grin. "Now stop changing the subject and answer me."

"You're bossy." Dani took a sip of her coffee. Hmm. Needed more sugar, even though it was probably too much. But she needed the courage, the extra jolt, if she was going to survive the next few hours. "But fine, I bailed after ten minutes because there wasn't a spark. It would have been a waste of time and money. At least I got out before he had to buy me dinner, right?" She added another teaspoon of sugar from the bowl beside the Keurig. "That was the considerate thing to do since I knew it wasn't going anywhere."

"Dani . . ."

Here we go. "I know what you're going to say. Just don't, okay? I know my standards are high—"

"Try impossible." Mia grabbed herself a donut and plucked off a stray sprinkle. "Not every relationship is going to end like your parents.'"

"I know." And she did. She believed in love. She'd seen it. For other people, like Mia and Troy. "But there's always the possibility that it will. And can I really live with that constant fear?"

"What fear is that, exactly?"

Dani stirred in her sugar. "The fear that loving someone so much will destroy me if the relationship ends." Her voice trembled and lowered as she set the spoon down on the counter. "Look at how vulnerable Dad became when Mom cheated on him. Look at what he *did.*"

"I know that whole situation was really hard for you, Dani, but there was probably so much more to the situation than you realize. Not that it excuses what Aunt Becky did. Or what your dad did afterward." Mia frowned and picked at the sugar coating on the apple fritter in her hand. "But who's to say that the guy you fall for would cheat on you? Does Liam seem like that kind of guy?"

"No." Dani sipped on the hot coffee, let it run down her throat and warm her through. "But Mom didn't seem like that kind of woman either. We were happy once, Mia. Or I thought so. But then Mom's high school sweetheart showed back up on the island—all done up in his fancy attorney suit—and Mom threw that happiness away. The same love that gave us such joy destroyed us all in the end. And I'm just not sure I'm strong enough to survive that kind of destruction again."

"Hey." Mia stepped toward her and grabbed Dani's hand, squeezing. "I'm not saying Liam is the one or anything. Other than cursory introductions, I haven't spent any time with him since we were kids, and I was too young to remember. But you're writing him off just like you've written off every guy who is a remote possibility. And don't you think it's time that you give yourself a chance?"

"Maybe."

Mia narrowed her eyes. "Maybe?" For someone who was four years younger, she sure had the mom look down—and the ability to put Dani in her place.

Dani laughed. "Fine. I'll think about dating again. Someday."

"No day like the present, you know."

"Ha." Dani took a final swig of her coffee, finishing it off with relish. "Today is not one of pleasure, but business. Today is, hopefully, the first step toward bringing Jonathon Island back to life. And maybe, once that's done—

once the economy is thriving and people have made their way back here—maybe *then* I can find time for my own happy ending."

"I only hope by then it's not too late." Mia smiled, something sage and sad in her eyes. "But I do wish you all the luck in the world today. You're feeling good about it?"

"A bit nervous. Okay, a lot nervous. But yeah, I think I've communicated my vision to Liam well enough, and I'm looking forward to seeing what he's going to present."

She could only pray that her mission to get her family back to the island wouldn't fail before it had even really begun.

The moment of truth had arrived.

Dani stepped inside the conference room, which buzzed with energy and movement. Off to one side, red-haired Janine Dirks pushed her glasses up on her nose as she chatted quietly with the ever-stylish Tara Chamberlain, who smiled and tossed her silver-blonde hair over one shoulder. Patrick Kelley sat at the twelve-person table, his thumb scrolling along the screen of his phone. Seb and Martha were in back, Seb grabbing a cup of Joe from the coffee carafe someone had supplied and Martha forking out a sticky bun from a Styrofoam container.

"Good morning, Dani."

She turned, and there was Liam, glancing up from his computer, which was hooked up to the projector. His navy, three-piece suit cut across his shoulders, across his whole figure, somehow emphasizing his muscles without being pretentious. Dani stepped closer to him. "Morning. How are things?" She glanced around him. "Where are the plans you're going to show us today?"

"Since I didn't have all the supplies to prepare a professional presentation board, I scanned the plans in via my phone and uploaded them to a PowerPoint last night."

"Fabulous. And . . ." She bounced on her toes. "And everything's ready to go?"

"We've got this." He winked at her, leaning in just a bit to squeeze her elbow. Good thing Mia wasn't here. She might be able to sense how Dani's heart hitched just a little at the contact. "You just sit back and watch the master at work."

Dani snorted. "The very arrogant master."

"The *charming* master, remember?" He flashed her his dimples as if, yes, he knew how dangerous those things were.

"You all ready to begin?" Seb cleared his throat behind them.

Dani and Liam turned to find the rest of the council seated. Tara's gaze bounced between the two of them thoughtfully, but the rest of the members were either looking at their phones or paying very close attention to their sticky buns and coffee.

"Yes, sir," Liam said.

Dani nodded her agreement and tugged at the bottom of her blouse. For this meeting, she'd worn her nicest blouse and a pair of slacks she'd had to drag from her closet just so she didn't look like a hag next to Mr. Stylish over there.

She glanced down at Uncle Seb, who gave her a smile, but she couldn't help but see the creases in his furrowed brow. Clearly, he was still worried over the fact Dani hadn't been able to convince Liam to show her his plans.

Well. Here went . . . everything.

"Welcome, everyone," she said. "As you know, Seb and I have been working on a plan to revitalize the island's economy, and it starts with the rebuilding of the Grand." Her throat grew thick. This really was momentous. "I've been working with a development company out of Los Angeles that specializes in renovations and rebuilds to draw up a proposal that will both honor our island's legacy and help us move forward into the future. Once we've presented you with the plans, we'll open it up for discussion and questions, and at the end of the meeting, we will vote whether we want to move forward with these plans or not. Majority will rule."

Everyone blinked back at her, expressions neutral. Dani's toes fidgeted in her black flats. "So, without further ado, let me introduce Liam Stone." Turning, she smiled at Liam—and she felt his returning grin to her fingertips. "Liam, take it away."

"Thank you, Dani." Liam grabbed his presentation clicker from the table while Dani slid into the chair farthest from Liam—a good way to view the crowd and their reactions. "I want to thank you all for taking time from your busy schedules to be here. It's been an absolute honor to spend time on your island this past week. I'm sure it comes as no surprise to you that I've been utterly captivated by the beauty of Jonathon Island—especially its hotel."

Oof, he was a charmer, wasn't he?

Janine nodded along, and Martha tucked a piece of her gray-streaked, dark hair behind her ear and leaned forward, her top-heavy frame pressed against the table.

"Now you might be asking, who is this Liam guy and what are his qualifications? And you might be skeptical of me too. I know some were." His gaze flickered to Dani—hopefully quickly enough that nobody else noticed. "But I want you to know that I'm fully qualified to be here and help you. I've got degrees in architecture and business, and over a decade of experience in the field. Here are just a few of the properties I've helped to take from old and worn to shiny and new."

Liam flipped to the first slide of an impressive beachside hotel. Then another and another, each one fancier and more luxurious than the next. Uncle Seb folded his hands on the table and studied them with extreme focus, as did the rest of the council. Janine frowned, but that was to be expected.

None of the properties had the historic glamour of the Grand.

"Now that that's out of the way, let's get to the reason we're all here. The future of your island."

Dani blew out a breath as Liam hit the clicker. An architectural rendering of the rebuilt Grand appeared on the screen—but this was not her family's hotel.

The Grand, a veritable bastion of history, had been transformed into a shining, completely modern shell of what it had been. Liam's drawing had the hotel painted red and gray. Gone were the familiar turrets. The curving terrace. Gone was the long summer porch. In its place were divided, individual porches for each ground-floor room, and a public porch where a hotel outdoor restaurant would now be. In the sketch, a grand staircase led down to an outdoor pool in the shape of Jonathon Island, and there was a whole new addition labeled "villas" abutting a separate pool where the gazebo currently stood.

Her eyes frantically searched the plans, finally seeing the gazebo moved to the waterfront where, sure, people might gain a fabulous view of the lake but would lose all the privacy and quiet currently afforded by the location.

"This is just the outside, of course. I'll get to the inside in a moment. But as you can see"—he mashed the clicker down, and a pinpoint of light appeared on the projector screen—"we've got three pools, one of which is an adults-only spa retreat pool, as well as a new garden, tennis and pickleball courts, a walking path that will strategically take visitors past the state-of-the-art fitness center and spa so as to encourage them to make use of such facilities, and of course, the golf course, which will be expanded from the current nine-hole course to a full eighteen holes."

If she'd been a cartoon character, Dani's jaw would have smashed straight through the desk, maybe even the floor, beneath her. This couldn't be right.

Her gaze swung to Liam, desperate for him to look at her. For him to confirm that he was joking.

He *had* to be joking, right? If not, how could he have gotten it so wrong?

But maybe . . . maybe the inside was better?

He flipped to the next slide and the next—and just . . . no. Dani hadn't blinked, and the dry air stung her eyes, so she rubbed them. Maybe she could somehow clear away what she was seeing. But it was still there.

"The indoors will boast a new and improved foyer, designed to impress and welcome visitors to their luxurious new home. There will be space for three restaurants and a conference center for larger events. What used to be the Grand Pavilion will now be the island's one and only movie theater. And I haven't even gotten to the rooms."

The rooms, at least, he surely wouldn't change. The Grand was known for its unique guest rooms, each one featuring a different style and color scheme, from the wallpaper to the paintings and curtains.

And then Liam flipped to the slide labeled "Accommodations," and when Dani saw a sleek room with black furniture, swanky wall hangings that looked like they belonged in a modern art museum, and lush dark carpet to replace the real wood floors and brightly-patterned carpets that were all part of the Grand's historical charm—she nearly couldn't hold it in any longer.

But Janine beat her to it. "I can't look at this anymore. What is this monstrosity you're showing us?"

Liam stopped talking mid-sentence. "I'm sorry?"

Janine pointed an accusing finger at the screen. "Did you even look at former pictures of the Grand? We never had fancy jet tubs in the bathroom or TVs above the desks. And we certainly never had tacky Andy Warhol paintings. We had Monet or Renoir on the walls—the perfect way for guests to calm themselves at the end of a beautiful day of stepping back in time. What you've done is just ruin the whole effect with your cookie cutter plans that degrade the historical integrity of our island."

Harsh, but Dani couldn't agree more.

"And you." Janine turned and glared at Dani. "You let it happen."

Dani opened her mouth to respond. But what could she say? How could she defend herself?

But the bigger question was—how could Liam have thought *this* was what she'd wanted?

Seb frowned. "Now, Janine—"

"Janine's right." Patrick pointed at the rendering. "That is a very nice hotel, young man. But it does not belong on Jonathon Island. And frankly, Dani, I'm surprised you support this."

"I . . ." The words got stuck in her mouth.

Liam's brow furrowed. "My primary concern here wasn't preserving the history. It was creating a luxury hotel that will be irresistible to the right tourists—the kind who will gladly spend thousands of dollars in your shops and restaurants during their stay." He turned to Dani and looked her purposefully in the eyes. "The kind that will get people back to this island."

Her insides squished together, her stomach bottoming out, and she honestly wondered if she was going to be physically ill. "But at what cost? *This* is not what we discussed."

Liam took a step backward, blinking as if to clear away a

cobweb from his eyes. He glanced at the projector screen, frowning. His jaw ticked tight.

"I, for one, think it's a fabulous hotel." Martha glared at Patrick across the table. "Mr. Stone is right. We need something big and flashy to draw people back to the island, and this is exactly the kind of luxury visitors will be looking for."

Beside her, Tara turned in her seat to look at Martha. "Yes, but nothing about this hotel is special or unique. I'd love to see a hotel that marries the desire to appreciate our past with the recognition that the future is upon us as well."

"That's a very political answer," Martha said. "Which is typical of someone in your position."

Tara's lips pursed.

"I agree with Tara." Patrick stroked his mustache.

"Surprise, surprise." Martha didn't do much to hide her comment under her breath. "You always have to fight me."

"Not everything has to do with you." Patrick shot her a glare. "It's very reasonable to ask to see plans that are more in line with history. That place is unrecognizable."

"Hear, hear." Janine rapped her knuckles on the table as if she held a gavel. "I am all for bringing our economy back to acceptable standards, but not if it means compromising our morals."

"Oh, please." Martha rolled her eyes. "There's nothing immoral about Mr. Stone's drawing."

"I most certainly think there is—"

"Ladies, please." Uncle Seb held up his hands. "Calm down, everyone. I know you are all very passionate about our home, but Mr. Stone has done great work here, especially given his background."

How could Uncle Seb say that? Was he just being nice? Then again, there was a certain gleam in his eye, one Dani almost didn't recognize. Mia sometimes talked about Uncle Seb's fast-paced job as a lawyer back in the day. About how ruthless she'd heard he could be. At the end of the day, he was a businessman first. It made sense that he would be all in favor of "progress"—if that's what this could even be called.

If it were up to her, Dani would call it *murder*. Hotel-cide. History-cide. That was a thing, right?

"Dani, you've been awfully quiet." Uncle Seb patted her arm, and she jumped. "Any questions for Mr. Stone here?"

Her gaze met Liam's. His was full of questions.

She sighed. Maybe he meant well, but in the end, he was just an outsider. How could she expect him to understand what this meant to them all?

Still, she couldn't stand to see her family's legacy reduced to *this*. And her brothers and sisters would never in a million years come back for a hotel like the one in the rendering. Certainly her father wouldn't. As far as they were concerned, this would only serve to put her family legacy in the ground once and for all.

"No questions." She felt everyone's eyes on her. "Just . . . I'm sorry, everyone." What else could she say? In the end, it was her fault for relying on someone so different, with different values, from a different world for help.

"No need to apologize, Dani," Uncle Seb said, the compassion—and maybe pity—clear in his eyes. "Look, everyone, it's clear we don't agree on this plan, so what we're going to do is take a breather and revisit things next week. How's next Monday?" He studied each person, waiting for their nods. "Meeting adjourned. See you all then."

His words were the death knell to all of Dani's dreams. Because there was no way to find a new developer to create plans by next week.

And Liam wasn't the man for the job after all.

Seven

HE'D NEVER FAILED THIS EPICALLY before in his life.

Maybe personally—first with Mom, then with Tiffany. But professionally?

How had he read the situation so wrong?

As Martha, Tara, Janine, and Patrick gathered their belongings and shuffled out the door with a little chitchat, Liam ran a hand through his hair and blew out a breath. Looked at Seb. "I don't know what to say. Or how this happened."

"I was afraid something like this might happen." Seb folded his hands, his expensive watch gleaming under the conference room's fluorescent lights. "It's not your fault, son. You were set up to fail by experience alone."

"But this has never happened to me before." He needed to unhook his laptop and get to work again on the plans, but all he could do was stand there, frozen. His eyes darted to Dani, who stared at the table, unmoving.

Clearing his throat, he moved to her side of the table, slid into the seat beside her. "Dani . . ."

Her gaze darted up to his like she was startled by his presence. Then her eyes narrowed. "What *was* that, Liam?"

"That was my best attempt at getting you what you wanted."

"What I want . . ." She trailed off, huffing and pushing away from the desk. Standing. "Liam, did you listen to me at all? This entire week, I've been telling you story after story about that place, trying to bring you into something special, to show you that Jonathon Island is different. But you still don't get it. And how could you?"

He tried not to wince at her words. As she began to walk toward the front of the room, he followed. "I *do* get it, Dani."

She whirled to look at him, folding her arms across her chest.

He continued. "I know how important this is to you. That's why I worked so hard on upping my game on this hotel. I created somewhere that I *know* people will want to come—a place people will want to spend time and lose themselves—just like you asked me to."

Dani studied him for a moment, then sighed. "It's not your fault, Liam. It's mine. Regardless of your process, I should have insisted on seeing those plans before the meeting like Uncle Seb wanted."

Speaking of Seb, he was now in the back of the room,

cleaning up the coffee and snacks—or pretending to, any-way.

Liam took a step closer, lowering his voice. "Come on, Dani. I still don't understand what's wrong with the plans I created."

"And that is precisely the problem." Dani stepped away, shaking her head. "Goodbye, Liam. Thanks for trying, but I just don't think this is going to work."

"Wait." Now she'd just plain insulted him. "You're just going to give this up without seeing if we can fix it?"

"I think my dad may have been right." Her shoulders sank. "Some things just can't be fixed." Then she turned and left.

And despite Seb messing around in the back, the room felt empty without her.

She'd released him.

He'd done what he came here to do, all that Dad had demanded—his best for the client. Even if that wasn't enough.

Liam should be happy.

Instead, he rubbed a hand over his sternum.

"Don't worry, son." Seb walked over, his voice breaking into Liam's thoughts. "She'll be all right."

"I'm not so sure about that. She's really upset." Liam moved to the computer setup. Shut the lid. Pulled out the cord connecting it to the projector.

Now what?

Liam looked at the ceiling for a moment, contemplat-ing his words. "It sounds like she's ready to be done with me. With this project."

Leaning against the table facing Liam, Seb unbuttoned his shirt sleeve and rolled it up to his elbow. First one, then the other. "Son, the thing you need to know about Dani is that she lives and breathes this island. This whole thing was her idea."

"I knew that. She's clearly passionate about the rebuild, about this town. I didn't understand at first how much was riding on this, but once I did, I slaved away at the plans. I tweaked and restarted. I even got advice from a few colleagues of mine, which I never do. But I wanted it to be perfect."

For her. And not just because she was a client.

Because she was . . . Dani.

The realization hit.

Oh man, he liked her. How had he let *that* happen?

Liam loosened his tie. "Anyway, I really thought I'd nailed it. Clearly, I was wrong."

Seb considered him before nodding at the now-blank projector screen. "I actually think you did a bang-up job. I love the facelift you gave the hotel, including the addition of the villas and the more modern lobby. But that hotel doesn't mean as much to me personally, and Dani's got a whole host of memories tied up in that place, in growing up there. If Dani's motivations are what I suspect—to get her siblings all back here—the way to do that isn't to change the offering. It's to remind them of what they've given up."

"That makes sense. But given your understanding of today's tourists and their expectations, do you really think that building an exact replica of the past would be as successful as what I've designed? Because as much as I want to please Dani and the entire council, they aren't my only concern."

"I know. Your father has staked a lot on this project. I respect that you want to create plans that are going to speak well of your company."

"I'm glad you understand. I wish Dani did too."

"Maybe you can get her to come around. And I think with a few tweaks, Tara and Patrick could probably be persuaded to approve your plans. Janine is likely a lost cause."

"I figured that too." Liam paused. "So you agree that for the most part, my plans would be successful here?"

Seb stroked his fingers along his smooth chin. "As popular as the Grand was in its heyday, there were always travelers looking for the latest amenities. I mean, the rooms didn't even have a television, and some guests loved that. Others didn't. Some wanted a spa to relax in. Room service. A private porch they didn't have to share with their neighbors."

"So . . ." What was Seb getting at?

"So, do I think sticking with the old will have as much success or even fetch the kind of price that a more modern version would—especially if Daniel Sullivan decides he doesn't want to buy it back after all? And that's always a risk, knowing that man and his hot-headed temper." Seb paused. "No, I don't."

"I don't either." And that would mean Liam's dad would be out a significant amount of money when it came time to sell the property.

It was quite possible that going the way that Dani might

want things to go would result in a huge risk. And for what? He loved history as much as the next person, but preserving it didn't always pay the bills.

"What can I do? Dani pretty much told me things were over."

Which should be fine if only there wasn't that internal tug, that desire that had only grown through Liam's little bit of time with her. The desire to help her. And according to Dad, Stone Development was Jonathon Island's only hope for getting this project accomplished.

"Guess you've got to convince her otherwise." Seb stood again, snatching his cell phone and stuffing it into the clip on his belt. "You always were a charmer, Liam, even as a little tyke. Find a way to show her that modern doesn't have to be the enemy."

After gathering the last coffee carafe, Seb walked out of the conference room, leaving Liam in the silence that buzzed with the white noise of the heater whirring in the background. How was he supposed to show Dani something modern while they were in this town that oozed history and everything she was familiar with?

An idea came to him, so sudden he almost wondered if it was divinely inspired. But was it too big a risk? Maybe it was better to just walk away.

Then again, he'd never know if he didn't just try.

Pulling his cell phone from inside his jacket, Liam dialed the Los Angeles office.

"Stone Development, this is Marianne speaking. How may I direct your call?"

"Mare, it's me."

"Well, hi, shoogs. How ya doin'?" The sounds of keyboard typing filled the phone receiver. "We haven't heard hide nor hair of you in a few days."

"I'm okay. Having a little bit of difficulty convincing this client to go the more modern route." He paused. "Is Douglas Kutcher still giving Dad grief in Minneapolis?"

"Yes, in fact. He just called again this morning, but your dad's been in meetings all day. Why?" she asked. "Surely you aren't calling to get the scoop on that when you're knee deep in problems yourself."

"I actually thought that maybe I could kill two birds with one stone. You willing to help me?"

"Are grits the most delicious breakfast food known to man?" At Liam's pause, she chuckled. "Yes, sugar. The answer is yes. Anything. How can I help?"

Maybe she should just face the inevitable.

Getting the Sullivans back to Jonathon Island wasn't in the cards.

"Are you sure there isn't anything I can do to help, Aunt Elise?" Dani dragged a chip through a bowl of guacamole on Uncle Seb and Aunt Elise's butcher block island counter, which was spread with a full-on Mexican food feast, including chicken enchiladas, homemade refried beans, and flour tortillas. The smell of taco meat rent the air, spicy and full-bodied. It was Dani's favorite meal.

But not even that could cheer her up tonight.

"No, dear, thank you." From her spot standing at the stove, Aunt Elise pushed a spatula through the ground beef as it sizzled in a skillet. Even though she'd been cooking and probably cleaning for the last hour or so, she looked as put together as always in her beige slacks and powder blue sweater, her dark bobbed hair coifed without a strand out of place. "The girls and I have it handled."

Dani's family bustled all around her—her fifteen-year-old cousin Nora setting the table, Mia washing lettuce, Uncle Seb in and out grabbing fajita meat to toss on the Traeger, and her oldest cousin Evie chopping tomatoes.

Dani's fingers itched to do more than snatch chips. "Seriously. After the day I've had, I'm happy to do anything to get my mind off things."

"What happened today?" Evie piped up from the other side of the island. Tonight she wore a silky purple jewel-neck tee that, paired with her shoulder-length dark hair, somehow made her look elegant and older than her thirty-two years.

"The town council met to approve plans for the Grand Hotel rebuild." Dani made a face. "Or rather, to not approve the plans."

"Oh, that was today? The whole thing is so exciting." Evie—who had worked at the hotel years ago, before it closed—brought the knife down on the tomatoes. "But I'm sorry the meeting didn't go well."

Mia shook out the lettuce and patted it with a paper towel. "How'd you even know about it, Evie? This is only your second time back on island this year since the ferry started up again."

Evie's banker husband Kyle Munson worked in Port Joseph, the small town across Lake Huron, so they'd lived there for much of their nine-year marriage. But Evie eventually wanted to purchase a home right up the road from the ancestral Jonathon estate located on the northern tip of the island. And who could blame her? With its sweeping lawn that overlooked the lake, huge porch with a handful of Adirondack chairs, and enough space for them all to gather every week, it was an ideal place to raise kids.

"I still keep up with local chatter, sister dearest." Evie hip bumped Mia. "Everyone's been all abuzz about the new guy in town. Is he really as handsome as they say? What's he like?"

Mia grabbed a glass bowl from one of the paneled green cabinets and moved back to work beside Evie. "You should ask Dani about that. She's spent the most time with him."

Oh brother. "I don't—"

Thankfully, Finn chose that moment to sweep through the crowded kitchen making airplane noises, and Evie's five-year-old Cora chased after him along with Maggie, who dragged one of Evie's old Cabbage Patch dolls behind her.

"Chloe! Chase! Come play with the littles, please," Evie called toward the den, where her eight-year-old twins were watching television, enjoying the beginning of their spring break.

But the ragtag group headed out the back door all on their own, leaving the adults in relative peace again—for now.

"Don't you remember Liam Stone from our visit to California when you were a teenager?" Aunt Elise asked, continuing the conversation as if nothing had happened.

"He and his family came out several times to visit us in New York too."

"I remember some scrawny kid running around playing with swords. Was that him?" Evie asked.

"It was. And I believe he's grown into quite the handsome young man."

"Gross, Mom." Nora spoke up from the dining room. She stuck her head fully into the kitchen and scrunched her face, accentuating her freckles, one last plate in her hand. "He's like, half your age."

Mia tsked at her younger sister. "Just because she's old doesn't mean she doesn't have eyes."

"Who are you calling old?" Aunt Elise came after Mia with the dirty spatula.

Laughing, Mia hid behind Evie, who just kept chopping tomatoes as calm as could be. Not surprising, as she was used to three kids and their crazy antics.

"You're not old, Mom," Evie said. "Just oh so wise."

Dani sighed. She missed this in her own family. Missed feeling a part of it. It wasn't their fault—the Jonathons always did their best to include her. It was just something in her own soul.

"That was a very loud exhale." Aunt Elise flipped off the stovetop burner and moved the skillet of taco meat to another before covering it with a lid. Then she turned and slipped into the seat beside Dani. "I'm sorry the meeting didn't go your way."

"What happened, exactly? You said Liam was working hard on the plans." Using a cutting board and lettuce knife,

Mia started in on the lettuce, cutting willy nilly, unlike Evie's perfectly proportioned tomato slices.

Dani reached for another chip and dipped it in the guac. "Liam's proposed plans for the hotel weren't exactly what I'd pictured." She bit into the chip, the crunch filling the sudden silence of the kitchen. "And by that, I mean he proposed something completely new and modern—it was nothing like what the Grand ought to be. The man somehow managed to remove every ounce of historic charm and replace it with cold sterility."

Mia groaned. "How frustrating."

"I agree." Aunt Elise tucked her hair behind her ear. "But your uncle seems to think a hotel like that would make the island a lot more money."

"He said that?"

"Mmm hmm. But I told him that some things are worth more than money."

"Yeah, but money's nice to have," Evie said, finishing with the tomatoes and scraping them into a bowl, which she positioned between the olives and shredded cheese. "Still, I get why you're upset, Dani. Some people just don't understand the draw of history that makes the island special."

"I tried telling Liam." Dani sat back and tugged her hair up into a ponytail, fastening it with a hairband that had been on her wrist. "He just didn't get it, I guess."

"It's too bad that young man didn't get to see the island at the height of its popularity," Aunt Elise said, her expression dreamy and far off. "All the charm of it, with the summer storefronts open, the walking tours, the smell of fudge as you walked down Main Street. Some things just need to be experienced."

They all smiled, remembering.

"It's charming even in the spring though." Mia set down her knife. "So many lovely and romantic spots. Troy used to take me to . . ." She trailed off, frowned, cleared her throat. "Anyway. The point is, even now, a shell of what it was, Jonathon Island is still the most enchanting place in the world. A big fancy hotel would ruin that."

"It would, wouldn't it? And my brothers and sisters would never come back to run a hotel like that." Oops. Had she said that out loud?

"Is that your goal?" Evie sounded surprised. "I thought you merely wanted to revitalize the economy."

"I do. But . . ."

"That's a pretty tall order, dear." Aunt Elise patted Dani's knee.

"I know that. I do. But if anything would get them back here, it's a rebuilt hotel. James would be the first one to return. You know he always dreamed of running the hotel someday."

"All things are possible with God. But there's a lot of hurt here for your siblings. Do you think it's realistic to place all of your hopes in them returning?"

"I just want us to be a family again."

"You can be a family even if you aren't all in one place." Aunt Elise dropped her voice. "But even being five miles from someone doesn't mean anything unless people are willing to forgive."

As if sensing their need to be alone, Evie and Mia finished up their tasks and headed out the back door to check on their dad and the kids.

"You're talking about Mom, aren't you?"

Another squeeze to her knee. "You say you want family back, but you aren't willing to try with the one member of your immediate family who *is* close by and *wants* to be here."

"If that's true, then where is she?"

"You know where. The same place she's been. Waiting."

Dani sighed and opened her mouth to respond, but her phone vibrated on the counter in front of her. She frowned when she saw Liam's name pop up on the screen. "What does *he* want?"

"To talk, I imagine." There was amusement in Aunt Elise's tone.

"About what? I told him the project was done."

"Guess you won't know unless you answer." Standing, Aunt Elise headed for the back door too. "Hey, all! About time to eat!"

Dani should just ignore the call but then she'd spend all evening wondering. Ugh. Fine. "Hello? Liam?" She headed for the front porch.

"Hey, Dani. Do you have a minute to talk?"

Once outside, she leaned against one of the porch posts, where a flowerpot hung just overhead. Right now, the plant inside sat dormant, but come summertime, it would bloom into something beautiful.

"Okay." A breeze filtered in off the lake, and she shivered. It may have been warmer than usual lately, but it was still chilly when the sun went down. "Go ahead."

"Thanks." Liam cleared his throat. "I've been figuring some things out all day. And frankly, working up the nerve to call."

"I figured you'd be long gone by now."

"Then you don't know me very well."

"I guess not."

"That's not . . ." He groaned. "Look, I know we've hit a snag. But I think there's still a chance we can fix this."

"Are you saying you're willing to redo the plans?"

"I'm not going to say no to that, because it wouldn't be fair in light of what I'm asking of you."

"And what's that?"

"I want you to take a trip. With me. Tomorrow."

"What?" Was he asking her out? "That's not what I expected you to say."

"Let me explain. I have a client meeting at one of our luxury hotel projects in Minneapolis. I thought I could show you around. Maybe explain my vision for a modern hotel a little better?"

Oh. "But I don't *want* your vision." She pressed her lips together, making sure to school her tone into something professional. Because despite what she'd thought, she and Liam weren't becoming friends. They were colleagues— colleagues with different opinions. But she was the client, and wasn't the client always right? "Why can't you just draw up the plans for the hotel the way I see them?"

"Because as I've told you, my company has a lot at stake here too. And two of the five people at that table today loved the plan I presented. They—and I—believe it would be in the best financial and economic interest of the town to go the more modern direction."

"You need a majority though."

"Seb thinks with a few tweaks, Patrick and Tara can be convinced to approve my plan."

And then Dani would lose all control over the project that was hers to begin with.

Unacceptable.

Her left hand formed a fist, but she released it slowly along with a breath. "Let me make sure I have this right. You want me to come to Minneapolis so you can convince me that modern is the way to go?"

"Essentially, yeah. My secretary booked us flights for tomorrow. But if you don't feel comfortable with that, I understand. I just thought it would be a good way to show you my perspective instead of trying to explain it with words."

"You have a lot of nerve after what happened at that meeting. Maybe it's just best to let this whole thing go."

"Is that really what you want? I thought I was the only developer even willing to touch this project."

She frowned. "Maybe Uncle Seb didn't look hard enough."

He sighed. "Look, Dani. I'm not asking for a commitment here. I'm just asking for you to give this one more shot. Let me show you what I do—what I can really do, if you give me a chance—and if you want to can the project after that, fine."

"Why are you doing this? I got the impression that

you'd gladly wash your hands of this project and walk away because it was too risky to your bottom line."

It was a moment before he answered. "To be honest, Dani, I'm asking myself the same question. But basically, it comes down to the fact that I promised my dad—and I promised you. There's a disconnect somewhere between us, and I want to see if it's possible to bridge the gap."

"You mean bring me over to your side."

"If you want to phrase it like that, fine."

"What if I want to bring you over to my side instead?" Now, hey, there was an idea. What had Aunt Elise said? *It's too bad that young man didn't get to see the island at the height of its popularity. Some things just need to be experienced.*

That was it. Just like Liam wanted to show her his perspective, she wanted to show him hers. And it went so far beyond the hotel—which wasn't a true assessment of Jonathon Island, being half burned like it was.

She had to show him *more.*

And if she could convince an outsider like Liam Stone to love and cherish this place, then maybe her dreams really were possible.

It was her last real chance to find out.

"I'll go, on one condition."

"And what's that?"

"I'll go with you if you come back to the island with me afterward and let me show you *my* perspective, my island in a way you haven't seen it before. After our little drive through town and the tour of the hotel, you got right to work on your plans, but there is still so much to show you.

So I'll give you a chance to convince me, but only if you let *me* have a chance to convince *you*."

"Do you think you can keep an open mind about what I show you?"

Dani hesitated. Could she? But it was only fair if she expected the same of him. "If you will."

"Good then. It's a deal. May the best convincer win."

Eight

DANI HAD NEVER FELT SO COMPLETELY small-town in her whole life.

Minneapolis traffic raced by at her back while she craned her neck upward, taking in the sleek building towering over her, its multiple rows and columns of tall windows creating a prism reflecting the noonday sun. Bright blue and white in color, the hotel seemed to take up the entire skyline, bold and sure of its place in the world. An enclosed pedestrian footbridge shot out from the hotel's second level, traveling over the intersection and connecting to the building across the way.

"Well?" Once again, Liam wore a three-piece suit under his coat, this one gray and slim fitting. He looked every bit the city dweller and completely comfortable with navigating around, unlike Dani who hadn't even known where to go to grab a taxi when they'd landed at the airport. "What do you think?"

What *did* she think? Of course it didn't compare with the feelings she had for the Grand, but how much of those were wrapped up in her memories, her love of the place where it resided? If she studied the Lucian Hotel on its own, no comparisons to be made, she had to admit it was beautiful in its own right. And there was something attractive about the idea of staying at a modern hotel dripping with such prestige.

But she couldn't let Liam know she was impressed. Not yet, at least. Besides, she hadn't even seen the interior yet. Maybe it was dumpy—a case of something being flashy on the outside but rotten on the inside.

Fine, it wasn't likely. But a girl could hope. Especially a girl who hated to be wrong.

She lifted her eyebrows. "That remains to be seen."

"Ah, a tough nut to crack." He pretended to pop his knuckles and move his neck from side to side. "Challenge accepted."

She wanted to laugh as he strode forward and held open the door for her and said, "After you, milady," but she refused to let Liam's charm get to her. This was a business meeting, nothing more.

"Thank you." She wheeled her suitcase through the doorway then pulled it alongside her and stopped just inside the lobby, which was massive.

The reception desks were along one wall behind a granite waterfall counter. Two attendants stood there, and a concierge in a suit stood at the side. Elevators extended all the way up in gold from the main area, and three stories up drifted two massive chandeliers, their tear-drop crystals glittering with light against the gold accents of the room.

The floor was travertine, but massive Turkish carpets covered the lobby area upon which sat deep blue velvet sofas in groupings around glass tables with gold legs. On each table sat a gold vase filled with a spray of fresh flowers: roses, hydrangeas, fuchsia, freesia, and white lilies. Smooth jazz played from the speakers in the room, softly lending an ambiance of ease along with the fresh fragrance of the flowers.

At the sound of trickling water, Dani searched and found a giant waterfall running down the wall at least two stories high, gentle and dropping softly into a pool of water covered with lily pads.

She'd stepped into paradise.

Wow. "How much does your company have to do with the decorating once the hotel is built?"

They walked toward the desk and stopped behind an elderly couple being helped by the only receptionist.

"I help advise on the decor once the building is complete, but just like the building itself, I don't get the final say." He cleared his throat. "Normally, that is."

Right. Because the deal with the Grand was different. The stakes were high for both of them. That's why she was here, after all. To keep an open mind.

But there was one thing she was confused about. "I thought this property was under renovation."

"We're doing a section of it at a time, and all of it is complete except for the back corner. We've tried to minimize the disruption to guests and events so the hotel doesn't lose as much money as it would if it was shut down completely. In fact, that's what I'm thinking we'd do with the Grand once we begin. Renovate in stages, one wing at a time, so we can begin opening it sooner."

Dani swallowed. Of course, they'd discussed the timeline before, but to see it lived out here, in person, was remarkable. They'd done a fabulous job of ensuring guests weren't disturbed by the work going on somewhere upstairs.

She tapped her fingers along the extended handle of her suitcase and allowed her gaze to wander. She'd missed the bar when she first walked in and now saw it tucked away around the bank of elevators. A long leather bar top stretched along one wall, and small groupings of golden chairs held guests of the hotel—clearly guests that had a lot more money than the people that visited Jonathon Island. Or maybe Jonathon Island was just used to a certain type of tourist.

These people were businessmen and women dressed in suits and dresses and heels. She suddenly felt a little bit dowdy in her jeans, tennis shoes, and sweater. Piano music lifted from the bar, and she spotted a baby grand with a couple of circular sofas surrounding it. A man in a tuxedo played "Piano Man" for the crowd, many of whom were drinking wine, a few singing along. Another group sat in front of a crackling hearth on a leather sofa—epitomizing both opulence and coziness.

Much as she hated to admit it, Liam's team knew what they were doing.

For Minneapolis, at least. Not for Jonathon Island.

"Okay, so *now* what do you think?"

"It's lovely. Exquisite, even."

Liam smiled. "I'm glad you think so."

"I do. But that doesn't mean I think this type of treatment is right for the Grand. Our clientele is different."

"Is it really, though? Aren't the people who visit your island looking for the same thing as those who visit this hotel? Rest, rejuvenation, relaxation . . ."

"But look at all the business travelers."

"You know who spends a lot of money?" Liam angled her shoulders toward the bar and pointed. "Those kinds of people. And with the conference center I proposed building on to the hotel near the ballroom, your hotel could host business travelers too."

Huh. "I hadn't thought of that."

"You're thinking about what the Grand means to you, all the memories wrapped up in it, right?"

"What's wrong with that?"

"Nothing. I just want to expand your horizons. To show you that sure, you can have the tourists who come to step back in time, but most tourists overall want the same thing—an unforgettable experience where they're treated well and pampered."

"But all of this"—she waved her hand around the room—"is still so modern. It's opulent in a way that makes you feel like you should be wearing a fancy dress or suit just to fit in."

"The old-timey pictures of the Grand show people pretty dressed up too."

"That's because there was a dress code after six p.m."

Dani smiled at the memory of Mom forcing her into her Sunday best to join Dad at the hotel for dinner. "But the style of the Grand is a lot brighter than this. Where are marble black-and-white checkered floors adorned with crimson and lime-green floral rugs, the average-height ceilings that make you feel tucked in and safe? The white pillars throughout the lower level, the gorgeous wainscoting and custom crown molding? You can't see those details when the ceiling is so high. And it's hard to feel welcome in a place that overwhelms you."

"Even if it's overwhelming you with awe?"

"Even then."

Liam pursed his lips together and studied her. "I'm trying to understand here, okay? But you promised me you'd open your mind too."

"You're right. I'm not trying to complain." She pivoted, now facing the reception desk again. "It really is a beautiful hotel, Liam. And you've done a great job here."

"Wow. Two compliments in the span of a few minutes. Now was that so hard?" He elbowed her playfully and smiled at her with those boyish dimples, tucking his hand into the pocket of his slim-cut gray suit.

He looked at her expectantly, as if waiting for a reply. But much as Dani wanted to joke right back with him, she still didn't know how much she could really trust Mr. Handsome. Being in his world only served to show her how much *this* wasn't her.

But it was Liam.

It was no wonder he'd drawn the plans he had. Of *course* he had.

"Dani? What's wrong?" Gone was the teasing, and in its place was concern. Real and true and genuine.

But she couldn't allow that to cloud her judgment. "I'm fine." Dani's chest loosened as the older couple in front of them finally moved on from the desk, and the receptionist waved her and Liam forward. "Oh, look. It's our turn to check in."

Liam greeted the receptionist with a warm smile. "Hi"—he glanced at her name tag—"Stacy. I'm Liam Stone and this is Dani Sullivan, checking in for the night. I've got a meeting with Mr. Kutcher this afternoon if you could tell him I've arrived."

Stacy, a twenty-something with her blonde hair pulled back into a flawless, tight ponytail, seemed to straighten in her chair. "Hello, Mr. Stone. It's a pleasure to finally meet you." Even the collar of Stacy's white uniform blouse sat starched and crisp at Liam's attention. "Mr. Kutcher got called into a meeting and wanted me to let you know he won't be available until three. But I've got your rooms all ready for you, and of course, there is the pool, the spa, and the restaurant open for your relaxation and enjoyment."

Her eyes flitted first to Dani then down the length of her and back up. At least from here, she shouldn't be able to see Dani's Converse sneakers. Oh, why hadn't she thought to wear something business casual at least? It's not like she didn't have the outfits—she just didn't have much occasion to wear slacks and nice blouses on the island.

"Thank you for your help, Stacy. We are so appreciative."

"Of course." Stacy moved her gaze back to Liam, who

waited patiently for their room keys. She scanned them through the system and handed them over. "There. I got you both moved to the best suites available, Mr. Stone. Yours is on the ninth floor, and Ms. Sullivan's is on the sixth. And you'll each find a bottle of complimentary wine in your room to say thank you for visiting."

"That's very kind of you," Dani said.

Stacy pulled a map of the hotel onto the counter and circled a room with her pen. "Here's your room, Ms. Sullivan. Just take the main elevator to the sixth floor and follow the signs. It'll be at the end of the hall. And Mr. Stone—"

"I know the way, Stacy." He slipped a twenty-dollar bill across the counter. "Thanks again for your assistance. Who do I talk to about making a dinner reservation?"

Stacy beamed. "Normally the concierge, but I'm more than happy to do that for you. What time?"

Liam glanced at Dani, who shrugged. This was his show. And, much as she hated to be impressed, he was quite good at it.

"Let's say six."

"Sounds great," Stacy said.

"Thanks again, Stacy." Liam grabbed the handle of his suitcase. "Ready to go?"

"Sure."

They wheeled their suitcases toward the elevator, which allowed a view of the lobby as they ascended to the sixth floor. When they stepped out, even the hallway smelled luxurious, like eucalyptus and lavender, and the plush carpet must have been twice as thick as that of her apartment. Dani was halfway tempted to kick off her sneakers and walk barefoot, but managed to hold off as they approached Room 628.

"You didn't have to walk me to my room, you know."

"I didn't mind. Do you want to drop our stuff and grab some lunch?" Liam leaned against the wall. "I have some time before my meeting, though I do need to go over my notes and check in with the office."

A yawn popped out before she could stop it. They'd gotten up quite early and taken two different flights to get here.

"On second thought"—he smiled—"why don't you take a nap? Order room service. You work so hard. Take the time to relax a bit."

"Room service is expensive. And some of us can't afford fancy food." She ran her hand down the length of her body. "Or, clearly, fancy clothes."

"Fancy clothes are overrated. If I could just wear joggers and T-shirts all the time, I totally would."

"I call false on that one. I've never seen you in anything but a suit."

"You're right. I even sleep in them."

"Ha ha, funny man." She rolled her eyes.

"And as for 'fancy food'"—he used air quotes—"the hotel will comp any food we eat while here, so live it up. I want you to get the full picture of the good life."

Ah, now she understood. Dani crossed her arms. "The Grand had room service too, you know." Sure, it was only available on the weekends and during limited hours, but it had been there all the same.

"Good for them." Liam eased himself off the wall. "Seriously, Dani. This isn't about convincing you of anything. I really just want you to enjoy your time here. You deserve a break just like anyone else. And a nap."

His words were sweet, but could she trust them? "I'm here to work, same as you."

He frowned, then nodded. "Rest up for our meeting, then. We'll do dinner and then I'll give you the grand tour. There's so much I want to show you." He glanced at his watch. "Since dinner's at six, how about I swing by here around five forty-five?"

If this had been any other situation, she'd be tempted to say "it's a date" in reply. But tonight was about so much more than a date. She just had to get through his tour, and they'd be able to return to Jonathon Island—where she could give him a tour of her own.

Dani smiled at the thought. "Five forty-five works. See you then."

Normally after a client meeting, Liam was exhausted. He'd head "home" to whatever hotel room he was living in, order room service, and turn on baseball or basketball or whatever sport was on and drown out the loneliness with a cheeseburger and a Coke.

But despite the rather poor reception he'd been given by Douglas Kutcher—and all the ways he'd been forced to grovel and soothe away the guy's worries about the project's timeline—Liam found himself energized tonight.

And it all was because of Dani.

"And this"—he swept his hand in a grand motion around the hotel's enclosed courtyard—"concludes the tour."

She snuggled deeper into her white jacket, which she wore over a casual dress and leggings, her hair down and curled. Though she hadn't been half as dressed up as others eating dinner in the hotel's steakhouse, Liam never would have noticed if she hadn't pointed it out.

Because to him, she was perfect.

Not that it mattered. Though he hadn't meant to, he'd broken trust with her. Trust he desperately wanted to rebuild—for their partnership's sake. Maybe their friendship's too.

He was in no position to give her more than that anyway.

Dani's eyes swept the courtyard, which was strung with thousands of lights. They hung and burned brighter than the stars above, which twinkled just enough to show themselves. No, it wasn't the view that Jonathon Island afforded, but for a big-city sky, the inky jewel-studded backdrop was still a beautiful one.

"It really is pretty." Dani and Liam walked along the stone pathway that cut through the courtyard and veered off in various directions—one toward an open firepit lined with padded couches and chairs, one toward a bank of rooms, another toward a stone fountain that stood in the very center.

"That's all you have to say?" he teased.

All evening, from the time he'd picked her up at her room and taken her to dinner until now, she'd been fairly quiet, taking it all in. He'd tried to rein in his enthusiasm as he'd shown her the spa, the ballrooms, the penthouse suite—which was undergoing renovation but was almost complete—and all of the other amenities that had the Stone stamp all over it. Before they'd started the renovations, this hotel had been nice but nothing special. But now? Rooms sold quickly and at a premium. He was proud of that fact, if only because the Stone name meant something.

"What do you want me to say?" She smiled, but there was something a bit adrift in it as she lowered herself onto the edge of the fountain and leaned over to dip her fingertips in. A shiver coursed through her body, and she quickly flicked the excess water away and stuffed her hand back into her jacket pocket. "Yes, it's lovely, and I can see why so many people love it here."

He sat down beside her. The cold stone pressed through his slacks, and he had to hold in a shiver himself. "But you don't?"

"It's not that. My room is really comfortable and relaxing. I love the huge bathroom and tub. The down comforter is really something. But the whole place is so . . . big. So much."

"In what way?"

"I don't know. Like, the television, I guess." She moved her hand through the air. "The rooms at the Grand never even had televisions, and the ones here take up half the wall space."

"Well, I did advise against such large screens, but Douglas insisted on going bigger than his competitors. Still, people come here to relax, to indulge, to treat themselves to things they never would at home."

She lifted an eyebrow. "And that can be accomplished with introspection. The chance to escape from reality. How can they do that with so much to distract them? The Grand always had a lot of spaces for that introspection. The gazebo, the community porch, the walking path around the golf course, benches along the grassy bluff. Space to just sit and breathe in the relaxation." And then she smiled for real, at the memories, he presumed. "*That's* what a vacation should be."

He didn't disagree, not completely, but was she seriously suggesting they provide hotel rooms without the latest, and most basic, amenities? "Times have changed. Some people would go crazy without technology to distract them."

She pursed her lips and looked at him sidelong. "*Some* people?"

He heard what she didn't say—*or you*? Standing again, he offered her a hand up. "I'm just saying we need to allow for differences. If you want to attract a broader clientele back to the island, you need to think bigger than how things used to be."

She considered him a moment before taking his hand and joining him in standing. Electric currents pulsed through his fingertips for the few seconds before she dropped from his hold. "We'll have to agree to disagree on that. Or maybe I'll just have to convince you."

"You'll have your chance, but right now, it's my turn—

and I've got one more place to show you." And if they didn't hurry, it would be closed.

Dani gestured down the path toward the hotel entrance. "Lead on."

With a wink, he took her through the doors and down a hallway toward his favorite place in the entire hotel.

Dani's eyes widened when he held the door open to her. "An ice cream parlor?"

"Yep." They stepped into Donna's Delights, where only a few patrons currently took advantage of the warmth inside the 1950s-style shoppe with its high-class red booths, checkered floors, and gleaming black tabletops. Behind the counter, a twenty-something woman greeted them and offered them samples of a dozen different flavors. "The peanut butter pretzel is my personal favorite," he said.

"Sounds amazing. I'll try that one, please."

The woman handed Dani a tiny spoon containing some of the creamy delicacy, and Liam couldn't help the dryness in his throat as he watched her take it between her lips, close her eyes, and sigh. "Oh my goodness, that's amazing. I will definitely have one of those, please."

"Make it two, but I'll take mine in a waffle cone."

"Right away, Mr. Stone." The woman set to work getting their ice cream served up, and within minutes, they were tucked away in a corner booth.

Somewhere above them, a speaker played an Elvis Presley ballad.

"I'm not sure I've ever had ice cream in April." Dani dipped her spoon into her cup and held it up, as if examining it from every angle. "But I'm highly in favor."

"You and my mom both." Liam licked his cone, the bits of chocolate finding the sweet spots on his tongue. "She always said ice cream should be a year-round thing."

"Sounds like my kind of woman." Dani cocked her head. "Her name wouldn't happen to have been Donna, would it?"

How had she figured it out? Liam stared at every ridge of the cone. "Every hotel we renovate gets a Donna's Delights. It's part of our normal contract. Kind of our signature thing. Of course, our contract for the Grand is a bit outside the norm, so no worries about being forced to add one."

"I'm not worried." Dani reached across the table and placed her hand on his forearm. Squeezed. "I think it's amazing that you've found such a great way to honor her memory."

His gaze shifted to her fingers, each one long and thin. Her teal fingernail polish was chipped around the edges, but it didn't seem to bother her. He knew plenty of women back home who had their nails done every week or so, but he'd never seen a hand as beautiful as hers. "Thanks, Dani."

They ate in silence for a few long moments, but it wasn't uncomfortable. More like she was sitting with him in the memories. Then she finally spoke. "I'd love to hear more about your mom. If you don't mind telling me."

Liam inhaled a shaky breath. "I don't mind." But what could he say to really describe how amazing his mom had been? How could he really do her justice? "She . . ." He watched a drip of ice cream slide down the side of his cone and plop onto the table. "She always had a snack waiting for me after school. We'd sit and talk about my day, or about her day. She was a freelance editor. Really smart. And she was always doing things for other people, you know? Taking them meals when they'd had surgery, watching their kids for them when they had doctor's appointments, that kind of thing. And she loved me and my dad like . . ." His words choked him. He coughed. "Like we were the best things in her life. Like we mattered more than anything. She'd drop whatever she was doing and just be with us. And she made our house a real home. Decorated it with all of these knickknacks she'd get garage saling. Drove my dad crazy, and he'd tease her about it."

Liam blinked against the memories. Oh man. He hadn't meant to talk for so long. His ice cream had dripped more than once all over the table, and he grabbed a fistful of napkins from the silver dispenser. Wiped away the mess before he got the courage to look up at Dani.

Her eyes were watering. Was she crying?

"You okay?" he asked.

"Sorry, yeah." She tugged a clean napkin from his pile and dabbed her eyes. "It's just really beautiful to hear about her."

"She was a really great mom. And she gave me a great childhood home. Things were never the same after she died, you know? Dad and I moved from the suburbs to downtown L.A. A friend of his and our biggest client owns a hotel there and lets us rent the penthouse for dirt cheap."

"You live in a hotel?"

Her question didn't come across as judgmental, just curious. Maybe with a touch of surprise too.

"It's weird, I know. But not so bad. I'm not home much anyway. Always running off to manage the next job. I'm never in one place for very long. Though I do hope to change that."

"You mentioned something about that last week. How are you hoping to change it?"

"I've got a project in the works with a buddy of mine. We're hoping to get Dad to buy a hotel and renovate it ourselves."

"So you'd be your own client?"

"Basically. It's in Los Angeles, and it would be a strong asset to add to our portfolio. I'm thinking that once we have one under our belt, maybe we can buy others in the area. Kind of create a new revenue stream, you know? And that would keep me there, in one place. I could maybe get Dad to retire."

"Does he want to retire?"

"He should, for his health." Liam took a bite of ice cream. "But I need to be in L.A. for him to even consider it."

"Hmm." Dani swirled her spoon in her ice cream cup. "So, your mom. How . . . how did she die?"

He shifted in his seat and set his cone down on the dirty napkins. His appetite had fled. Because after all the memories came the dreaded emptiness—the memory that Mom had gone and taken any semblance of home with her. "Um, childbirth. It was . . ." The words got stuck in his throat.

"It's okay." Dani's voice was quiet, soothing. "You don't have to tell me."

He just sat there, staring at the table, blinking. Because it wasn't that he didn't trust her enough to tell her. It was just that, well, what was the point? Liam cleared his throat. "So, what about you? Are you and your mom close?"

"We used to be." Dani stood and tossed her ice cream bowl and spoon into the nearest trash can. "Not so much anymore."

"Sorry to hear that." Standing, he threw away the rest of his cone and pile of napkins. "What about your dad? And you said you had six siblings, right?"

"I do." Dani hauled it out of the parlor like she was being chased. Then she turned in the hallway that led to the lobby, cocked her head. "But you don't want to hear about my family drama."

"Actually, I do." And he found that he meant it. He wanted to know more about what had made this woman into the fascinating, loyal, passionate person she was. And he wanted more than that. Wanted to draw her to him, to soothe away any pain others had caused her. That he'd caused her. Liam took a step closer. "I *really* do."

Her vanilla scent wrapped around him, and she looked up at him with wide eyes. Dani's mouth opened, closed, and for a moment, both of them were still.

Liam leaned in just a hair.

But Dani blinked and drew back, breaking the spell. "Um, hey, so, I'm pretty tired right now. I think I might head to bed if that's all right. But thank you for sharing about your mom."

He shook himself from his stupor. "Thanks for listening."

"Sure." They stepped onto the elevator and rode in silence. When they reached Dani's floor, she stepped off and turned to face him, arms folded over her chest. "Night, Liam."

"Night."

And then she was gone.

What had just happened? He'd wanted to kiss her, that was what. More than he'd wanted to kiss anyone in a long time. No woman since Tiffany had even come close to capturing his interest, and he'd known Dani exactly a week.

He needed to get focused. Did he like Dani? Yeah, fine, okay. But that was a non-factor. Because he was needed back in L.A. and was leaving in a week.

There was no future here.

And yet, even as he hit the button for the ninth floor, a part of him stayed back with Dani on the sixth.

Nine

T HERE WAS NOTHING SO ICONICALLY Jonathon Island than a horse-drawn carriage ride through Blueberry Hill Park.

Even if there was only one horse instead of two. And a four-wheeled contraption that hadn't been used in probably a decade.

All she needed now was Liam.

Oh, Liam.

"When is he supposed to get here?" Mia pushed Maggie on the park swings beside the path where Pegasus—who was one of the only horses still on the island and had been personally loaned to her by the reclusive Quinn nephew, Asher—waited patiently.

Meanwhile, Finn ran hooting and hollering along the playground set with another boy about his age. Dani had been surprised when her cousin had shouted a hello a few moments before, but then again, lots of families were at the park today, enjoying the sixty-degree weather that had decided to show its face.

"Any minute now." Dani took a sip of her coffee.

"Okay, so then there's not much time for you to spill. What happened between the two of you in the Twin Cities? You look different. Almost nervous."

"I do?" She dug the toe of her tennis shoe into the playground sand. "I don't know, Mia. He gave me a tour like we'd planned. We ate dinner and ice cream like we'd planned. He told me a little bit about his family, about his goals for the future."

"Ah, so you got personal?"

"He did."

"And let me guess." Maggie squealed as Mia pushed her extra high in the toddler swing. "You stayed close-lipped because 'he's an outsider'?"

"I guess. Or maybe I just didn't want to go into it. To bring the whole mood down." She sighed. "But then there was this moment at the end of the night when I swear he wanted to kiss me. But I panicked and basically ran away."

"And how do you feel about that now that it's a few days later and you've had time to process? How do you feel about him?"

Dani stared into her coffee, gathering her thoughts. "I think . . . I think I want to tell him about my past. About my family and what this town means to me. I want him to understand."

Mia reached out and squeezed Dani's hand. "I think that's a great idea, Dani. It's time to take a chance and let him in. Really in."

"Stop it. This isn't about romance. It's about getting him on my side. We're just business partners."

"Are you sure?" Mia pointed to the horse-drawn carriage. "Because you sure picked a heck of a romantic ride for a business meeting."

An hour later, Dani could see Mia's point so clearly.

Because could the man *look* more handsome and carefree beside her on the bench, the sunlight bringing out the lighter bits of his hair as it filtered through the hole in the carriage's white canvas top? Today, Liam had worn his navy suit but no tie, and he'd discarded the jacket on the back of the red leather front seat and even rolled his sleeves up his forearms. And every time a breeze rustled his hair, it carried the scent of his spicy cologne her way.

What had she been thinking?

Thankfully, Dani had been able to launch into tour guide mode until this moment, which had led them back to the park after traversing one end of Main Street to the other. The information she gave him this time around was much more complete as they clopped along at a snail's pace.

"I must say, you're really bringing your A game today, Ms. Sullivan." Liam took a swig from his own Good Day Coffee cup. "I feel like I know all the secrets of every family and every building on Main Street now."

"To know the people of Jonathon Island is to know the island." She waved at two moms and their jogging strollers as they passed. "During the busiest parts of the season, we use this park for everything from food and art festivals to farmers' markets to summer concerts. On the weekends in the summer, this place bustles with townspeople and tourists."

"It's a really beautiful park."

"I think so too. And that"—she pointed to Pinnacle Drive, which overlooked the northern edge of the park via a ridge—"is the public school. See? Even our schools are quaint." The one-story brick building was surrounded by trees and ideally located just south of the Blueberry Hill neighborhood where a large majority of kids on the island lived. Not that anyone lived all that far from anything, since the entire island was only about four square miles.

"It's definitely cozier looking than the school I went to in the city. How many kids go there?"

Pegasus stopped to munch on a dead bush. Asher had warned Dani that if she didn't know how to control the beast, the beast would control her. Dani flicked the reins and tutted, and Pegasus finally started moving down the path again. "It serves kindergarten through twelfth grade, and I think there are about twenty or twenty-five kids right now. It was at least double that when I attended."

"I can't even fathom going to a school that small." Liam adjusted in his seat, and his leg brushed up against hers. The warmth seared through the material of her jeans.

"It wasn't so bad. Actually, it was kind of cool. You know all the teachers, they know you. Kind of like this town in general."

Liam laughed and took a sip of his coffee. "I'm just a visitor, and yet I feel like everyone knows me already."

"It's spring. There isn't much else of interest going on. So when a handsome guy from the West Coast comes—"

"You think I'm handsome, do you?"

Oops. She jutted her chin up and focused on the clip-clop of Pegasus's horseshoes against the pavement. "Some might say that."

"*You* said that."

"I was speaking for the other ladies of the town." She peeked out of the corner of her eye and found him smiling against his drink as he took another sip. Why did he have to be so adorably good-looking? He made it kind of hard to remember this was supposed to be a business meeting. "Anyway, I think part of the charm of the island is the close-knit bond that residents have. People here help each other out. They watch out for one another. It's not just a place to live. It's a community. A family."

Liam's thumb stroked the edge of his black coffee lid. "That sounds really nice, actually. Kind of like my dad's company."

Interesting. "Your dad's company? Not yours?"

"Well, yeah, it's mine too. But he put his blood, sweat, and tears into building it from the ground up."

"He sounds like an accomplished man." Dani eased the reins to the right so the horse turned down the winding sidewalk. They were now heading south along the eastern loop of the park, the one that faced Lake Huron. Today the sun sparkled off the water, almost inviting despite how cold she knew it to be. She pulled the horse to a halt so they could enjoy the view.

"He's a good guy. Does a lot so that the employees and our clients have the best." Liam sighed and stared at the calm waters. "But he works himself to death—almost literally."

"Sounds like someone else I know." Dani nudged Liam.

But he didn't laugh at her teasing. "I only work hard because I want him to be able to retire. And he never will if he doesn't think there's someone capable enough to take over for him."

Oh, wow. "You said something about wanting him to retire for his health?"

A quick nod. A sigh. "Two years ago, I was home from a business trip and came out of my room for a snack. Found Dad on the couch sleeping. His laptop had fallen off his lap onto the rug below, and I came over to right it. But something just seemed off, so I tried to wake him up and . . ." He shuddered. "Turns out he had extremely low blood sugar because he hadn't eaten in hours. He's diabetic and doesn't take care of himself like he should. If I hadn't been there . . ."

"Oh, Liam. How scary." She turned, rested the reins in her lap, and set her free hand on his. "But you were. There, I mean."

"Thank goodness. But I can't always be there, which means the only real solution is to take things off his plate so he retires and lives his best life, away from the stress of work." Liam glanced down at her hand, then back up, into her eyes.

He was such a good son. Still . . . "Don't you think you're taking too much on yourself? Your dad's an adult, after all."

"Of course, but with Mom gone . . . well, family takes care of each other, right? And that means it's up to me to make sure my dad's okay." His gaze explored hers, as if searching for something there. "That's why I couldn't let someone else take this project. Why I'm pushing back on things. Because . . ."

"Because if it fails, then your company will be in the red. I know."

"But it's more than that. If the company is set back, my dad won't hesitate to use his own retirement fund to make sure everyone is taken care of. To turn things back around. Which means he won't be able to retire."

Dani sat back against the bench and blew out a breath. She hadn't realized just how much of a risk Mr. Stone was taking in agreeing to this deal. Still, didn't Liam understand? "This deal means a lot to me too."

"I know. You want your family to come back."

She licked her lips, glanced away. A breeze off the water blew through, and the horse's tail flicked at it as if it were a fly. "Like you, it's more than it seems."

Now Liam's hand covered hers. Squeezed. "Tell me." His voice, like honey, filled the empty spaces in her heart. Warm and soothing, and sticky in a good way. Like it wasn't going anywhere.

Even though it was.

But for right now, Liam was here. And he wanted to know. She didn't have the heart to get into all of it—Dad burning down the hotel, and the aftermath that ensued—but she could still share her heart without all of that. Tell him why this mattered so much.

She turned her palm up, and his fingers slid around

hers, locking them together solidly. "My parents split up when I was fourteen because my mom had an affair."

"Oh, wow. I'm sorry. Is that why you aren't close with her?"

"That's part of it." She sighed. "When I was eighteen, the hotel burned. My dad left for Florida at that point. He started over with a new hotel there. Mom and my stepdad at the time moved to Port Joseph. Mom is still there, divorced again. And my older siblings—all six of them—left one by one. Now they're scattered across the country, and I'm the only one left."

"That must feel lonely."

"I have Uncle Seb, Aunt Elise, my cousins. But it's not the same."

"I understand loneliness."

She believed him. "I think the first time I was ever lonely was when I was eight, and my oldest brother, James, went away to college. Out of all my siblings, I was always closest with him, even though he's ten years older. But he was never too cool for me, you know? He let me tag along everywhere, even when his friends were there. And then he left for Boston. I know that's not that far, but for a girl with as small a world as mine, it might as well have been another country."

Liam's thumb moved along the curve of hers, drawing delicious shivers down her spine. "I always wanted a sibling. I'm glad you had that."

Poor Liam. His mother had died in childbirth, which meant he must have lost the sibling he so desired.

She pressed her shoulder against his and nodded. Her

gaze took in the rocky shore, the expansive lake, the trees that were dead but would one day soon be brought back to life. "I'm glad I had that too. But sometimes I wonder if my heart would be whole if I didn't." Dani bit the inside of her cheek. "That probably sounds so silly. But after James left, and I cried and cried buckets of tears, my mom took me aside, dried my eyes, and said, 'When people leave us—whether temporarily or for good—they take a piece of our hearts with them every time.' And I know she meant it to comfort me, but I have never been able to get that picture out of my head."

"What picture is that?" Liam's warm breath tickled her ear. He was solid, and here—so close.

"The image of my heart, breaking off little bit by little bit every time someone leaves. Scattering to the corners of the earth, following them wherever they go. Sometimes I wonder if I'll ever be whole again. This project feels like my only chance to be. And that's why I need the hotel to be rebuilt exactly the way it was. Don't you see? If it's anything but that . . ."

"Thank you for telling me all of that, Dani. I'm sure that wasn't easy." It took Liam several long moments before he spoke again. "I'm not trying to disrespect your memories or your dreams, but shouldn't the hotel rebuild be about what's best for the island?"

"Well, yes. But the two aren't mutually exclusive. I really do believe that changing things won't be good for the island."

Liam sighed. "And I still believe you're wrong."

Dani sat up, inched away from him. "Isn't there any

part of you that wants to see the grandeur restored?" She tugged her hand free.

"Of course I do." Liam pinched the bridge of his nose. "But in my mind, that means making improvements."

"You mean changing it. And we don't want it changed. We want to keep what's special about it."

"Dani, I'm not discounting how special it is. How special this town is. It's like Mayberry, caught in time. It's an escape. It's the thing that people always long for, a dream really, something that people can have for a brief moment in time. I get that."

"Then if you truly see how special it is, what's the problem?"

"The problem is, my firm specializes in the tourist of today, and somehow, I have to figure out how to create a hotel that caters to people from today's world who want to step back into the past. The problem is that we can't live in the past. We have to step into the future to prosper, even if our hearts long for the world that you have here."

His words sliced through her. Lips pursed, Dani picked up the reins and flicked them. The buggy made its way around the final bend of the park.

"Dani? Would you say something, please? Please tell me you understand my predicament here."

"I do." Dani pulled the buggy to a stop in front of the livery, where Asher had helped her lug the contraption from storage earlier today. "But I just can't see a way forward. While I appreciate you hearing me out, I clearly haven't convinced you to change your mind, and you haven't convinced me to change mine. I think . . . I think we're at an impasse."

Liam just sat there, staring at her. "So what now?"

She inhaled a trembling breath. "Now, you go home." The thought shouldn't hurt the way it did. "And I'll see if I can find another developer willing to help me make my vision come to life."

Why couldn't he just get on that ferry?

Liam stood on the dock and watched the last ferry of the day pull away. It wasn't even that late—just two o'clock on this Friday afternoon—but at this time of year, the schedule was still very limited.

He should have been on it. But something had kept him here.

With one hand rolling his suitcase behind him, Liam strolled the shoreline that would lead him back to his inn. Bicyclists whizzed past him on the lakeside path, and joggers waved hello and flashed him curious looks—maybe because they recognized him and wondered why he was walking *away* from the ferry landing with his suitcase.

You and me both, guys.

Sighing, he continued trudging along until he approached the bustling marina. Boats were going in and out. People were grilling and dining together on the back of boats still tied to the dock. Families took advantage of the walking path, and some gathered beside a small dog run where they allowed their pets to play. Everyone seemed to be enjoying this week's warm snap, likely afraid the weather would decide to change its mind and go cold again.

Maybe Liam should try enjoying it too.

As he took one of the docks out toward the water, Liam inhaled deeply, struck once again by the differences between the Pacific where he lived and the lake here. The scent wasn't briny at all, but instead emitted a faint earthy smell mingled with a hint of fish. Closing his eyes, he listened to the lapping water, the hum of a motorboat, the cawing of seagulls somewhere overhead.

No angry honking of cab drivers. No hawking of food by vendors crowded along a busy street. No hissing and groaning of oversized buses blowing plumes of exhaust into the air.

Dani was right. Jonathon Island was the perfect place to think. Maybe they *should* use the location to their advantage. Maybe if they could each swallow their own vision for how things should be—swallow their pride—they could come up with some compromises that would work for them both.

The trouble was, Dani didn't want to seem to do that. Yesterday, she'd made up her mind that they couldn't work together, and he'd given her a full twenty-four hours to change it.

He hadn't heard a peep from her since.

"Liam! Hey!"

Liam turned his head and shielded his eyes against the sun. Not five feet away stood Cody Hart on the deck of a fishing boat with peeling white paint. He wore faded jeans, an old flannel shirt, and a backward baseball cap. "What's up, man?"

"Just working on something." Cody cocked his head, squinted. "You headed to the ferry?"

"I missed it, actually."

"Bummer. Although I'm hurt you weren't going to say goodbye." Cody placed a hand over his heart in dramatic fashion. "After all the things I've fixed for you."

Liam grinned. "You never did get to the squeaky ceiling fan."

"Was planning to come by in the morning to fix that one." Chuckling, Cody cocked his head. "Do you need to go work right now?"

"Nope. I'm free as a bird, considering Dani fired me yesterday."

"Ouch." Cody winced. "Well, wanna help me with something then?"

"Sure." Better than holing up in his room with nothing to do but think about why he wasn't on the ferry. He walked to the boat landing and climbed on board, suitcase in hand. From here, he could see that the back end was damaged. Not that he knew much about boats, but the splintering looked fairly extensive.

Cody stood at the top of a descending staircase. He had a dirty rag tucked into his back pocket and waved Liam after him. "This way."

Liam left the suitcase on deck and followed him down the dark space, ducking so his head didn't hit the top of the stairwell. "This boat yours?"

"Nah, a client's." Cody led him through a small kitchen

galley, which was covered with a fine layer of dust, and a dark dining area with two large tables and a wall mounted with a TV suffering from a cracked screen. "He's off island at the moment and bought this at a steal off Sam Caruthers, a guy who moved to Arizona last year."

Pushing open a door on the opposite end, Cody ducked into what looked like a storage pantry of sorts. Half-empty Costco-sized boxes of various food items—round crackers, beef jerky sticks, nuts, and more—filled the shelves. A few individual packages of cheesy chips lay on the ground near Cody's feet. "Anyway, the new owner hired me to get it season ready for him."

"How can I help? I know absolutely nothing about fishing or fishing equipment, but I'll do what I can."

Cody lifted a hand and knocked against a big plastic container of pretzels. "Don't worry, I'm not expecting you to help swab the poop deck or anything like that."

"Ah, good. I would have worn my ratty shoes if so." As it was, his white sneakers probably weren't the best thing to wear on a dusty old ship, but it was better than his work loafers.

At that, Cody laughed. "At least you're not wearing a suit."

"It was supposed to be a travel day with no client meetings. I do own other clothes, you know."

"I didn't, actually." Cody laughed. "Anyway, what I *could* use some help with is clearing out this storage. All of this food has been here a while. Might even be salvageable if the due dates haven't passed. We can donate that stuff to the church. Or we can junk it all. Whatever you think." Cody leaned against the doorway. "You sure you don't mind?"

"Put me to work." It would be good for him to focus on something other than his failed hotel plans.

With a nod, Cody left for a moment, returning with a box cutter that he handed to Liam. "So you can break down any of the boxes." He started to turn toward the door again.

Liam pushed up the sleeves of his sweater. "And what are you going to do?"

A grin curled the edges of Cody's mouth. "I'm gonna go swab the poop deck, of course."

"Ha ha. What are you *really* doing?"

"Working on the engine."

"Oh, sure. Leave me with the pantry cleaning while you get to do the cool, manly stuff."

"Sorry, man. You wanna join me?"

"I'm just joking." Liam held up his hands in mock surrender. "I'd be looking over your shoulder completely confused and asking dumb questions. Plus, I could use the manual labor. Leave me to it, Captain." He saluted Cody, but instead of a laugh, he got a frown in return.

What had he said? Seemed like he was doing a lot of unintentional hurting lately.

Like Dani.

Sweet, beautiful Dani, whose sad, disappointed eyes had gut-punched him yesterday. He hated that he'd hurt her.

And maybe that was why he hadn't been able to leave.

Because deep down, this island was starting to mean something to him.

She was starting to mean something.

Liam hauled a stool over, climbed up, and snagged a box of ramen packets from the top shelf. Checked the expiration dates. Started organizing boxes in the galley into piles of things to keep, things to toss. He sneezed when he pulled down a particularly large box and a pile of dust fell from above, going everywhere.

His phone buzzed in his pocket. He pulled it out. Travis.

Ugh. His friend had been calling him all day for an update. Liam was supposed to be working on the Bertram proposal, but he hadn't had any spare time.

And now that he did, he hadn't been able to get his mind back to L.A.—not when Jonathon Island had it so thoroughly captured.

He hit ignore and stuffed the phone back into his pocket.

Before he knew it, an hour had passed, and it was time to break down the pile of boxes littering the galley. He grabbed the box cutter and started hacking away at the tape, ripping the seams so he could fold the boxes flat on the counter.

One box gave him more trouble than the others, the tape thick, the cardboard unyielding. Why wouldn't it just lie flat like the others? Why did it insist on being so difficult?

With a grunt, Liam leaned heavily on it in an attempt to put it in its place.

"What's got you so riled up?"

Liam turned as Cody strode toward the galley sink. His hands were covered in dirt and grime, his face dripping with sweat. "Just a dumb box that won't cooperate."

With a lifted eyebrow, Cody washed off his hands and dried them on some paper towels he found nearby. "Uh huh. It's a woman, isn't it?"

"What? No, dude, it's just a box."

Cody tsked and moved toward a small cooler on the ground near the fridge. He popped the lid and pulled out a couple of water bottles. Tossed one to Liam. "You sure about that?"

"Thanks." The dirt on his hands left behind streaks in the cold bottle's condensation. "And yeah, maybe I'm frustrated, and maybe it has to do with a woman. But not like *that*."

"So what's it like?" Twisting the cap on his own bottle, Cody settled back against the counter and waited. "Is this about you getting fired?"

Liam tore into his water and took a few long drinks before answering. "Partly." Maybe it was unprofessional to talk with Cody about this, but maybe it would feel nice to unload on someone who wasn't involved. He couldn't very well tell Dad about his worries. That would only stress his father out and make him question his faith in Liam. He'd rather have that conversation face-to-face. "Guessing the whole island probably knows by now that things did not go well with the town council on Monday."

"Heard something about that, yeah." Cody took a sip of water.

"Despite my best efforts, I really messed up that meeting and came up with plans that more than half the council—plus Dani—hated. So I thought I could get her on my side by showing her a hotel my company's renovating in Minneapolis."

"And did you? Get her on your side?"

"No. In fact, when we returned, she went right back to trying to convince me to rebuild an exact replica of the hotel that she used to know and love. I just wish she would trust me, you know? Trust that I know this business, that I can get her the tourists she needs, that I could have them eating out of the palm of her hand, if only she would accept my vision of things. But she is so stuck in the past." The plastic bottle crunched beneath his tightening fist. "Yesterday, she realized we're at an impasse, and I guess she'd rather fire me than even consider compromising."

"Does compromising mean doing everything your way?"

"What? No."

"Does she think that's what it means?"

Oh. "Well, I'm not sure."

"Okay, then." Cody finished off his water and crushed the plastic down flat with the palm of his hand. "Look, from what you're telling me, and from what Mia's told me—"

"Dani's cousin? Why would she tell you anything?" Liam set his own water down. "Wait, are you guys together?" Maybe Cody was an interested party after all.

Cody blanched. "No, it's not like that with us. She and

I . . . we've been friends since we were kids. She married my best friend."

"Oh, wow." Liam chuckled. "Didn't mean to make that weird." Except, wait. Hadn't Dani told him . . . "I thought I remembered hearing her husband d—" He winced.

"Yeah, he did." Cody turned a one-eighty and looked out the galley window. "He died."

Shoot. He'd gone and made things awkward. But the thing about grief was, a person couldn't ignore it. When Liam's mom had passed, some people had tried to pretend like things were normal. They never even said they were sorry for his loss. Liam had asked Dad about that once, and his father had just said, *Some people think that bringing up your mom will make our pain worse. What they don't realize is that pretending she never existed is the worst pain there could ever be.*

Liam stepped forward and clapped a hand on Cody's shoulder. "Sorry for your loss, man."

Cody's frame shook with a few deep breaths. "Thanks."

Liam dropped his hand. "Guess I'll get back to work. Thanks for the water." He started back toward the pantry.

"Liam."

Liam turned. "Yeah?"

"You going to the bonfire tonight?"

"The bonfire?"

"It's kind of last minute, to celebrate the nicer weather. Don't tell me nobody's invited you."

"I haven't really talked to anyone today." Liam shoved his hands into his pockets.

"You should come." Cody grinned. "I have it on good authority that Dani will be there."

"I don't think she wants to see me."

"And I think you owe it to both of you to see if compromising is an option. That is, if you're willing."

"I'm not sure what that would look like. Or if she'd even be willing."

"You'll never know if you don't ask."

"And what if she just ignores me?"

"She might. But she loves Jill's peanut butter cookies. Haven't you ever heard that the way to a woman's heart is through her stomach?"

Liam crossed his arms over his chest. "Pretty sure that's dudes."

"You must not have had Jill's cookies yet." With a wink and a light punch to the shoulder, Cody sauntered out of the galley.

Huh, okay. Liam had never used cookies as a persuasive tool before, but there was a first time for everything.

Although, maybe Cody had a point.

Maybe it wasn't so much about persuading Dani over to his side of the table but figuring out a way to meet her in the middle.

Ten

HER BRILLIANT PLAN TO FIND ANOTHER developer was going swimmingly.

Not.

"You really don't know anyone else?" Wood piled high in her arms, she trailed Uncle Seb from the side of his house toward the pit where he, Cody, and some of the men of the town were preparing for the bonfire. It was the perfect night for it—a darkening velvet sky, slight glimmers of the northern lights playing coy with them all, and cold enough to need blankets, cocoa, and a fire, but not so freezing as to make them miserable.

But as much as Dani loved community events like this—when the town came together with food, songs, and laughter—tonight she had other things on her mind.

Like how to get another developer in here, stat, since she'd maybe fired Liam too quickly.

She'd tried doing research on her own all of yesterday

afternoon and today on top of her other town duties, but she just simply didn't have the contacts that Uncle Seb did.

When she got to the firepit, she dropped her pile of wood and dusted her hands off on her jeans. "Please, Uncle Seb. Try to think." She tried to keep her voice low because townsfolk had already started to gather around the pit with their camping chairs. Children ran across her uncle and aunt's expansive lawn, through the grassy knoll, and onward toward the shore in the direction of the lighthouse.

As new families pulled their golf carts into the yard, women and men carried Crockpots and trays up the front porch steps. There would be quite the spread tonight, and with nothing else going on, there would be a lot of townsfolk in attendance.

Not Liam, though. There had been at least three ferries out since their meeting at the park yesterday, and no doubt he'd been on one of them.

Seb frowned and tugged the knit cap from his head. He scratched behind his ear. "Dani, I'm sorry. I exhausted my contacts during our first round of searching. I told you, we were lucky to get the Stones' firm." He replaced the cap on his head and took off for more wood.

Dani rushed after him. "But what if this time, you focused on finding a firm that specializes in refurbishing and restoring historical landmarks? That's who we really need on the job."

"Dani." Her uncle stopped in front of the neatly stacked wood pile and turned to face her. Despite the dim light, she knew the look he was giving her. Pity. And she despised it. It made her feel like a victim, but she wasn't a victim. She was responsible for this whole mess in the first place—at least, the scattering of her family. And she was finally doing something to fix it. Didn't he understand that?

"What?" Her chin trembled, but she lifted it anyway. Seb the businessman admired strength, didn't he? But maybe in her brokenness, she was too weak for this battle.

Her uncle sighed and pulled her in for an unexpected hug. At first, Dani stiffened, but then she melted and let his arms embrace her the way her dad's hadn't in a while because *he* wasn't here.

But she wouldn't cry. No. She wouldn't.

Finally, Uncle Seb pulled back, placed his hands on her shoulders, and looked her straight in the eyes. "The reality is that the hotel will never again be what it once was."

His words . . . they didn't compute. "What do you mean? Isn't that the whole point of all of this?" To restore what had been.

"No. The point is to build a large enough hotel to house temporary island staff and guests who want to visit Jonathon Island. Honestly, if it was up to me alone, I'd demolish it all and start fresh." As Dani started to protest, he held up a hand. "But I would never allow that, because I know what that place means to you. And I can recognize that it's important to maintain some historical integrity for the island's sake. But that doesn't change the fact that it can never be exactly what it was. It can be just as good, maybe better. But time and progress don't stand still."

"That's basically what Liam told me yesterday." Dani

folded her arms over her chest and felt her shoulders deflate.

"He's a smart kid." Someone called for Seb, and he peeked around her. "I've got to go help get things started. Just try to work with Liam again, all right? Give the boy a chance. He might surprise you." Then he strode away, leaving Dani feeling numb and alone.

And too late.

She'd have to find a way to tell Seb—and the whole council—about firing him. Or find a way to ask him back.

But the last thing she wanted to do was grovel for his help.

"Dad's right, you know."

She turned to find Mia standing there, hands on her hips and head cocked. From beside her, Finn and Maggie shot away, zooming off in the direction of the dock, where Nora was watching some of the kids skip rocks across the surface of the lake.

Dani's eyebrows raised as her cousin approached her side. "Did you just admit your father is right?"

"If you ever tell him I said so, I'll deny it."

They walked together down the gentle sloping grass toward the shoreline. "What's he right about, exactly?"

"You *should* give Liam a chance."

"He didn't mean romantically. He meant with the project." She sighed. "But I can't give him a chance because I kind of sort of fired him yesterday."

"What? Why?"

"We couldn't come to any sort of agreement on the

hotel project. He thinks everything needs to be super modern, and I still want to take the traditional route."

"Yikes."

"I know. But when I told Uncle Seb that, he said the hotel wasn't ever going to be the same. And now I'm all conflicted. What if I was too hasty in letting Liam go? What if I've ruined everything?"

The sound of splashes filled the air, along with children's laughter.

"Aw, Dani." Mia hugged her jacket tighter around herself. "The hotel will never be the same because *you're* not the same. You have so many wonderful memories attached to it, but what if you were to rebuild it exactly as it was, and none of your family returned? Don't tell me it would feel the same to you."

"No. But I have to try, don't I?"

Without looking away from her kids on the dock, Mia grabbed Dani's hand in her own. "I know you want your family back, but don't forget that family is more than just siblings, a mom, and a dad. Even if I weren't your cousin, we'd be family."

Dani's eyes burned, and she blinked back the tears.

Mia continued. "So are Cody and Jill and Tara and Henrietta and every islander. This town . . . we are a family. And whatever happens with the hotel—whether you put everything back exactly as it was or not—won't change that."

Whew. Her cousin's words landed right in her gut. Dani still wanted her family back. And the best chance of that happening was to play on their nostalgia. But what if they *did* say no to returning?

Worse, what if the project never got off the ground in the first place because Dani was too stubborn to risk it?

She swallowed hard, squeezed Mia's hand. "I have to compromise, don't I?"

"Yep."

Her cousin's voice was now infused with pep and some sort of glee—a welcome change from her demeanor for the better part of the last year. Of course, it was coming at Dani's expense, but she almost didn't care. "Don't sound so happy about it," she teased.

"Of course I'm happy about it." Mia flashed her a quick smile. "You'll have to keep working closely with the good Mr. Stone in order to hammer out the details."

"It's too late." Dani shivered, and it wasn't from the breeze floating off the lake. The idea of being alone with Liam again, working closely with him for potentially long hours at a time . . . well, it sparked more joy than it should. "He's got to be long gone by now, if not on yesterday's ferry, then today's. There's no point in entertaining the idea of more."

"But you want to." It was a statement, not a question.

No point in hiding her feelings from the friend who knew her best. Dani groaned. "Ugh, yes. I want to. But I can't imagine things ever working out between us, even if by some miracle I convinced him to come back here. He's planning to take over his dad's job as CEO in Los Angeles. I belong here. And my heart is already so . . . Well, I just can't afford to lose any more of it to someone else who is just going to leave me."

She glanced up at the sky filled with hints of green and yellow. Some said the northern lights were always there but they weren't always visible. On nights like tonight, it felt almost cruel of God to keep the full beauty of His creation from them. Like He was dangling a carrot she desperately wanted. The same was true of Liam. He was everything she'd want in a man, really. Loyal, kind, hard-working, considerate. And of course, he wasn't terrible to look at either.

But he couldn't ever be hers.

Without a word, Mia rested her head against Dani's shoulder. Finally, she spoke, and her words were soft but fierce. "You've been trying to protect yourself from being hurt again, and I understand that. It's why you haven't sought out dates. The perfect guy for you literally landed on your doorstep, and you're still not giving him a real chance. But maybe it's time for you to take that leap of faith and see what happens." She drew in a shuddering breath. "Troy wasn't perfect. We had our problems. But if I could have Troy here with me for twenty-four hours, *knowing* he would die again the very next day—that I would have to go through all this pain again—don't you know what I would choose?"

A tear snuck past Dani's defenses and fell hot down her cheek. "Love. You'd choose love."

"I would. And so should you."

The sky had darkened even more now, so much so that

the adults were calling the kids in to eat. "I wouldn't even know where to start."

Mia gave her a hug, then pulled back with a grin. "How about you just turn around? That's a good start."

"What? Why?"

"Because." Mia pointed over Dani's shoulder. "It looks like Liam didn't leave after all."

Dani turned.

Liam stood ten feet away, impossibly handsome in a dark jacket, jeans, and a blue cap—the first time she'd ever seen him in anything but a suit. One hand was shoved into his pocket and the other held some sort of small bag. He was tall and broad, like a rescue ship coming into harbor.

"What's he doing here?"

"Why don't you go find out?" With a quick squeeze to her arm, Mia hustled off toward the house to join her kids.

Her whole body felt frozen, rooted to the ground, but Dani managed to lift her hand in a small wave.

Liam strode toward her.

And then, just behind him, overhead, the aurora borealis finally revealed itself in full. Streaks of color danced across the sky, a painting on a canvas so beautiful it hurt. But hurt in a good way, in a way that reminded her that a broken bone sometimes had to be reset in order to heal properly.

And she couldn't deny the whisper in her soul from the Creator, nudging her forward a step. One, two. Toward Liam, until they stood toe-to-toe.

The look in his eyes matched the one she'd seen in the

Minneapolis hotel earlier this week. Was that the same desire, or had she imagined it then too?

Dani swallowed. "I'm sorry for giving up yesterday."

Liam drew back and then a smile inked across his face. "I'm sorry too. I shouldn't have been so stubborn." He paused. "Does that mean I'm not fired?" The question was soft and teasing and filled with something else. Longing, maybe.

"I'm willing to bring you back on a probationary basis," Dani teased back. "If you think we can work this out."

Liam leaned in just a bit. "I'm counting on it."

"Good. Me too."

He studied her in the moonlight, gaze drifting over her features like the softest caress. "Good."

She laughed. "I already said that."

"I'm saying it again." Then he held up the bag, which looked suspiciously like it had come from Good Day Coffee. "Just in case you needed more convincing, I've brought a peace offering." He handed it to her.

She peeked inside. "I could kiss you right now." Oh, wow. Oops. She was sure her cheeks were on fire. Thank goodness for the darkness.

He coughed. "That must be some cookie."

"Don't tell me you haven't tried one?"

"Can't say that I have."

"Then you have to split this one with me." Reaching into the bag, she drew out the cookie that was nearly as big as her hand. Without another thought, she broke it in half.

"You don't have to do that."

"I want to do that." She gave him his half and held hers up close to her mouth. "Ready? On three."

He matched her posture. "One."

"Two," she said.

"Three," they said together.

Dani bit into her cookie and groaned as the pastry melted against her tongue, making a sweet night even sweeter.

Because one of Jill's cookies eaten alone was good.

Eating one with Liam?

It was pure magic, just like the sky above them.

Just like she hoped to create with him, now that they were on the same team.

"I don't think I've ever been so stuffed in my entire life." Liam set a hand against his stomach.

"Never let it be said that the ladies of Jonathon Island don't know how to potluck." Dani's eyes danced from her spot beside him. Or maybe that was the flickering of the firelight. Either way, her smile dazzled.

And it moved something inside of him. Something that made him want to stay right here beside her.

He still couldn't believe she'd rehired him. Thought he'd have to do some real cajoling and begging, but she'd seemed almost relieved to see him when he'd shown up tonight. It seemed they both had come to the realization that compromise was going to be necessary for them to complete this task.

And then, she'd gone and been all kinds of irresistible

and teasing in the moonlight, and once again, he'd had the strongest urge to kiss her.

What was happening to him? Since when would he rather spend a Friday night cozied up beside a fire instead of at an art gala or a corporate event in the city?

Maybe this island was changing him.

Maybe Dani was.

"I wouldn't dare say such a thing, because that was some of the best eating I've ever done." Laughing, Liam stood with his empty plate—which had recently been filled to the brim with potato casserole, deviled eggs, pulled pork, and cherry pie—and offered to take Dani's too. She sat adorably tucked into her folding chair, one leg pulled up all casual, the other flat on the ground. "You want some hot chocolate?"

"Ooo, yes, please." She turned her attention back to the massive bonfire that was the center of the gathering where at least forty or fifty townspeople had gathered. After they'd made up and decided to meet tomorrow to hash out their new joint plan for the hotel, Dani had taken Liam around and introduced him to most of them. Some he knew already, but whether they'd met before or not, each one welcomed him with a smile. Peggy Martinez had even patted him on the cheek and called him a "dear boy," and Stuart "Mac" MacBride—a grizzly bear of a man— had given his hand a squeeze with his big beefy paw and no words. And many others smiled and nodded, accepting him with friendliness in their gazes.

And he couldn't forget how most of the residents had

looked between him and Dani with curiosity and expectation.

Now Liam walked his trash to the large garbage can near the Jonathons' front stoop, then trudged up the steps and swung open the door to the house, where he was greeted with warmth and chatter. He made his way into the kitchen only to find Elise Jonathon and Nancy Hart—Cody's mom, who he'd met before dinner—along with a few other women. They all straightened and stopped speaking immediately, a few of them looking away from him. Hmm. Subtle, they were not.

"Ladies." He nodded as he moved toward the hot chocolate station, where someone had set up small mason jars filled with various accompaniments, from toppings like crushed peppermint, marshmallows, chocolate chips, truffles, and coarse sea salt to caramel sauce, dark chocolate syrup, and whipped cream.

"Liam, we were just talking about you," Elise said. "Nothing bad, I promise."

"That's a relief to hear." And rather surprising, actually. What was so interesting about him? When he'd first arrived, he'd felt like a fish out of water in his three-piece suit and big-city ways. But apparently nearly two weeks in Jonathon Island was all it took to bring out the casual in him, to become one of them. Because here he stood in his boots and jeans, even more comfortable than he'd imagined. He rather liked it too.

The other women resumed talking, though not about him. Their voices buzzed through the kitchen like a bunch of bees working away, but Elise joined him at the cocoa station.

"This is a superb party, Elise." Liam reached for two Styrofoam cups, placed them side by side, and filled them with cocoa from a Crockpot. It smelled divine. "Thanks again for having me."

"Of course. I'm thrilled you could come."

"Nowhere I'd rather be." He added a dash of sea salt to his own cup, placed a lid on it, then paused. Dani liked things sweet, but which toppings were her favorite?

"Trying to decide what to add to my niece's cup?"

He glanced at this woman, who wore a red sweatshirt, a knowing look on her face. Ah. Maybe that's what the women had been discussing. Not him, per se. But him and their favorite small-town tourism director.

Were his feelings for Dani so obvious to everyone? Or were they simply being nosy and making assumptions because the two of them were both single and working together?

Clearing his throat, he pointed to the chocolate chips. "She'd want some of those, right?"

"I'd think so."

He sprinkled some into her drink. "And marshmallows?"

Elise took a dish rag from the sink and started tidying up the area around the bowls, where sprinkles had spilled, likely by one of the many children he'd seen running around the property. "I've never known her to drink cocoa without them. Might want to add some peppermint too."

"Thanks." Adding a dash of peppermint, he then placed

a generous dollop of whipped cream on top of Dani's cocoa. "That oughta do it."

"I do believe it will." Elise swiped the counter where some hot chocolate had spilled. "I notice yours is very savory while hers is very sweet."

"Good observation." He chuckled and stuck a lid on Dani's hot chocolate, then took a sip from his own.

"I think the two are a good balance, don't you think?" Elise smiled, something secretive in it, and looked at Liam with expectation.

Ah. "We aren't talking about the cocoa anymore, are we?"

Elise winked. "You always were a smart one, Liam. Even as a little guy."

"I sometimes forget you knew me as a child. That you and Mom were friends." Settling back against the counter, he took another sip from his drink. "A lot of those memories are gone for me, unfortunately. And Dad doesn't really talk about them."

"That's understandable, given all you've lost." Elise set the rag down and turned to face Liam. "We didn't see you often, but I always knew you'd grow into quite the catch. And from what I've seen, from what Seb has told me, I think your mother would be very proud of you."

Not what he'd expected, and a lump formed in his throat. "Thanks, Elise."

"And I know I'm biased, but my niece is quite the catch too."

He smiled. "And your point?"

"Just that your mom would want you to be happy." Elise

squeezed his shoulder. "And if Dani makes you happy—better yet, if she makes you want to be an even better man than you already are—then don't be afraid to pursue her."

Aw, man. But what could he say? "You're right. Your niece is a catch. I'd be blind not to see that. And I'm not afraid to pursue her for my sake. More for hers." He frowned. "I'm not sure what I can really offer her."

"Like I said, you're a catch too. Offer her your heart. That's all she needs."

If only it were that simple. "I appreciate that, but we live in different time zones. And I don't have the best track record with relationships."

"Then it's a good thing that God is in the business of working out those kinds of pesky details like where people live." Elise said. "And as for your track record, I am fully confident that God will give you exactly what you need to rise to the occasion if He's calling you toward something new."

With another squeeze to his shoulder, Elise offered him a final smile and rejoined the other ladies, who were now discussing Mia and how they wished she would start dating again. Apparently, once women reached a certain age, all they wanted to talk about was matchmaking for the younger generations.

But that didn't mean they didn't have a lot of wisdom too. What Elise had said . . . well, he knew her words would probably keep him awake tonight.

Clearing his throat, Liam grabbed up both cups of hot chocolate and hustled out of there and back into the chilly night air. His and Dani's seats were near the back of the multi-layer circle, but because the fire was so large, its effects could still be felt from their spot. When he got back to the seat, Dani had bundled herself in a blanket.

"Here you go," he said as he lowered himself into his seat beside her and held out her cup. "Hopefully this will warm you up more."

"Took you long enough." Then she removed the lid from her cocoa and smiled at what she saw. "All of my favorites. Yum. Thank you."

Score one for Team Sweet. "No problem. And it wasn't my fault it took so long. I was waylaid by Elise."

"My aunt is quite the talker. I'm surprised she wasn't surrounded by her friends chattering away."

"Oh, she was when I first came in. A whole Gossip Brigade accompanied her."

Her lips curved upward. "Ah, yes. What poor souls were they talking about today?"

He rubbed the back of his neck and coughed.

"Oh." So she understood. If he'd been able to see the color of her cheeks, would they be pink? Did she like the fact the two of them were being lumped together? "Sorry about that. You know how small towns are."

"I actually don't." He sat back in his chair and stared at the fire, which was at this point taller than Seb and Cody, both of whom were stoking it with more wood. Someone on the other side started playing a guitar, and a few kids started singing "Ninety-Nine Bottles of Root Beer." "I mean, in theory I do. And I understand based on my oh-so-long stay here."

"Really. Like what?" Her tone had turned amused as she sipped her cocoa.

"Well, of course, there's all the stuff you've told me. But I've also picked up a few other facts. Like the Quinns are the stable owners and keeper of the horses on the island, but there hasn't really been a need for horses and buggies since the pandemic. And the Barretts own a construction company that used to be on island but now is off, but some of the brothers still live here, and they've not got the best of reputations. Oh, and Cody and Mia claim to be friends, but I'm sensing more there."

Dani laughed. "And just how did you pick up on all of this?"

"Hey, the coffee shop is a bastion of information. You sit there long enough"—he tapped his right ear as he turned his gaze to her again—"you hear things."

"And Jill Kelley is part of said Gossip Brigade."

"That too. I'm not sure she liked me at first, but my many purchases over the last few weeks have worn her down."

"That and the fact you're a sweet talker."

"What can I say?" He lifted his drink. "It's a gift."

She rolled her eyes playfully. "Well, color me impressed."

"You should be impressed. Did you know that Lyle and the gang even let me in on a round of gin rummy last night at Martha's?" He paused, fixed her with a meaningful look. "I think they could tell I was depressed after our ride in the park, and for some reason, they wanted to cheer me up."

"You sound surprised."

"I am. Back home, I don't even *know* my neighbors.

Of course, I live in a hotel, but still." He blinked, shaking his head. "And here, people who are practically strangers treat me like this."

"Like what?" Dani shifted in her seat so she faced him a little more. Her knee bumped into his—and didn't move away.

And suddenly everything inside him couldn't keep his brain off the desire to hold her hand.

He swallowed the lump in his throat. "Like they care about me. And not just as a new face, something interesting. But as a person."

"They do care." Dani paused. "*We* care."

"That means a lot." The singing grew louder around the campfire, so he leaned in a bit closer. "And I care about you too." Oops. "The town, I mean."

She drew nearer also, and her eyes searched his, a question in her gaze. Did she feel this pull toward him like he did to her? "*Just* the town?"

"No." How could he deny it? His fingers itched to trace every inch of her face—the faint creases in her forehead, the contours of her cheeks, the dimple right beside the lower bow of her lips. Would those lips taste as sweet as he imagined, like chocolate and cream? If he leaned in and kissed her right now, would her breath catch? Would his kiss elicit the same groan of pleasure as when she'd tasted that cookie earlier tonight?

Suddenly, he had to know.

Setting his drink on the ground, Liam reached up and grazed his thumb along her jawline, up, up, until he caught a strand of her silky hair between his fingers and brought it behind her ear. His eyes never leaving hers, he felt, more than saw, a shiver shake her as he leaned in closer, closer.

Finally, her eyes closed and so did his as he leaned in and skimmed his mouth against hers.

The kiss was soft, testing, and Liam sank into it, allowing himself the pleasure of this single moment with her, of his mouth moving against hers. Dani's sweetness carried through from her very essence to her lips, and she tasted of chocolate and decadence.

He'd never sampled anything so delicious.

How could he have ever thought just a taste would be enough? The *what if* rose inside him. Suddenly he didn't just want to test. He wanted to dive in. To belong to her, and her to him.

Liam's hands cupped her cheeks and pressed closer.

"Ow!" Dani broke away and looked at him, stunned, before leaping up from her seat.

"What? Did I hurt you?"

"Not you." But she was swiping at her pants, which were covered in a dark-brown liquid and—melted marshmallow? She pointed at the overturned cup on the ground at her feet. "My drink spilled during…" Her cheeks were red.

"You okay, there, Dani?" Seb approached, looking concerned.

"Oh yeah, just being clumsy." She glanced at Liam quickly, then back at her pants.

Seb leveled him with a hard stare. Had he seen them kissing? Did he approve?

But then the consequences of the kiss crashed over Liam. Honestly, what had he been thinking? No matter how welcoming the people of Jonathon Island had been, after he and Dani got the hotel plans completed and the council's approval, well, no matter what Elise had said, Liam was leaving.

Maybe God *was* in the business of working out details. But Liam couldn't take a risk that things would just magically work out.

Seb cleared his throat. "Maybe you should grab some paper towels, there, son."

"Right." Liam took Dani by the hand. "Here, let's get you inside." Turning, he led her up the steps into the house where the kitchen stood empty, then assessed the damage. The spot on her pants didn't appear too large, but she might have burns underneath. Then again, the cocoa had probably cooled considerably since the time he'd taken it out of the slow cooker. "Are you okay?" he asked as he gathered a fistful of paper towels from the dispenser near the sink.

"Fine. Mostly embarrassed." Dani took the paper towels and dabbed at the spot. "Um, that was—"

"I know. A mistake."

She looked up. Frowned. And it was a spear to his heart. And he hated the look on her face. The frown. A slack jaw. The wrinkles in her forehead pronounced. Why shouldn't she be confused? "Dani—"

"No, it's fine. You're absolutely right." Turning from him, she tossed the paper towels into the garbage. "We need to work together and get this job done and compromise. We can't let ourselves get confused, can we?"

Then she met his eyes. There was something unreadable in her expression.

Throat thick, he nodded. "Thanks for understanding."

"Of course." She pointed to her pants. "I think these are a lost cause, so I'm gonna go scrounge up some sweatpants from Aunt Elise's closet. I'll see you outside in a bit, okay?"

"Sure."

And she left the room, taking all the air with her.

Blowing out a breath, Liam pushed his hands through his hair, and they settled on top of his head.

"Everything okay?"

He turned to find Cody entering the kitchen via the back door. "Oh, hey. Yeah, everything's fine." He dropped his hands.

"Really?" An eyebrow raised, Cody headed to the stack of paper plates and served himself some chicken casserole. "I just saw Dani run upstairs, and it looked like she couldn't get away from you fast enough. You that bad of a kisser?"

Liam groaned. "You saw that?"

"I think the whole town saw it, man."

"Fabulous."

Cody rustled inside a bag of barbecue chips and plopped some onto his plate. "So what happened?"

"Kissing her was a mistake."

"And let me guess—you told her that."

"I screwed up, all right? But we've got too much at stake here to mess things up on a whim."

"You don't exactly seem like the kind of guy who does anything on a whim."

"Normally, I'm not."

"But she got to you. You're falling for her." It was a statement, not a question.

"Yeah, but I can't."

"Why's that?" Cody snagged a napkin. "And don't give me some lame excuse about how being with her would mess up the project, especially if you're both on board with compromising. There's gotta be more to it than that."

Liam sank against the counter and sighed. "Once we get the council's approval, the project will be turned over to someone else, and I'll move on to the next thing. Hopefully, getting my dad to let me take over as CEO in Los Angeles. Dani would never move there, and I can't be here, so it's a moot point."

"Ever heard of long distance, bro?"

"Been there, done that. It's not a good idea."

"Oh right, you mentioned something about that." Cody slid onto one of the barstools behind the kitchen island. "What happened?"

"A few years ago, I seriously dated a woman who lived in Los Angeles. Tiffany. But I was gone ten months out of the twelve we were together. I really liked her, and we did our best to talk every night, but you know how it is. Work would run late, or she'd be out with her friends when I'd call. I came home when I could, but she never wanted to travel out to my work site. Said I was too busy for her whenever she did."

"Sounds brutal."

"We did our best." Liam shrugged. "Though it wasn't enough for her. On our one-year anniversary, I took her out to this really great restaurant, one she'd been talking about for ages, and she told me I needed to ask her to marry me or break up with her."

"What'd you say?" Cody shoveled some casserole into his mouth.

"How could I ask her to marry me? I'd already signed up to take on a six-month project right after that and was up for a big promotion too, that would have required even more travel. It wouldn't have been fair to be planning a wedding while we were apart that whole time, and I knew I would have ended up disappointing her even more. So we decided to break up." Liam crossed his arms over his chest. "After that, I promised myself I wouldn't ever do long distance again."

Cody polished off his casserole and stood with his plate of chips, chucking his fork into the trash can. "I'm no expert by any means but sounds to me like you didn't want it badly enough. Neither of you did."

"Weren't you listening? My job situation just wasn't conducive to having a relationship."

"Nah, that's not it." Cody clapped him on the shoulder. "Because when you really want something, you go after it—no matter what obstacles stand in your way." A look stole over his buddy's face, almost like surprise at the words he'd spoken.

Then he blinked, shook his head, and carried his plate silently out the back door.

Leaving Liam in the kitchen, once more, alone with his thoughts . . . and absolutely no answers.

Eleven

TODAY, DANI HAD TWO GOALS.

Start the process of reimagining the hotel plans with Liam.

And not fall any farther for the man in question despite that incredible kiss last night.

She'd thought maybe once they'd gone into her aunt and uncle's kitchen, Liam might try to resume the kiss, but instead, he'd thrown proverbial cold water all over the place. Rejected her with a single word: *mistake*.

Didn't stop her mind from circling back to the kiss over and over again, though—or to the conversation she'd heard between Liam and Cody afterward. She hadn't meant to eavesdrop, but when Cody had asked Liam the very questions she'd wanted answered . . .

But his reasons for the rejection didn't matter. He was right. It *had* been a mistake.

And now, with Liam and Dani shut up in the same

room together—and plans to stay that way all weekend—she had to focus on the task at hand and the original pencil-drawn plans spread across the conference room table at the Tourism Bureau.

"It's been two hours, and we've made absolutely no progress yet." Dani sat back in her chair, which squeaked out a protest.

Liam tapped a pencil against the wooden tabletop. "I'm not trying to be difficult."

"I'm not either. But much as I like the idea of compromising, the reality of it is harder than I thought it'd be." Dani pointed to the plans. "Every time you suggest a change, I remember something I loved about the original way things were. I'm sorry."

"I get that. I'm not taking it personally. But if we have any hope of getting something together by Monday . . ."

"Ugh, I know."

A cloud covered up the sunlight that had just been streaming through the conference room window that faced the alleyway between the bureau and Great Lakes National Bank.

Liam frowned. "I hate to say this, but I'm wondering if there's any chance we could get the meeting postponed. We only have two days until the Monday meeting."

"No, that's actually a good idea. But can you afford more time away from the office? Isn't your coworker getting anxious for your return so you can pitch your project to your dad?" Liam's phone had buzzed when they'd first started working, and he'd said it was Travis looking for an update.

"He'll survive. I'll have to let Dad know about the schedule change, but if it means we have a bit more time to put together a killer proposal, I'm sure he'll be okay with it."

"All right." Dani picked up her phone and sent off a text to Seb. "I'll let you know what my uncle says about a postponement."

"Great." Liam stood and stretched, walking the room in his jeans and purple Henley that hugged his muscles. The man looked good in a suit, but all casual like this?

It was making Dani's second goal for the day that much harder to achieve.

"Great." Dani tried for a smile, but it felt forced. She fiddled with the silver foil ball in front of her that had once held one of Martha's breakfast burritos. "So, any ideas for how to get this compromise truly under way?"

Liam paced a few moments, then froze. "How about this? What if we do this kind of like a draft pick in sports?"

"A what now?"

"Come on, Dani. Don't tell me you've never watched a draft pick."

"Not exactly a sports enthusiast over here. I spend most of my free time watching the Travel Channel and planning all the trips I want to take someday." She flicked the foil ball across the table toward the trash can at the end. It flew across the room and hit the door instead. She winced. "Case in point."

Liam chuckled and bent to pick up the ball. With seemingly little effort, he tossed it into the can. "What if we just go back and forth, taking turns picking something we want to keep about our plan for the hotel? It makes us have to prioritize what's most important to us."

"That could work. Let's try it."

"Okay." Liam slid back into his seat and studied the plans.

Dani did the same, her eyes searching, mind considering—and doing her best to not let the spicy scent of his cologne wrap around her or sway her heart.

Finally, Liam sat back in his chair and swiveled to face her. "Ladies first."

"This is hard. And scary. What if your first pick is something I can't stand?"

"I'm open to suggestions if you've got a different way to go about this." There was no arrogance in his tone. He truly was trying to be objective.

And not for the first time she wondered why he was doing this. Why he'd stayed when he could have easily gone home. Was he truly falling for her, like he'd admitted to Cody? Or was it some sense of obligation, the promise his dad had given Seb?

She couldn't ask him though. It would definitely risk her ability to accomplish that second goal. Might derail them from goal number one as well.

Dani shook her head. "No, it's okay. We'll do it your way." Then she closed her eyes and allowed herself to remember the Grand Sullivan Hotel how it once was. What meant the most? Her eyes reopened. "I want the gazebo to stay where it is." It was too important to her—to her family's history—to ever see it moved elsewhere.

"Got it." Liam grabbed a yellow legal pad and wrote

down her choice. But what part of his monstrous plans would he insist on keeping first? "And for me, the rooms have to have televisions."

She nearly laughed with relief. "You and those TVs."

He winked and wrote his "demand" down with a flourish. "I've got to make a stand for my fellow modernites. What's next?"

"The community porch. It stays."

Frowning, Liam nodded. "Gotta admit, that one hurts. I really loved the idea of individual porches."

"And I have too many memories on that porch to let it go."

"Like what?" He looked up at her then cleared his throat and diverted his gaze. Tapped the legal pad again. "Never mind."

Her insides twisted. She hated him pulling away like that. But it was for the best. "Um, so what's your next pick?"

"The lobby as I have it designed here."

Ugh, no. "Does it really have to be three stories high? Aren't we losing out on valuable real estate we could be using for housing guests?"

"That's what the villas are for—to make up for that. The outside of a hotel has to be beautiful, but a lobby is a hotel's first real chance to impress guests. Why would we waste that opportunity?"

Dani swallowed against the loss of the lobby she remembered as it disappeared like a popped bubble. "O-okay." Her voice shook, but she plowed on. The faster they got this "draft pick" over with, the sooner they could be done here—and she could retreat to her couch and drown her sorrows in a pint of Ben & Jerry's and the Travel Channel. "Then speaking of the outside of the hotel, I want to rebuild it to keep the original architecture. The columns lining the veranda, the turrets, the twin low-lying dormers with multiple windows, the central open belvedere."

"The original is gorgeous, I'll give you that." Liam scratched his neck. "But we're keeping the colors I suggested."

"Red and gray? You can't be serious."

He shrugged. "White is so plain."

"And stately." She couldn't keep the indignation from her tone. Dani stood, walked to the window, and leaned her forehead against it. Breathed. "Sorry, I didn't mean to get worked up." When she turned back to face him, Liam was looking at her, frowning.

He opened his mouth to say something, then shut it. Sighed. "It's fine." Picked the pen back up. "Next pick?"

She wanted to move forward, to shake him, to shake back the teasing Liam, the one with the softness in his gaze, who asked her what was wrong.

But if he returned, then she probably wouldn't be able to stick to her resolve. This professional distance was good, and she'd do well to remember that.

Dani resumed her seat, shoulders straightened. "I want the rooms designed the way they used to be—all individual and unique, with charming bold patterns and antique furniture."

Nodding, he wrote it down.

They went on that way for hours, working out all the

little details, picking and choosing. And by the end of the day, they had a plan—and Dani hadn't flirted with Liam once.

But she still wasn't sure if she'd really succeeded at either of her two goals after all.

He and Dani finally had a plan. Liam should have been relieved.

But it was all wrong.

They'd concluded their meeting at seven last night, cross-eyed and exhausted, but he hadn't slept well.

And even though he'd just sat through a sermon by Pastor Arnie on peace, Liam's insides were as fidgety as ever.

It had been kind of nice to attend church though. Little Stone Bible—with its steeply angled A-frame roof, its twenty wooden pews with red hymnals that had clearly been handled over the years by multiple generations— was not at all like the mega church he'd attended as a kid with Mom and Dad, but despite its humble existence, love pulsed strong here. Liam could feel it in the greetings he'd received before service, in the sturdy presence of Seb and his whole family, including Dani, who sat on the opposite end of the pew next to her cousin Mia.

"That's all for today," Arnie Chamberlain said from the small pulpit. The fifty-something-year-old pastor closed his Bible, and the light streaming through the stained-glass windows lining the walls reflected off his shock of red hair. "Be sure to say hello to all of our guests and make them feel welcome."

And by that he meant Liam, because as far as he could tell, the fifty or so people here were all Jonathon Island residents.

The crowd stood and the din of their chatter rose, filling the small space. Laughter, pleasant and long. Hugs exchanged. Liam got up and moved to the wall, watching it all from the sidelines. His gaze narrowed in on Dani, so pretty in her long floral skirt and white top, her hair down and curled, looking like a spring flower.

How he'd managed to be in the same room as her yesterday and not kiss her again was a wonder.

"Mr. Stone."

He startled, and he looked to his left, finding Pastor Arnie there smiling at him in his black button-up shirt, his red hair slicked back. "Hi, Pastor." Liam straightened and fiddled with one of the cuff links on his suit jacket. It had seemed appropriate to wear to church, but after a few days of dressing down, the thing felt a bit awkward, even here. "Thanks for that sermon today. I'll be thinking about those verses on anxiety for sure."

"I'm glad, son. And happy to have you visit with us today." Pastor Arnie held out his hand and Liam took it, shook. "Finding peace is something some spend their whole lives figuring out. It's one thing to say 'trust God.' Another completely to actually learn how to do it."

Liam laughed, and it came out stunted. "I understand better than I'd like to."

"Well, we'd love to see you next week." He tapped his Bible against his chest. "We'll be talking more about it then."

"Wish I could, but I'm leaving Friday." Seb had agreed to move the council meeting to Thursday, which meant Liam's time here was running out.

And so was his time to figure out a better hotel plan with Dani.

"Too bad. Next time you're on the island, we'd love to see you though."

Like he could ever bring himself to come back. Not with how hard it already was to think about leaving Dani once. He'd never survive a second goodbye.

But Liam just smiled and nodded. "You got it."

As Pastor Arnie moved off to speak to an older woman, Liam blew out a breath and snuck a look at his watch, then again at Dani. Maybe he should just tell her he'd meet her over at the Tourism Bureau—

"Liam, dear."

This time it was Constance Franklin at his elbow—Mia's mother-in-law, the one who'd lost her son and husband in the boating accident a few years ago. "Hi, Constance." He'd met her at the town picnic the other night. "What can I do for you?"

"Oh, I was just wondering if you liked blueberry muffins." The woman smiled in a motherly way and pulled a Ziploc full of muffins from her large purse. Miraculously, they weren't squished. "I baked some extras and thought you and Dani might like to enjoy them together."

"That's really kind of you." Too kind, really. What would she say if she knew he'd kissed Dani and then called it a mistake? Probably lob all of these muffins in his face. Or maybe she was too nice for that. "Are you sure?"

"Of course I'm sure." She handed him the package of muffins and then shrugged, something frail in the motion. "They were my Troy's favorite. I always bake extras . . . old habits. So I'm happy if they can go to someone else and not straight to my hips."

Wow. "They look delicious, and I know for a fact Dani has a sweet tooth. These are gonna help fuel our next brainstorming session."

Constance nodded and patted him on the shoulder. "I'm glad, dear, I'm glad." Then she shuffled off, leaving Liam with nothing to do but lean back against the church's white wall.

This town really was something else.

"Are those Constance's famous blueberry muffins?" Seb asked as he sauntered up, rubbing his hands together.

"They are. Want one?"

Seb scanned the crowd, his gaze stopping on the spot where Elise, Dani, and Mia were chatting. "I'd better not. Elise has been after me to lessen my sugar intake. But you enjoy."

"I told her I'd bring it to my next brainstorming session with Dani this afternoon."

"Ah yes, she told me you'd be hard at work yesterday and today. Hopefully the extra time gives you a bit more flexibility in your schedule so you can really dazzle us with your presentation."

"Hopefully." Liam tried to infuse confidence in his tone, but judging by the scrutiny in Seb's look, he'd failed.

"Are things not going well? She told me this morning you had come up with a plan."

"We did, but . . ." Liam pressed his thumb along the Ziploc's seal. "Something about it just isn't jibing. It feels off."

"How so?"

"We're trying really hard to compromise our visions, and the way we went about doing that was to take turns selecting features we wanted to keep from our individual plans—or in Dani's case, the way the hotel used to be."

"Ah." Seb stroked his chin. "And that didn't go well?"

"It went fine in terms of us getting along and making decisions. But I think it feels off because it will create a really disjointed experience for guests. They'll arrive to a nineteenth-century building painted the wrong color and then walk inside to find a dazzling modern lobby. Then they'll go up to their rooms, which will have this vintage design but a sleek bathroom that doesn't match the charm."

"That sounds confusing."

"I know." Liam groaned. "But I honestly don't know how else to compromise."

"Let me tell you something I've learned after thirty-plus years of marriage, son. Compromise isn't just about picking and choosing things from your two individual visions of what life should be. It's about teamwork and blending your ideas so you create something new—together."

Liam straightened. Seb's words . . . they struck a chord. "That's where we've gone wrong. Seb, you're a genius."

Seb laughed. "I'm glad someone around here finally realizes it." Then he winked. "Now, go create something amazing with my niece."

Liam frowned. "We're just talking about the hotel, right?"

"Of course." Seb grinned. "What else would we be talking about?"

Ugh, not Seb too. "Thanks for the advice. I've gotta go." Liam walked toward Dani, who looked up from talking with Mia.

"Liam, hi." Her smile was fake—he knew her real one enough to recognize the counterfeit, and it still ate at him. "Are you ready to go?"

"If you are."

"I'll see you later." Mia gave Dani a hug. "Bye, Liam." She flashed him a meaningful look before leaving.

Without another word, he and Dani walked out the front, people waving bye and letting them know they were praying for them to work miracles on the hotel.

When they were finally out of earshot and on the road toward the Tourism Bureau, Liam spoke. "So I was talking to Seb, and something he said really sparked a thought in me."

"Yeah? What's that?"

"I don't know about you, but the plans we came up with last night—"

"They don't feel right, do they?"

He stopped, turned to face her. "You don't think so either?"

A breeze picked up the ends of her hair and blew them around her face. She swatted them away. "No. But I don't know how to make it better."

"I think I might."

"Really? How?"

"By creating something entirely new, something that's borne of the old, inspired by the old, but that brings the hotel into the twenty-first century."

Dani cocked her head. "And how do we do that?"

"By blending your design elements with the functionality and amenities found in my plan." At her look of confusion, he waved his hand in the air. "Like, for example, the community porch. That stays, but the terraces above it become individual room balconies. We can keep the colonnaded look—and the design of the porch that means so much to you—but we can also gain the amenity of a private view that so many modern visitors will love."

She tugged on a strand of her hair, considering.

"I've got a million other ideas, but that's just one example." A pause. "So, what do you think?"

"I think…" And then Dani flashed him a real and true smile, and his heart lurched inside his chest. "I think you're on to something, Mr. Stone. Let's go get our brainstorm on."

Twelve

DANI WAS EXHAUSTED–BUT THE GOOD kind. The kind that came from a hard day of work on a project that meant a lot to her, from a lot of progress made.

They still had a long way to go, but they'd begun the process of creating something new. To really get into a groove, to finally get on the same page. Which was wonderful for the project . . .

. . . and terrible for her heart.

It had been complete torture working alongside Liam, a guy she was having the hardest time not falling for more every day. Especially after his inspired idea to blend their ideas.

Which was why she probably should have said no when he'd insisted on making her dinner. But she'd been too tired from their all-day work session to argue. Now she was paying the price for that lapse in judgment, because the man was already attractive enough. But in the kitchen, making her a pizza?

Um, yeah. It'd be a miracle if she made it through the night without confessing her undying love for the food—maybe the man too.

"I know we still aren't finished, but I think we did good work today." Dani peeked into her oven and saw the pizza Liam had assembled after a quick stop at Doug's Market. Her stomach growled at the sight of the bubbling cheese, the crisping pepperoni, the crust starting to turn a golden brown. It smelled heavenly.

"I was really pleased with the headway we made too." Liam removed the apron she'd loaned him. It was dusted with flour and splatters of homemade sauce. "Our plans are really starting to shape up into something presentable."

"I agree." She yawned. "Sorry."

"Don't be sorry. You worked hard. Why don't you sit down, and I'll bring dinner to you in a few."

This man. "I'm not going to let you—" Dani's phone buzzed on the counter before she could finish her thought.

She picked it up and found James's name on the screen. "It's my brother. Mind if I take this?"

"Not at all." Sliding on a pair of oven mitts, Liam turned to deal with the pizza in the oven.

Dani slid her thumb across her phone and raised it to her ear. "Hi, James." She hadn't spoken with her brother in weeks—not since before Liam had shown up.

"How could you do this?" His voice, normally so staid and constant, grated against her ear with a hardened edge.

"W-what?" She glanced at Liam, who had pulled the

pizza out of the oven. Steam rose from it, and bubbles of cheese popped.

But instead of being focused on his work of art, Liam's attention was turned to her. His eyebrows knit together, and he mouthed "You okay?" to her.

"Dani." James's angry voice cut into her thoughts, and she jumped.

Turning, she walked to the couch and plopped down. Across from her, the television flickered the latest Travel Channel show on mute. "What's wrong?"

"Seriously? You have the gall to ask me that?"

Oh, her head hurt. This was her oldest brother, and he'd never been angry with her a day in his life. Not that he'd shown, anyway. "I…" Her voice shook. "I'm not sure what's going on."

He huffed. "What's going on is that Dad tells me you got him to sell the hotel."

"Not exactly. You see—"

"Oh, I see, all right."

Tears prodded the backs of her eyes, burning. "You don't understand—"

"He explained the terms of the deal to me, Dani, so I understand that." He plowed on, unaware, or uncaring, about what his words were doing to her. "What I don't understand is how you could trust Mom's side of the family not to screw us over."

She shut her eyes and rubbed her temple. Breathed in. Breathed out. "Uncle Seb wouldn't do that."

"Wouldn't he? He shares Mom's blood."

"Oh, come on. That's a poor argument. Don't you know

the man at all? And we all share Mom's blood—including me. Don't you trust *me*?"

"Honestly, Dani? I don't know anymore."

The words slapped her. Never had her big brother been this unkind. Then again, the hotel had always meant the most to him. He'd planned to stay on Jonathon Island forever, to take over the hotel when Dad retired.

But then, Mom had cheated.

Dad had burned the hotel to the ground.

And Dani had made a mess of everything—effectively setting into motion the final dissolution of her family.

"You still blame me," she whispered. Somehow, after all of these years, she'd hoped that her siblings had forgiven her lapse in judgment.

But James's tirade was proof that all was *not* forgiven.

"Don't make *this* about *that*." He sighed. "I just don't understand why you'd do it."

"Because." Eyes still closed, she felt the weight of Liam as he lowered himself onto the couch beside her. "I just want to fix all of this."

"I don't think you can." Then the line went dead.

Dani dropped the phone into her lap. All of her senses buzzed.

"Dani?" Liam slid onto the couch beside her. "What's wrong?"

"I . . ." Her eyes started to fill, but she blinked rapidly. "I don't think he's ever going to forgive me, Liam."

"Forgive you for what?"

"For . . ." She choked on the words, and a tear fell despite her best efforts.

"Hey, come here." Before she knew what was happening, Liam's arms gathered her close. She buried her head in his chest, inhaling the hints of bergamot and saffron emitted by his expensive-smelling cologne. "I'm here if you want to talk about it."

She couldn't answer him for a few long moments—she just let him hold her. Let him be still with her in this moment. Finally, she drew back, laying her head against the couch cushion behind her, facing him. Her body was still angled toward Liam's, and his hand cupped her elbow. "I'm so sorry about that."

"Hey." He placed his head against the cushion back too. "You *never* have to be sorry."

"Thanks," she whispered. Her eyes lifted briefly to the ceiling then back to Liam's handsome face. What was this guy doing here with her? She was such a plain Jane, small-town girl. He was Los Angeles. But he'd known pain too, and that connected them. If anyone would understand loss, it would be him.

Not that he'd understand her sense of shame—her guilt—but maybe he wouldn't judge her too harshly for that either.

"We were happy once. My family."

He squeezed her elbow.

"My parents used to be so completely in love. Like, they'd dance in the kitchen—and my dad isn't the dancing-in-the-kitchen type, you know? But he did it for her." Until it changed. "Somewhere along the way, I guess they grew apart. Maybe when Dad took over management of the hotel from my grandparents and they moved away.

Maybe when Mom got so busy running kids from activity to activity. Who knows how these things happen. They just do. And then Ryan came back to town."

She shuddered at the memory.

"Ryan?"

"Ryan MacBride. You met his older brother Mac—Stuart—at the bonfire." At Liam's nod of acknowledgment, she continued. "Anyway, Ryan was my mom's high school sweetheart until he moved away to Chicago to become a lawyer. He came back years later wearing suits and talking fancy and swept Mom off her feet."

Liam's eyes widened slightly, but he didn't say anything more.

"When Dad found out about the affair, they separated. All of my siblings were old enough to be living on their own. A few had already gone off to college. Others were here, working at the hotel. I was forced to go back and forth between Mom and Dad's houses. Mom eventually married Ryan. That was the last straw for Dad."

She was quiet for so long that Liam finally asked in that gentle way of his, "What happened?"

Dani fiddled with the small ring on the first knuckle of her forefinger. "One night, I found him drunk, walking up and down the lower balcony of the hotel—a huge bottle of vodka in one hand, a lighter in the other. Dad always smoked when he got stressed, and this particular night . . ."

She inhaled sharply at the memory of his bloodshot eyes. Of the utter despondency in them. At his words, repeated over and over. "He just kept saying, 'She left me, she left me.' I don't know. Maybe he expected her to come back to him. But then she got remarried. That must have been the thing he needed to realize it was never happening, even though they'd been separated for four years." Dani cleared her throat. "That night, he set that bottle on the floor and reached into his pocket, pulled out his pack of cigarettes, and stumbled into his vodka. It spilled everywhere. Soaked the old wooden floor. And when he lit the cigarette and accidentally dropped it . . ."

"Oh, no," Liam breathed.

"Oh, yes. Thankfully he wasn't standing right over the puddle, but then it caught fire right in front of him. I shouted at Dad to stomp it out, but it was too late. It was the perfect storm. Didn't help that the wind blew that night, but thankfully we got everyone out. Afterward, the insurance company had assumed it was an accident. Had been ready to pay. Nobody else saw what had happened. Nobody except me."

"That must have been a huge burden."

"You have no idea." She sniffed. "I was so upset in the following weeks, and in a moment of weakness, Mom finally got me to open up. She held me. I thought she cared. And when I told her Dad had done it . . ."

"She told someone?"

Dani nodded. "Ryan. And he told the insurance company, who then refused to pay for the damages. Dad couldn't afford to rebuild. Uncle Seb offered to pay him what the hotel was worth—which wasn't much, in the shape it was in—but Dad refused, saying he'd rather see the property rot then allow Uncle Seb to demolish it and rebuild something else on the property my uncle and Mom rightfully owned. He was just so angry with my mom."

"I can't imagine how tough that must have been to be in the middle like that."

"Don't you get it? I wasn't just in the middle. I am the *reason* my siblings all left. Why Dad left—found investors in Florida and started over with a new hotel." She straightened. "If I'd just kept my mouth shut, they'd all still be here right now. We might have figured out a way to make this rebuild happen much sooner. I might not be so . . ." She held back another sob.

"Alone?"

Her eyes watered again. Oh, nonsense. When had crying ever helped? And yet, finally sharing this load with someone—with Liam—somehow did.

"The thing you're not realizing here is that you told the truth. If you hadn't, your dad might have gone to jail for insurance fraud."

"I mean, maybe."

"There's no maybe about it. You did the right thing and probably saved your family even more heartache in the end." Liam reached for her again and pulled her close. She went willingly, and oh, how safe she felt, tucked in his embrace. "And I'm sorry that you feel so alone, but you're actually not. I'm here."

Oh, her heart. "Thank you, Liam."

"Always." His breath fanned against her cheek. "But wait. Your brother blames you for all of this? That's ridiculous."

She opened her mouth to protest.

But Liam only held her tighter. "No, Dani. Listen. You were just a kid torn between two warring sides. You trusted your mom to have your best interests at heart, and she failed you. That's not on you. It's on her. And it's on your dad, who let himself get so far gone that he burned down the place he loved best. The place *you* loved best."

"He was hurting."

"And it's understandable. But what's not understandable is how all of them left you alone here to pick up the pieces."

She knew they all had their reasons. But his words still hurt. Rather, the truth in them did.

"You know, one of the things I love most about you is your passion for this place. Your forgiving heart. The way you really see people and their faults and love them anyway. But you can't control what other people do, and you can't keep them from hurting you again, no matter how hard you try to protect your heart by taking the blame on yourself."

Her breath shuddered in and out. "Is that really what I'm doing?"

"I just want you to see how amazing you are. And if your family doesn't see it, that's on them."

"You're good for my ego, you know that?" She snuggled up against him, her arms tangled in his.

He chuckled, and the sound rumbled in his chest. "Hey, I've got an idea. The last two days have been really exhausting. How about we take a breather tomorrow? You could show me more of the island."

"I don't know. We only have four more days until the meeting."

"True, but I find that sometimes when my brain is too tired—when I've been noodling on a project too long—the best thing I can do is change up my scenery. Get outside, into nature. And maybe being here on the island, seeing the sights, will inspire something in us both."

"I like that idea."

"Good. Me too." He slowly pulled away. "Now, I also find that food is helpful in restoring balance after a nice, good cry."

"And how about some Travel Channel to go with it?" Dani picked up the remote and waved it in the air.

"Sounds like the perfect way to unwind."

She couldn't agree more—and that was the problem.

But apparently, it was a problem for another day. Because right now, Dani didn't want to be alone.

More than that—she didn't want Liam to go.

Liam inserted his hotel key card into his door and shoved his way inside. He set his briefcase down on the side table and then sank onto the edge of the bed, groaning.

He was in so much trouble.

Because he'd just spent the last two hours eating pizza and watching travel documentaries on the couch with Dani—pointing at the screen, laughing, and sharing—and he was fairly certain he was crazier about her than ever.

Especially after the way she'd spilled her heart to him, let him hold her.

How was he ever going to leave Jonathon Island?

And yet, how could he stay? He was needed back in Los Angeles—if not by Dad, then by Travis, who had been blowing up his phone all weekend.

And Liam had nothing to show him because he hadn't spent a lick of time on the Bertram proposal.

Speaking of Dad and work, he owed his father an update. They hadn't spoken since Seb had agreed to move the date of the council meeting back a few days. He checked his watch. With the time difference, it was only about six-thirty p.m. for Dad. Kicking off his shoes, Liam settled back against the bed's headboard and grabbed his phone, opening it to a video call. Then he dialed.

After a few rings, his father's face appeared on the screen. "Liam! Good to see you, son."

"Hi, Dad. You have a minute to talk?"

"I always have time for you." His father swiveled in his office chair. Instead of being "home" in their hotel room or out at a restaurant, Dad was working. On a Sunday night. Liam shouldn't be surprised.

"Just wanted to let you know that I'll be here an extra few days. I hope that doesn't throw our schedule off."

"Everything all right?"

"Yeah, just some differences in opinion we're working through."

"Is old Seb giving you trouble?" His dad laughed, but it turned into a hacking cough. Dad lifted an extra-large

Styrofoam cup from their local bodega and took a sip. It was likely filled with his favorite soda.

Liam held back a sigh. He needed to get back there soon. Or at the very least, text Marianne to beg her interference with Dad's diet. Make sure he was eating more than takeout junk.

"No, Seb's not giving me trouble." He couldn't help the smile that inched on to his face. "His niece, actually."

"Is that so?" Dad raised an eyebrow, and amusement filled his features.

Not him too. "Nothing like that." Not that he didn't *want* it to be something like that. He did. But as much as Dani fit perfectly in his arms, she didn't fit into his life. And he still couldn't figure out a way not to break her heart—or his own—at the end of all this.

"So, is that okay? If I stay a bit longer?"

"If that's what the client requires. I know you must be itching to get out of there though. You haven't spent time in a small town. Have we ever had a project in any place smaller than a million people?"

"Don't think so. But I haven't minded being here. It's a great place, actually." A place a guy could put down roots—if he didn't have other obligations.

But Dad wasn't just an obligation. It was Liam's privilege to help him. To make sure he had a nice long life after retirement. He'd promised Mom, after all.

His dad's mouth twitched the way it did when he was surprised by something. "I've got another project starting next month in Chicago that I was going to put you on, but other than that, you've got nothing else that's pressing, time-wise."

Wait. "You're sending me out again? But Travis and I are still planning to pitch our project to you."

"And I'm still planning to hear you out. But these things take time, and in the meanwhile, we have other projects on the docket."

"But Dad . . ." Liam sat up straighter on the bed. "It's not just about the Bertram project. I thought we'd talked about . . . well, one reason I want to stay in L.A. more is so you could start backing off. You know, begin to really think about retirement?"

His dad waved him off. "I've got time, son. Lots of time."

Seriously? "Maybe. Maybe not."

"Now what's that supposed to mean?"

"Just that . . . I don't know." Liam ran a hand through his hair. "Your doctor said you needed to reduce your stress. To take better care of yourself. And that was two years ago. Tell me. What's changed since then?"

"Now, son—"

"Nothing. That's what." Blowing out a frustrated breath, Liam turned his face toward the window. From here, he could see the streetlamps illuminated along Blueberry Boulevard and the harbor. There weren't any people out at this time of night, not that he could see, anyway. Most everyone was tucked away in their cozy homes. Their fireplaces were probably lit. Maybe they were eating pizza and watching travel documentaries with the people *they* loved.

Whoa. Loved?

He didn't love Dani.

But you could. If you'd only let yourself.

He blinked against the soul whisper.

"Liam." His dad's gentle voice filled the room. The same voice that had told him his mother and baby sister had died. The same one that had told him everything was going to be okay, all of those nights when nightmares had awakened him. The same voice that had cheered at every football game, that had cried out "That's my son!" when he'd walked across the stage to receive his college degrees.

Dad had always been there for him. How could Liam turn his back on him? He couldn't.

Not even for the possibility of love.

"Sorry, Dad." He turned his attention back to the screen, where his father leaned in, concern etched into every crevice of his face. "I didn't mean to snap at you. I just worry. I . . . I can't lose you too."

"Aw, son." Dad started to lift his drink then paused and set it back down. Pushed it away, out of the camera's view. "I promise I'll do better. Maybe you're right."

Liam perked up. "Right about what?"

"I'll think about it, okay? I just hate the idea of retirement. What am I going to do with myself all day, huh? Sit around alone and watch *Jeopardy* in my underwear?"

Liam snorted at the vision. "Or, you know, find a hobby. Golfing. Fishing. Reading." He waggled his eyebrows. "Going on dates again."

"Pshaw. It's too late for that." He patted his belly. "Besides, I'm too much of an old fuddy-duddy for anyone to be interested in me like that."

"Whatever, Dad. You're a caring, generous guy, and any lady would be lucky to have you."

"He's right, you know." A female voice intruded on their conversation, and before Liam knew it, Marianne was pushing Dad out of the way and waving at the screen. "Hi, shoogs. Good to see you."

Dad pushed right back against her. "Move out the way, woman. Can't you see I'm talking to my son?"

She smacked his shoulder and laughed. "Charles Stone, you just have a little patience." Marianne held up a plastic bag by its handle, a local restaurant's logo across the front in bright scrolling font. "I came all the way down here to bring you some dinner, so you'd best be nice to me."

His dad reached for the bag. "Have I mentioned lately how highly I value you?"

She held it out of reach. "Enough to give me a raise?" Her eyes sparkled behind her glasses.

"Don't push it." Lunging, he grabbed the bag from her and brought it greedily to his chest.

She just laughed.

Liam's jaw went slack. What. Was. Happening? Were his dad and Marianne flirting?

How had he never seen this? Holy cow. They were perfect for each other. But if his dad's words were true, he hadn't even dared think about dating.

Wow.

Marianne blew a kiss at the screen. "Would love to stay and chat, but I've got to get to bingo. I invited your father, but he claims he's got some all-important business to attend to." Marianne's eye roll told Liam exactly what she thought of that.

"Bye, Mare. Good to talk to you. See you soon."

"Bye, hon." Then the secretary hustled out of the room, and the click of the door said she was gone.

Dad started pulling containers out of the bag. "All right, where were we?"

"You were telling me that it's too late for you to ever fall in love again. But I don't think Mom would agree with you."

His dad's hand paused half inside the bag, and he lifted his head. "Don't bring your mother into this."

"Why not? Isn't she the one who taught us that love always wins?"

Love always wins, my boy. He remembered the soothing tone of her voice as she'd stroked his head one day when he was young, comforting him over something. He couldn't even remember what. He only remembered her words and the love with which she gave them. "Remember, Dad? 'Love is patient, it is kind. It does not envy, it does not boast, it is not proud. It does not dishonor others, it is not self-seeking, it is not easily angered, it keeps no record of wrongs. Love does not delight in evil but rejoices with the truth. It always protects, always trusts, always hopes, always perseveres. Love never fails.'"

"She did always love those verses, didn't she?" Dad pushed aside the bag of food and steepled his fingers, placing them against his closed lips. His forehead scrunched. Then he nodded. "And she used to say that love would find a way. That God would provide a path even when we couldn't see one. And that His paths always lead to love—often love we didn't see coming." His dad's eyes grew misty. "So maybe you're right. Maybe I shouldn't give up on love just yet."

"Maybe you shouldn't," Liam said. "Dad?"

"Yes, son?"

"I think maybe you've got a bingo game to get to."

Dad sat up straighter. Blinked. "I think maybe you're right."

"Win one for me, all right?"

"Will do. Love you, son."

"Love you back." Hanging up, Liam set his phone on the bed beside him. Huh. Imagine that. Dad was going to take a chance on love after all.

And if he could do it, maybe Liam could too.

Thirteen

TODAY HAD BEEN EXACTLY WHAT DANI needed.

To be outdoors, to get away from the desk, out into nature on the island that was more than home to her.

The weather was finally nice enough to take her fat-tire bike off her patio and pump the tires up, and she'd asked Cody if Liam could borrow his. And now, here they stood at the top of Sunset Cove, watching as the sun descended from the sky. Bidding them farewell with the last vestiges of its rays that looked like melting lava across the lake's surface.

"Other than the Grand, this might just be my favorite spot on the whole island."

"I can see why." Liam leaned forward against the stone wall built at the edge of the lookout. A blue spring jacket had replaced his fancy coat, and he wore sneakers instead of his loafers. He looked every bit the islander, his cheeks and nose red with the chill of riding into the breeze, his eyes full of wonder at the beautiful sight before them.

No doubt about it. He was the most handsome man Dani had ever known. And after the way he'd listened, held her, told her she wasn't alone last night . . . well, he was the kindest too.

They'd spent the entire morning biking around as she showed off the best parts of Jonathon Island—Lovers' Leap, Archway Boulder, Bones Cave—and he'd let her put on her tour guide hat without too much teasing.

He'd told her all about his dad and how he thought maybe he had a crush on the company secretary. They'd brainstormed silly ways to get them together if bingo hadn't done the trick, and they laughed in the process.

That was the other thing—the laughter. He made her laugh more than anyone else.

If only he didn't live on what might as well be the other side of the world. But she knew why he had to go back. The fact that family meant so much to him was another reason she loved him.

Well. Not *loved* loved. She wouldn't be so foolish as to have fallen in love with someone who was leaving. Dani shivered at the thought.

Liam bumped her elbow with his. "It's getting a bit colder now that the sun's going down. Should we get back?"

Dani shook away her dreary thoughts and focused on the magnificent view in front of her. "Come on, city boy. You can last a little longer." Her knees hit against the cold wall as she leaned forward for support. "We can't miss the best part of the show."

"And what's that?" Liam's voice had grown quiet, almost husky.

She glanced up at him, smiled. She would miss him when he left. They only needed to finish their presentation, pitch it to the council on Thursday, and then he'd be gone. But for right now, she was going to enjoy every moment she got with Liam Stone. "That moment just before the sun disappears is always the most beautiful."

He blinked at her, opened his mouth as if to respond. But instead of saying something, he turned and slipped his arm around her shoulders, and together, in the silence, they watched the last blip of light as it dropped from the sky. Just before it was gone, it seemed to radiate out, to reach beyond its bounds, like a blinding flash of shimmering diamonds.

And then . . . darkness.

But oh, how gorgeous it had been before the flame had gone out.

"You were right." Liam smiled, gave her shoulders a squeeze, and stepped away, leaving warmth in his wake. "That was beautiful. Thanks for sharing it with me."

"Thanks for being here."

An owl hooted somewhere in the distance. The moon took over the sky, illuminating the dark even after the sun had retreated. It cast a different light over the island, and it was beautiful in its own way.

"Where to next?"

She shrugged. "That's the end of the tour."

"Well, it was a fabulous tour." He cocked his head. "But there's one more place I'd like to visit, if you don't mind."

"I don't mind. Lead the way." Because even though he'd only been here for just under two weeks, Liam had become one of them. He knew his way around. The townspeople accepted and loved him. She couldn't count the number of people who had approached her after church and said they were "rooting for them."

Wouldn't they all be surprised when he left and never returned . . .

Don't think about that now.

Dani and Liam walked a little way through the trees until they reached the path where their bikes were parked. They climbed on, and Dani followed Liam the short distance to downtown. She almost wasn't even surprised when he turned up the large drive toward the Grand. For how often the place had been a topic of conversation lately, they hadn't spent much time here after that initial meeting.

But Liam didn't head for the half-burned hotel building. Instead, he bypassed it and continued on the grounds until they reached the small gazebo, which stood in a little clearing of trees whose branches were sprouting back to life.

She stopped the bike, grounding herself. "What are we doing here?"

Liam climbed from his bike and reached for her hand. "I thought we might be hungry at the end of our tour."

Hungry? She didn't know what the man was talking about—the nearest restaurant was several blocks away on

Main—but she didn't have to know. She just had to trust him. And she did.

So she followed him toward the gazebo, which, despite the years, still stood in the exact same spot. Sure, it could use a fresh coat of white paint, but the eight pillars set in a circle, the intricate woodwork along the top, the sweetly pointed roof—all of it had remained strong.

And when she stepped up the three stairs and entered the place that had been her haven on more than one occasion, she gasped at the black-and-white, wool blanket on the ground, the electric space heater tucked neatly away, the picnic basket, the LED lanterns illuminating the place with magic. "What's all this? How . . ."

"Maybe some island fairies left this here for us." He leaned over and flipped on the space heater, which, in moments, took the chill out of the air surrounding them.

She lowered herself to the blanket and sat cross-legged. Laughed. "More like you charmed your way into a favor."

"I knew you thought I was charming." He sat beside her, and they both laughed. "No, I wanted to surprise you and may have asked Mia for some ideas early this morning. And help."

"Ah." Dani watched Liam dig in the picnic basket, withdrawing a thermos, two mugs, and a few wrapped sandwiches. "That was really sweet of her. And you."

"You told me when we first met that the gazebo was really special to you." He offered her one of the sandwiches. "I hope I didn't overstep or intrude on your special spot."

"You didn't." She took the sandwich, the wax paper crinkling beneath her fingertips. "I come here a lot. To think. To get away. To remember why all of this matters in the first place. What I'm fighting so hard to save." Dani sighed, setting the sandwich on her lap. "It's where my parents got married. Where they first met, actually. This place is literally my origin story."

"That's really neat, Dani." A pause. "I hope you don't mind that I brought all of this stuff into your sanctuary."

She looked around at the lantern, the heater, the blanket. "You know, it's different. But I don't mind. In fact, it's actually really cozy. Usually I can't stay out here all that long in the winter because it's too dark and cold. Even some summer nights are too cool."

"Hmm." Liam unwrapped his sandwich and took a bite, chewing and looking thoughtful.

"What are you thinking about over there?"

"Nothing I'm ready to talk about. Yet." He winked.

"So mysterious." She smiled and reached for the thermos. Unscrewing the lid, she poured cocoa into each mug. "Do you have a place like this back home? Somewhere you can retreat to?"

His silence caught her attention. Ugh. Why had she asked that? She knew he felt like he didn't have a real home. Maybe that meant he didn't have a sanctuary either.

She quietly slipped a mug into his hands.

His face softened. "Thanks."

"You're welcome."

Dani sipped on the hot cocoa, which warmed her insides.

"Sometimes I drive out to Claremont. That's the smaller suburb where I grew up." His words punctuated the silence. Soft. Something aching in them. "I park near our old house. I stand across the street, lean against this old gnarled tree."

Dani set her mug down on the wooden bench above her, turned, placing her hand on Liam's knee. Squeezed in a show of support.

He glanced down. Setting his mug beside Dani's, he covered her hand with his own. Then, "Some of the neighbors are the same. They say hello. Ask how I'm doing. How Dad is. It's pleasant. They're pleasant." He swallowed hard. "It's like I'm drawn there because it's where we were happy. Just like this place for you." Liam blinked. "But I know I don't belong there anymore. And that's never more apparent than when I see the new family who lives there. A mom, a dad, a sister, a brother. All together. All happy. Whole. And I can't stay. But I can't leave either. And then, the memories come."

"What memories, Liam?"

He shuddered, but he didn't shut off like she expected him to. "The night my mom . . ." Liam pursed his lips. "I was ten. My baby sister wasn't due for another two months. Dad was out of town on business. I was begging Mom to hurry up and get me to my baseball practice. She was racing around, trying to finish up something around the house to make it on time."

Oh, Liam. She longed to scoot closer to him, to lean her head on his shoulder. But they were just friends, and she didn't want to confuse the situation. So she pulled her knees into her chest and fixed her attention fully on him. The lantern light flickered for a blip of a moment. "What happened?"

"Thinking back, she'd had a headache and been acting tired, really stressed for a few days, since Dad had been out of town. But I was too distracted to realize something was actually wrong." His voice had turned mechanical, as if it was all he could do to get through this. "Then, she tripped as she was going down the stairs, hit her head, which bled really bad. I was terrified. Managed to call 911. They came for her, and as they wheeled her out of there, she grabbed my hand and told me she loved me, that it was all going to be okay." He looked up at Dani. "It wasn't okay."

"I'm so sorry." Dani wasn't surprised to find her own eyes had begun burning with tears. "Pre-eclampsia?" Her older cousin Evie had had a mild form of the condition with her youngest child, so Dani knew the basics.

"Yeah. I just wish I'd known what to watch for. Wish I'd paid more attention to her needs than my desire to get to that stupid practice."

"You couldn't have known. You were just a kid. And pre-eclampsia can sneak up on you. It's not like even your mom would have known."

"Maybe. But I was old enough for Mom to say one last thing to me as she left and my neighbor came over to take care of me."

"What was that?"

"'No matter what happens, you and Dad have to be there for each other. He needs you, sweet boy.'"

Wow. And Liam carried the weight of her words with him even to this day. "It's like she knew what was coming."

"I've often wondered."

"Whatever the case, you've done an amazing job fulfilling her wishes. Though I don't think your mom meant for you to carry so much."

"What do you mean?"

"Just that she never meant for you to become responsible for your dad and his health and his choices. Do you even want to be CEO?"

"Not especially."

"You'd rather stick with the architecture, being on site, right? I see how you come alive when you're working on your plans. And yet, you're planning to give that up so your dad can feel okay about retiring."

"I don't think he'll retire with anyone else at the helm. It has to be me."

"But would your dad want you to give up your dreams for his sake?" She said the words gently, because she didn't want him to think she was judging him. Just that she wanted to help.

"That's what you do for family." He studied her then lifted a hand to tuck a strand of hair behind her ear. The motion surprised her, but she welcomed his touch. "Isn't that what you're doing here with the hotel?"

"Regardless of my reasons, it's literally my job to restore the hotel, to rebuild the economy." Dani's hands fell from her knees, and she sat cross-legged, leaning forward, intent. "And there's nothing else I'd rather be doing."

"You sure about that? Because, so long as we are lobbing truth bombs, you could have any job in the world. For someone who loves the Travel Channel so much, you haven't really gone anywhere." His words sliced, though the tone with which he said them offered a healing balm. "I know you love it here and love your job, but how much of that is wrapped up in this hope that doing that job will bring your family back?"

"To be honest? I don't know. Maybe . . . maybe more than I want to admit." Dani looked away. "Thankfully, I think with our plan, we have an amazing shot at that happening. If we can just get the proposal right. Get the council to agree."

"We are definitely going to give it our best shot. But Dani, you're banking everything on them coming back. Your happiness most of all. And what happens if they don't?"

"You're not the first person to ask me that." Something in her heart throbbed at the thought. "And my answer hasn't changed. I'm not sure."

"Would you . . ." Liam cleared his throat, and that brought her attention back to his face. Reaching out a hand, his thumb traced her jaw all the way to her ear lobe. What was happening? This was not a friendly touch. It was more.

And she should move away for both of their sakes, but she was caught, completely derailed, with no desire to move away. "Would I what?"

"If your family didn't come back, would you ever consider leaving the island?"

Why was he asking her? Oh. His eyes held a desire that reached inside, took hold. Oh.

"Oh, Liam, I don't know. I've honestly been holding

so tightly to this dream that I haven't allowed myself to consider another possibility. But . . ." Was he saying what she thought he was? "I . . ."

"Okay, how about this." Bringing his face closer to hers, Liam touched the tip of his nose to her own. "What if I told you I was thinking of staying past Thursday?"

Be still her heart. "For how long?"

"Well, I have to go back to pitch the Bertram project to my dad along with my coworker, Travis. But Dad said I don't have any other projects scheduled for the next month. So I could stay through the weekend for sure and then maybe come back after that for a bit? I'm not positive. I only know I'm not ready to leave you. Dani, I . . ."

"Liam," she breathed. "Are you serious right now?"

"More serious than I've ever been. So. What do you think? Are you willing to try with me?"

In reply, Dani closed the gap between their lips and kissed him. And this was no ghost of a kiss. At first, it was sweet, tentative. She wound her hands up and around his neck, running her fingers along his hairline. One of his hands fell to her waist, and he tugged her closer. The other plunged into her hair as he deepened the kiss.

She sighed at the taste of cocoa on his lips, at the sweetness of Liam, at the kisses he feathered along her cheeks and jaw. How had she gone her entire life without ever feeling so cherished? Liam was . . . well, maybe he wasn't as big-city as she thought. Maybe deep inside he was small-town too, and maybe he'd awakened more in her also. A bigger life. Or maybe it was just that with him she was more courageous, more willing to see a different tomorrow.

So she leaned into the kiss, and with it, awakened something in him. He seemed to groan, deep inside, and deepened his kiss and no longer was he touching her with the same care he'd give a glass ornament, but breaking her apart with his kiss.

Breaking, and remaking, and suddenly she saw herself as more.

The person free of the haunting of her past.

Finally, he pulled back, both of them out of breath. He set his forehead against Dani's, and for a moment, neither spoke. Then, his lips lifted into a grin. "So I guess the feeling's mutual, huh?"

"Oh, it's more than mutual, buddy." Because the idea of him staying—whether long enough to figure out what this was between them, or maybe even longer . . . "Do you really think you could stay?"

"If we get the council to approve our proposal and move forward with the project, yeah, I think so." He paused. "For a few weeks at least. And maybe . . . yeah, maybe more."

"Seriously?" She grasped his hand tight. "How? I thought you'd committed to helping Travis with the Bertram project long-term."

"I could still help him from afar if Dad lets us move forward with it."

"Wait. You'd do that? Stay for the length of the project?"

"Maybe. If we thought this had the potential to be

something more between us." He paused. "To be what I think it can be."

"I think it can be something great too." A thrill ran through her. "But I thought the rebuild was supposed to take two or three years."

"Well, I think we can have some parts done by Christmas like you wanted. Not all of it, of course, but maybe the first phase. I could commit to that, and we could see how things go from there?"

"That would be amazing. But are you really willing to stay that long? To be away from your dad? I thought he was getting ready to retire and you had to be in Los Angeles. That you didn't want him to be alone anymore."

He played with a strand of her hair, rubbing it between his thumb and forefinger. "Honestly, he's not thrilled by the idea of retiring. And as for being alone, I have a sneaking suspicion that things might change in that area."

Dani laughed. "Well, if you did stay, I happen to know of several homes available for cheap rent at the moment."

She didn't expect her words to have such an effect on him. He actually stilled, then swallowed. "A real home?"

"A real home."

"I wouldn't hate that," he said softly. His gaze roamed her face.

"Me either," she said, taking a breath.

Like Mia had said, it was time for Dani to take a leap. And she might fall on her face or end up with a broken heart. Or she could fly.

Either one was possible. And wasn't the beauty of life in the surprises, anyway?

"Okay, for any of this to happen, though, we need to finish up our presentation." Liam gave her another soft kiss before standing and holding out his hand. "Which means you need to stop distracting me."

"But I like distracting you." Dani hopped up and smiled up at him.

"And you're really good at it too." He pulled her into his arms. She hadn't realized how well she fit there until now. Leaning his head down so his lips touched the shell of her ear, Dani shivered. "You're also providing me with some fabulous motivation to get this job done, and done well."

"Happy to be of service." She pulled back and tapped her forefinger against her mouth.

"Good," he said as he leaned down and kissed her again. Too soon it ended. "Then let's get to work."

"Lead the way, Mr. Charming."

This had to work.

But if the looks on Martha, Tara, Janine, Patrick, and Seb's faces were any indication, he and Dani had their work cut out for them.

"And as you can see here"—Liam pointed to the projector screen in the conference room—"we plan to keep the current pool but add a poolside restaurant that will allow for convenient drinks and lunches."

"But"—Dani interjected from her spot beside him, every bit his equal in this project—"it will be as small as possible, tucked away so it doesn't ruin the view that is the main draw of the porch and pool area." She flashed a grin his way, because that had been a point he'd conceded, and she'd won.

Her confidence and beauty took his breath away. It wasn't as if she'd dressed much differently—maybe a little fancier because her blue, long-sleeved blouse had a ruffle around the collar. But there was something different in her shoulders, pushed back but also relaxed, as if she wasn't worried or trying to prove something.

Her eyes radiated her passion for this project. It was something he'd seen over the weeks but especially over the last few days as they'd worked tirelessly together on the last piece of the puzzle. Their grand finale. The thing they were both sure would tip the scales in their favor. Liam really hoped it would, anyway.

Because he didn't like the frowns on several of the faces before him. The only one whose lips weren't turned down was Seb, and that could have merely been support for his niece.

"That's right," Liam continued. "And you may have noticed the balcony situation—"

"I hate that you took away the upper community deck." Tara Chamberlain fiddled with a pen as she studied the slide pulled up on the screen. "Not only is that a great space for guests to gather, but it provides such a wonderful view of the harbor."

Dani nodded. "I had the same concern, but we made sure to keep the community feel alive by maintaining the long lower deck. And the view from there is plenty gorgeous." She looked at Liam again, smiled. "We also agreed that having private balconies with a stellar view would provide the opportunity to have premium suites available for those who don't mind paying more."

We. Liam couldn't help but notice Dani's repeated use of the word. And what a fabulous *we* they made. All the dinners together, late nights spent perfecting their plans and this presentation. And yes, maybe snuggling and kissing too. Making plans.

He still hadn't asked his father about being the lead on this project after the council signed off. He wanted it to be a done deal before he broached the subject. Besides, any time he'd tried to contact his dad this week, Marianne had been surreptitiously vague about his whereabouts.

Liam cleared his throat and his mind. He needed to focus, or they'd never get this pitch signed and sealed.

Turning on his inner charming businessman, he continued. "Janine, I know one of your biggest concerns was losing the historical integrity of the hotel. So we've done our best to keep the Colonial Revival and Queen Anne-inspired architectural elements, especially on the outside. From there, other than a few tweaks like the upper terraces, it will look like a replica of the original."

"Well, that's definitely an improvement." She folded her arms over her chest. "But how can you justify that miles-high lobby?"

Liam chuckled. "Just a few stories high, and I assure you, we plan to keep the decor—even there—in the style of Dorothy Draper, just like the most recent design of the hotel before the fire. We want to combine the elegance of the past with the modern amenities—like a working elevator, a gorgeous water feature, a baby grand piano—in order to impress those looking for a little step into the past as well as those looking for luxury."

"And what about the grounds?" Patrick asked. "The last thing we need is something overcrowded. The place needs room to breathe."

"I'm so glad you asked that, Patrick." Liam flipped to the next slide, showcasing the proposed grounds, including their "grand finale"—the thing they'd show them at the end of the presentation. "Dani convinced me that less is more, and that the real amenity here is the setting. So, while we will be upgrading the golf course to an eighteen-holer and putting in a small set of pickleball courts, we nixed the idea for a movie theater, basketball court, and villas. Oh, and"—he smiled at Dani—"the gazebo stays where it currently is."

The brilliant grin she flashed him was a shot of confidence right to his veins.

Together, they really had created something great.

By the end of the presentation, he had Patrick and Seb nodding. Tara drummed her fingers along the tabletop but was no longer frowning, which was progress. Janine still sat back in her chair, arms still over her chest. Maybe she really was a lost cause. But Liam couldn't charm them all—and he was okay with that.

So long as Dani still found him charming.

He smiled at the thought.

And then there was Martha, who had been uncharacteristically quiet for the duration of the presentation but finally spoke up. "I like where you're going with this, but

I'm having a hard time picturing this supposed marriage of the true-to-history and modern approaches."

"I'm glad you asked, Martha." Dani clapped her hands. "Might we propose a little field trip?"

Martha opened her mouth to protest, but Liam swooped in and offered her a hand up. "Would you accompany me in my fine chariot, milady?"

The older woman rolled her eyes, but a good-natured smile filtered through. "If you mean Seb's golf cart, then fine."

His lips twitched. Behind him, Seb bellowed with laughter.

They all walked out of the Tourism Bureau onto Main Street and divided between Seb's six-passenger cart and Patrick's four-seater, which were both parked in back.

Liam got behind the wheel of Seb's, and Martha climbed in beside him. "Don't drive too quickly now."

"Yes, ma'am. Everyone good?" He pulled his sunglasses off the dash and set them on his face. The sun shimmered bright, and Liam prayed it was a foreshadowing of their success today.

Martha gripped the grab handle with white knuckles—did the woman ever give up control without protest?—and the rest of the passengers called their readiness, so Liam started up the cart and headed west on Main toward the Grand, Patrick and his passengers following behind, toward the gazebo.

Their grand finale.

When they arrived, Liam parked and rounded the cart

to help Martha while the others got out. The moment of truth had arrived.

Dani met him at the front of the vehicle. "Ready?"

Her bright eyes chased away any doubts he had. He wished he could drop his head and kiss her like he'd gotten used to doing, but right now was time for professionalism. "Ready." Then he turned to the group, who looked at them both with interest, and nodded toward the gazebo. "We obviously couldn't show you what the hotel would look like with our two visions blended together."

"But we could show you a small example with the gazebo," Dani said.

Murmurs went through the group as Liam pointed toward the octagonal structure, with its shingled dome roof, its white pillared columns, and its turned spindle railing encircling all but the front, where three steps led to its elevated spot off the ground.

"Dani told me how meaningful the gazebo is to the community. How long it's been around, how it's been a favorite spot for weddings and gatherings. And we didn't want to do anything to change that."

"Only to enhance people's ability to make use of it." She waved her hand in invitation. "Let us show you."

They all walked the brick-laid pathway toward the steps, where Liam and Dani stood at the top.

"As you can see, we got an electrician out here and made sure the wiring on the gazebo worked," Liam said. "Thankfully, it only took a bit of work to get things up to snuff."

"And that's when we hung the lights." Dani pointed to the tasteful bulbs now hanging from the ceiling. When they'd tested them last night, they'd provided a warm, romantic glow that had only added to the clearing's natural beauty. "Because as anyone who has ever been out here at night knows, it's pitch-black, and you have to use your phones as flashlights."

Tara tapped her chin, nodded. The hint of a smile danced around her mouth.

Arms crossed over his burly chest, Patrick walked closer, peering up at the lights. Inspecting. Martha and Janine did the same. Meanwhile, Seb smiled as he watched Liam and Dani.

They were hooking them. Now to reel them in. Liam continued. "Anyone who's been out here also knows how cold it can get. We wanted guests to be able to enjoy the gazebo at all times of the year, so we installed an infrared heater. It's nonintrusive but will provide consistent heat during certain hours of the day and evening." He nudged Dani, and she hurried to flip the small switch. The heat was immediate, and the group oohed and aahed at the difference.

"And Dani here even had the thought that the hotel could place a basket with blankets under the bench. Maybe even place a firepit and chairs over there"—he pointed to a spot in the clearing—"and hold evening gatherings out here for guests with complementary beverages and appetizers."

"Speaking of that . . ." Dani turned to the back of the gazebo, where she'd had Aunt Elise leave two thermoses of hot chocolate, some cups, and fresh-baked cookies. She grabbed up a cup and one thermos. "Who wants refreshments?"

Everyone said yes—even Janine—and Liam helped distribute the treats while Dani prepped them. They really did make a good team, didn't they?

"You've outdone yourself here." Patrick took a giant bite of his cookie and munched while his eyes roved the gazebo once again.

"Agreed. I love it." Tara shook her head. "You really have managed to enhance the convenience without destroying the historical integrity of it. If this is what you're going to do with the hotel, well, then I'm offering my full support."

"Thank you, Tara." Liam squeezed Dani's hand, determined not to let his excitement show. "And what about the rest of you?"

"What about the added cost of the heat and lighting?" Seb asked. "The added cost of all the extra amenities, in fact."

"I can show you the numbers when we get back to the conference room, but it will be minimal, especially when you consider how much more we can charge for rooms and services than in the past because we can bill this as a luxury resort."

Seb put out his hand for a shake. "If that's a fact, then you've got my vote."

"Mine too," Patrick said. "I like the feel of this. Seems it'll attract tourists with deep pockets, which will be good for all of us. But it won't be some modernized resort that isn't fully Jonathon Island." He turned to his sister-in-law.

"Come on, Martha. Say you agree so we can grab something to eat. I'm starving."

Martha scoffed. A breeze blew through her gray curls. "You're always starving." Then she wiggled her fingers in the air toward the gazebo. "I suppose you've done a nice enough job compromising so we are all happy."

Liam nearly chuckled. The woman couldn't give a compliment to save her life. "So does that mean . . ."

"Yes, yes." Martha huffed. "You've got my vote too."

"And what about me?" Janine asked. "I know you've got your majority, but does my vote mean nothing?"

"On the contrary, Janine." Liam approached her, hands folded. He glanced at Dani, whose eyes had widened. "We would covet your vote, though I've heard how averse you are to the addition of technology."

Janine harrumphed. "I am that. But . . ." She pursed her lips, looking at the gazebo. Then something softened in her eyes. "I suppose I can also appreciate innovation when I see it. And while I am not wild about the changes you've made, I recognize that most developers wouldn't do as much as you have to immerse themselves in our town and become one of us in order to understand what's important here."

Whoa. "That is high praise coming from you." Liam pressed a hand over his chest, which ached just a little. "Thank you."

"It doesn't mean I won't be carefully watching the construction to ensure things remain as historically accurate as possible." She pointed a finger at Liam. "But I suppose you've got my vote anyway."

The group cheered and Seb held up his cup of cocoa. "Here's to the revival of our home. And to Liam and Dani, who worked so hard to make this happen. I'm very proud of you both. And thankful."

"Hear, hear!" Tara said with a smile as she tapped her cup against Seb's and then Martha's cups.

"Thank you, Seb. Everyone." Liam's voice had grown thick, and when he looked at Dani, she offered a wink and a sly smile. "It's been an honor to work with you on this."

The group finished drinking their cocoa and ate their cookies, talking about life as they headed back toward the golf carts.

Dani slipped closer to Liam. "We did it," she whispered into his ear.

"We did." And he didn't care who was watching. Liam leaned down and kissed her. Just a peck—but a peck in front of prying eyes meant the whole town would see them as good as engaged by sundown.

But Liam didn't care.

The measure had passed. Their plan had worked.

And as long as Dad approved, Liam was staying. At least until the project was done, which could be two years. And by then, well, who knew. Maybe he'd come to love this island as much as Dani did.

Maybe he already did.

When he pulled away from Dani, her cheeks were pink—maybe from embarrassment or maybe from the breeze that had kicked up. But when she headed down the steps and joined Tara, who took her by the arm and off a way, a huge grin on her face and head bent in to speak to Dani in low whispers, all Liam could think was how lucky he was.

Seb found his way to the steps, eyebrows lifted. "So, you and my niece, eh?"

Liam chuckled and leaned back against a post. "She's an amazing woman."

"That she is."

The man glanced at where Dani stood beside the golf cart, now surrounded by both Tara and Martha. Probably fending off questions. Liam would rescue her, but she was smiling, so maybe she didn't mind.

Then Seb faced him again. His expression sobered. "But how is this going to work, with you returning to California?"

"Well, that's the thing." Liam shoved his hands into his pockets. "I'd like to maybe stay, oversee the project. Or the first phase of it, anyway."

"Would you now." It wasn't a question. But a smile tugged at the corners of Seb's lips. "Elise was right then."

"Isn't she always?" Liam chuckled. "I still need to check in with my dad, make sure it's all right. But yeah. I'd like to see what happens."

"Just don't break my niece's heart. She's had a rough go of it."

"I know she has. And I won't." Liam swallowed hard, praying he could keep that promise. After all, he wasn't anything special. But Dani was, and she was worth holding on to. Worth the effort. And now that it had worked out for him to stay here, he didn't have to worry about long distance.

He could just focus on *them*.

Only two things stood in his way: talking with Travis about being more behind the scenes on the Bertram project and putting in his official request with Dad.

"Speaking of that, I should make that phone call. Would you mind driving everyone back? I'll walk myself over later."

"Sure, sure." Seb called to the group, told them to pile in. Then he turned back to Liam. "You've done great work here, Liam, and I know your dad will be proud."

Before Liam could thank him, Seb was bounding down the steps, every bit as spry as a man twenty years his junior.

Dani joined him on the steps. "You're not coming back?"

"I need to call my dad, let him know what's going on." He gave her another kiss, this time on the cheek. "But let's celebrate tonight, yeah?"

"Okay. I can cook something." When he raised an eyebrow, she smacked him, laughing. "Hey! I can cook. I just usually choose not to."

"All right, I'll give you a chance to prove it then. Your place? Six?"

"Sounds perfect." She lifted up on her tiptoes and kissed him, this time long and sweet, a promise of so many good things to come. Then she was flitting off, waving. "See you then."

Even from his perch on the gazebo, he could hear the group's good-natured teasing as they pulled back down the drive, leaving him alone. A few birds called as they passed overhead, and a boat horn blew in the distance. Liam turned his face toward the sun and relished this feeling.

He'd felt accomplished before, after a good pitch, but there was nothing like this. Because the success of this pitch meant he was finally coming home, maybe for the first time since Claremont.

Coming home to Jonathon Island.

To Dani.

And beyond that? Who knew? Maybe he'd spend the next two years here, and Dani's family would return. Maybe they wouldn't. But by the time the Grand project was wrapped up, he and Dani would know where they stood and whether their future would be together. And then that's how they'd make decisions.

Together.

Liam pulled his phone from his pocket and dialed Dad's cell, fully expecting to get his voicemail and having to try Marianne at the front desk.

But then, Dad answered. "Hi, Liam." There was something in his voice. A tremble?

"Hey, Dad. Everything okay?"

"Oh, yes. Nothing that can't wait until you get home tomorrow. We can talk then."

Talk then? "About what?" He swallowed. "Dad, what's going on?"

"Liam, you were right. I'm not immortal." Dad sighed. "And I think it's time for me to retire after all."

Fourteen

THIS WAS REALLY HAPPENING.

But instead of pinching herself, Dani practically floated around her small kitchen, tossing tomatoes and cut up cucumbers into a bowl of torn lettuce. The scent of garlic and mozzarella conjured an image of the Italian countryside, just like the one that had gotten this whole project rolling.

And she decided then and there. No matter what job she was working, she needed to get out more. To indulge her desire to travel. Because Liam was right. She'd been holding back, afraid that her family would see her traipsing around the world and think that she'd given up like the rest of them.

But they couldn't think that now.

Her phone buzzed on the counter, and Dani wiped her hands on her apron, picking it up. A text from Dad:

<u>Dad</u>
So proud of you, honey.

Emboldened by the council's approval, she'd emailed a copy of the slides to Dad and her siblings with the message: *What I've been working on the last few weeks . . .*

She dashed off a response to Dad's text:

<u>Dani</u>

Thanks, Dad. It won't be the exact same as before, but hopefully we can build something even better. Wish you were here to see it.

Three bubbles popped up in reply then disappeared. Finally, a message came through:

<u>Dad</u>
Have you told your mother yet?

Uh, no. Despite Uncle Seb's promptings, Dani had no desire to open those old wounds. She was moving forward, not letting the past weigh her down anymore. "Way to ruin the moment, Dad."

Roma mewed from the couch, and Dani sighed. Talking to her cat again.

But this time, she wasn't doing it out of desperation or loneliness. Because right now, she was making dinner for the man she loved.

Yes, loved.

And together, they were about to have lots of time to explore that love, to see what would happen. What they both wanted.

Though she knew already.

She resumed making the salad, humming to herself

while a special on the Travel Channel droned on in the background and the lasagna she'd lovingly—though not so expertly—crafted baked in the oven.

Her phone buzzed again, but this time, with a call.

Dani reached for it and froze when she saw James's name on the screen again. It had been less than a week since James had reamed her out over the destruction of their family legacy, and neither of them had reached out. She was tempted to let it go to voicemail, but what good would that do? Whether James came home after the hotel was rebuilt or not, she still didn't want distance of any sort between them.

"Hello?"

"Hey." His gruff voice was quieter than usual.

"Calling to yell at me again?" She couldn't help the snark. Well, maybe she could. Dani leaned a hip against the counter and sighed. "Sorry. I shouldn't have said that. But our last conversation—"

"I was a jerk, Dani."

"You kind of were." Her own words surprised her. She'd never spoken so freely like this—had always been so afraid to offend. But maybe healing could only happen when truth was spoken, no matter how much it hurt. "But I still love you."

"I know. Because you're good like that. And I still need to say I'm sorry."

"For what, exactly?" And this time, she wasn't being snarky. She really needed to know.

"For everything. For saying you were ruining things by rebuilding the hotel, for not trusting you." James sighed.

"And especially for blaming you for what happened ten years ago. It was never your fault, Dani. And I'm so sorry I said it was."

A tear snuck down her cheek. "Thank you, James. That means a lot."

"Look, I've got to run, but take care of yourself, okay? Maybe I can get down there for Christmas or something. Check in on how the rebuild's coming. The plans you sent—they're really good. I'm proud of you."

"That would be amazing. Come anytime. Maybe we can get the whole gang back here sometime for a visit." First a visit, then maybe more.

But whatever they decided, Dani's future would be okay. Things were looking up.

Dani said goodbye to James and set down her phone. At the scent of something burning, she rushed to the oven, pulled it open, and groaned at the sight of a very burned lasagna. Throwing her hot pads on, she got the lasagna out. It steamed and bubbled, the dark-brown substance on top looking more like chocolate shavings than cheese. "Way to go, Dani."

Maybe she should have called her chef brother Zachary and gotten a foolproof recipe for her first real venture into cooking more than ramen and spaghetti. But she'd wanted to one-up Liam and his fabulous pizza that had tasted amazing even cold.

Oh, well. Too late now.

She reached for her phone so she could let Liam know to pick up Martha's on the way—her treat, of course—but then there was a knock on the door. Her eyes flitted to the clock. If it was Liam, he was fifteen minutes early. Flipping on the oven fan, she untied her apron, flung it onto the counter, fluffed her hair, and rushed to the door. A glance through the peephole confirmed it was Liam.

Her heart sped up at the sight of him. Every moment spent in his presence this last week—especially since that first real kiss—had given her the same shot of adrenaline. Dani was in deep, but no longer was she afraid.

It turned out, a person's heart could be whole again after heartbreak. Healing was possible. And she had this man right here to thank for it.

Her hand shook slightly as she threw open the door. "Hi."

But one look at him—one real look at him—and her forehead was creasing. His hair was a mess, as if he'd been dragging his hands through it, and his eyes were bloodshot, as if he'd been drinking for days. The collar of his button-down shirt was popped up on one side, and his shoulders slumped.

He held a bottle of sparkling cider as if he was prepared to celebrate, but everything else indicated that Liam Stone was a man unhinged.

"Hi." Stepping forward, she slipped into his embrace. "What's wrong?"

His arms wrapped around her so tight, she nearly had trouble breathing. When he finally let go, he shut his eyes and shook his head. "I'm sorry."

"You're scaring me." She snatched his hand and tugged him inside, closing the door behind them. "Here." She indicated the stools at the kitchen island, but he just shook his head.

Well she, for one, needed to sit.

Letting go of his hand, Dani slid onto one of the stools and studied him. "Liam?"

He set the cider on the counter and began to pace. "Dani, I . . . I tried. I called my dad and was going to put in my formal request to be put on this project, but he . . ." Then he stopped, a nearly wild look in his eyes. Panic. That's what it was. Panic, pure and simple. "I haven't been able to get a hold of him the last few days, and it's because he's been thinking. He went to the doctor on Monday and . . ."

"Did he get a bad diagnosis?"

"Yes. No." Liam looked up at the ceiling, then back at Dani. "He didn't get a *new* diagnosis, but he had a follow-up with his endocrinologist, who told him his sugars were off-the-charts bad."

"Oh, that's awful. I'm sorry, Liam." Dani cocked her head. "Isn't that something he can fix with medicine?"

"Usually, yeah. If he remembers to take it. But also, he has to start exercising. Changing his diet. Lowering his stress. All things I've been telling him."

"But he's finally hearing it?"

Liam nodded. "I guess it helped that Marianne went with him to the appointment." Then a glimmer of a smile crested. "He told me they've been doing a lot together. I guess our talk last weekend got him thinking about love again. He said he looked up, and there Marianne was. And that he was surprised, because she'd been there all along."

Dani reached for the saltshaker in front of her, ran her fingers over the ridges of the container. Smiled. "So they didn't need our intervention after all, hmm?" Then she sobered, put down the salt, and moved to stand in front of Liam again. Reached for his hand. "His resolution sounds like a good thing, but you look like you received bad news. Is it just that his sugars were bad?"

"No, because like you said, that's fixable." Liam frowned, looked off somewhere over Dani's shoulder. "But I guess he's been processing—with Marianne's help—exactly what he needs to do to fix the things he needs to fix. And he's decided that the best course of action is to do the one thing I've been trying to get him to do for months."

Oh. "Retire."

"Yes. He's decided to retire."

"And let me guess." She couldn't keep her voice from trembling. "He wants you to take over."

"Yes. But—"

"Did you tell him? About us? About wanting to stay here?"

But the pinched look on Liam's face gave Dani her answer before he confirmed it with words. "I didn't get a chance before he told me he wanted to retire."

"Can't he get someone else? Surely there's someone at the company who—"

"He's family." Liam ran a hand through his hair, his fingers following the exact path of the grooves already there. "You should have heard him. 'There's nobody I would trust with this but you. I'm so proud of you, son.' It's up to me, Dani. It always has been, and I was fooling myself to think things could be different."

His words sliced, but surely he was just talking about taking the job here and not being with her. "That's pretty hard to say no to." And Liam was a good son for saying yes. She knew that. This was part of the reason she loved him.

But now that reason was taking him away from her.

Still, this didn't have to mean the end of them. It just put them right back to where they were before that kiss—except, now he'd admitted how he felt about her. Told her that if given his choice, he'd gladly move here. And yes, long distance would be difficult, but plenty of couples did it all the time.

She wasn't going to give them up so easily just because things had gotten more complicated. But what about him? What about what she'd overheard him telling Cody about his last relationship?

Okay, then. "I understand."

"You do?" Liam exhaled slowly. "Thank you, Dani. I promise, I'll get the best person we have to handle this project."

"I know." She traced the back of his hand with her thumb. "But maybe you could spare a few days here and there to come check up on it? And I'll come to California too. I've always wanted to visit the Hollywood sign, the Pacific Ocean, Disneyland—"

"I don't think that's a good idea."

"I know you'll be busy, but if we're going to make this work between us, then we've got to both make an effort."

But the look in his eyes—pained, unwilling to stay focused on her—shut her words off like a faucet.

"Dani . . ."

"You can't be serious." How could he throw everything away just because they'd be in different places? "Nothing's changed from this morning except where you'll be living. And I know you hate the idea of long distance because of things not working out with Tiffany—"

"How do you know about that?"

"Oh. Well, I accidentally heard you talking about it with Cody after our first kiss. When you were in my aunt and uncle's kitchen. I was in the other room still. I'm sorry. I really didn't intend to eavesdrop."

"It's fine. It's not like I wouldn't have told you about it." He sighed. "But I still stand by what I said then. Long distance doesn't work."

"And what about what Cody said? I think he's right. You go after the things you really want. And I thought you wanted this. Unless it was all a lie?"

Flashes of smooth-talking Ryan MacBride crowded out her reason. He had never really cared about Mom. He'd fooled her, preying on her deep desire to be loved and cherished when her own husband had gotten too busy.

Whoa. How was she actually having compassion for Mom in this moment?

Dani shoved the thought aside and focused on Liam, the man who was breaking her heart. Again.

"Of course it wasn't a lie. But if you heard what I said to Cody, then you know that my last long-distance relationship failed so miserably."

"I'm not Tiffany."

"I'm not saying you are. But I'm still Liam, and this job is going to require more of me than any I've ever worked. The stakes are higher than they've ever been. I don't want to promise you something and then fail to be the guy you want—or need—me to be."

"Liam, you're letting fear control you again." She dropped his hand and fisted his shirt before realizing how desperate she looked.

"I'm sorry, Dani. I care about you. I do. But I just . . ."

"You have to go."

Just like Mom. Dad. Her siblings.

Why should Liam be any different? And why had she been dumb enough to believe that he would? To believe that broken hearts could ever really be mended?

Chest tight, Dani pulled away from Liam and turned, moving toward the couch. Pacing. Ugh, this apartment was way too small. She headed right back for the kitchen, and her eyes narrowed in on the lasagna.

Once full of promise. Now burned.

Dani touched the glass. No longer hot. Good. She took the pan and marched it to the garbage can, which she opened with a mash of her foot against the step. Overturning the pan, she shook the food into the trash. It took a moment, but it finally slid out into the can with a plop.

"Dani . . ." Liam moved closer, as if to help.

She must look crazy, throwing away what he thought was perfectly good food. "I can't believe you're just leaving. That you're not even willing to try. But that's what you do, huh? You leave when things get hard."

"That's not true. I don't want to leave you. I was willing to stay. But if I don't go now, I won't leave. And I have to."

Dani placed the pan in the sink and leaned against the counter. "Don't you get it? I'm not mad that you're leaving. Sad, sure. But not angry. I understand your need to be in L.A. I really do. But the fact that you're letting this play out just like you did with Tiffany—"

"It's not the same at all." Frustration edged his voice.

"It's exactly the same!" And she couldn't keep the shout out of hers. "Tiffany asked you to commit, and you broke up with her. You get close to somebody, and then you run. That's what you do, Liam. You're just a coward pretending to be a hero."

She hated the look of horror on his face—disbelief— but she couldn't find it in her to apologize. Not when he was determined to leave her alone . . . again.

"Sheesh, Dani."

Her insides felt numb. "You're going to go, Liam. So just . . . go." Then she pointed at him. "But one day, you're going to look back and see that this was the biggest mistake of your life."

Then again, it didn't seem like anyone else who had left her regretted it. So maybe Liam wouldn't either.

She'd survived before. She'd survive again.

But why did survival have to hurt like the dickens?

Dani stood on the ferry dock Friday morning, watching the first ferry of the day pulling away.

From afar, she'd seen Liam boarding it and hadn't been

able to stop herself from walking out here. Halfway hoping for a fairy-tale moment where Liam would realize the error of his ways and dash down the gangplank toward her, picking her up and twirling her around before kissing her senseless and living happily ever after.

The boat's horn blew, signaling the boat's departure, and a bitter wind signaled a turn back to the normal chill of the season. Dani turned from the water and tossed her empty coffee cup into a trash receptacle nearby. No matter how much her eyes burned, she would not shed another tear for a guy determined to leave her.

Time to get back to work—the perfect distraction.

"Dani!"

She glanced toward Ferry Street and found Aunt Elise approaching along the boardwalk in a blue sweatsuit along with Constance Franklin and Jack the town dog.

Dani waved and walked to greet them. Their cheeks were flushed, but their smiles as bright as the sun cutting through the mid-morning chill. "Morning, ladies."

"Morning, dear." Elise leaned in for a quick hug. She smelled of roses. "We were just getting in a walk together."

"Fun! I'm headed back to work. Was just taking a break."

"It's a lovely day out, even with the drop in temperature. Can I walk with you?" Aunt Elise asked.

"Oh, I don't want to interrupt you guys."

Constance swatted the air. "I've got to skedaddle anyway. Mia's got to work, so she's dropping the grandkids with me."

"Lucky." Elise winked. "I get them Monday, though, so I guess I can't complain."

They laughed and exchanged a hug, and Constance hurried off toward her home behind downtown. Aunt Elise turned to Dani. "How are you, sweet niece of mine?"

"Fine." Dani dropped to a squat and petted Jack, who sat like a little gentleman beside Elise, panting a bit. He gave her hand a lick, and his brown eyes studied her, a bit sad, almost like he knew something was wrong.

"Seb told me Liam is leaving."

Dani's hand stilled. "He just left."

"It was quite a surprise to Seb," Elise continued. "The last conversation he had with Liam just yesterday seemed to indicate he was planning to stay for a while."

Dani gave Jack another pat before standing. "It was a surprise to me too."

"How are you doing with that? Seb also seemed to think there might be something brewing between the two of you."

She cleared her throat and forced a smile. "I'm doing fine. Liam and I decided . . . well, things just didn't work out. But it's okay."

Her aunt just looked at her, those wise eyes saying more than her lips ever could.

"Really. Am I sad that things didn't work out with Liam? Yes. But I'll survive." Dani swallowed against a thick throat. "I'm sorry. I should get back to work."

"Do you mind if we take the long way around? I'd love to finish my walk and could use the company."

No sense in arguing with her aunt. "Sure."

They continued west down the boardwalk, where it would eventually meet up at the corner of Main Street and Lake Shore Drive, right by the public library and Martha's diner.

A few moms and kids whizzed by them on their bikes, children waving as they went. Jack's claws clicked on the wooden boards at their feet.

Aunt Elise stuck her hands into the pockets of her sweatshirt as they sauntered together. "I just wanted to say how proud I am of all the hard work you've put into the hotel project. It's hard to believe after so many years of downturn, we finally have a plan to rebuild the island."

"Thank you."

"You don't sound too excited about it."

There her aunt went, being perceptive as usual. "Of course I'm excited. This is everything I've worked for." And it was hard to believe the groundbreaking would happen so soon. Dani and Uncle Seb had meetings scheduled next week to discuss the process going forward, as well as the next steps in finding business owners willing to move to Jonathon Island—and fast. Ideally, they'd be opening a handful of new businesses this summer. "But it'll be a lot of work. I'm a bit overwhelmed, I guess."

She just couldn't take her eyes off the prize. Her family. All together again.

Though if Liam's leaving had taught her anything, it was that people didn't always do what they said. Or, at the very least, they changed their minds.

"I'm confident in your abilities. But heartbreak does have a way of being overwhelming."

"What?" A breeze kicked up, and Dani used the elastic band around her wrist to tie back her hair—an action she hoped her aunt would find nonchalant, casual. As if what she'd said hadn't shaken Dani to the core. "That's not what's overwhelming. There's just a lot to do."

"And you'll have to do it all without him, when you'd planned to have him by your side."

"He'll send someone new to take over. Nothing's changed in that regard."

"Don't you think that everything's changed?" Aunt Elise pinned her with a look. "Dani, you don't have to pretend with me."

"I'm not pretending." At her aunt's arched eyebrow, Dani sighed. "Fine, maybe I'm pretending. But it's only because if I don't . . ."

"You might fall apart?"

Dani scoffed. "I've been falling apart for years, Aunt Elise. And just when I thought I was finally being put back together . . ."

"He left."

As they walked along the road, Dani couldn't help but turn her head, craning her neck for sight of the ferry. But the harbor was now as empty as her heart. "Yes. He left. And he's not willing to try long distance, so we're done."

Her aunt touched her arm, and they stopped right where the land curved, lending a view of the Grand in the distance. Once the hotel was rebuilt—once the island had been revived—things had a shot at going back to normal.

And yet.

Her family really still might not come back. Just like Liam had said.

"He was right."

"Who was right about what, dear?" Elise grabbed her hand.

"Liam. He said I was banking on my family coming back, on us all being together again if I could just get everything to fall into place. But life isn't like that. Things don't always work out, no matter how hard you try. And I can't keep living my life hoping that someday I'll finally feel happy and whole again."

"Ah." Her aunt nodded. "Yes, if I've learned anything in my life, it's that we cannot count on people and circumstances to make us happy."

"So is happiness just a myth then? Are dreams meaningless?"

"Of course not. But happiness *is* fleeting, especially if we are relying on anything or anyone but God to give it to us. He never changes, and that's why instead of happiness, we can find joy in this life no matter what storms swirl around us." She squeezed Dani's hand again. "No matter who leaves us. Because the truth of the matter is, God's love for us is the anchor in the storm. And He will never abandon us."

Oh, sweet truth. Her aunt's words reverberated in her soul. "I've been thinking that my heart will never heal. Then with Liam, I felt hope for the first time that it could. But now it feels shattered again, and I'm trying to be brave, to move on, but this time, I don't know how to fix it. To fix everything that's been broken." She hated how her throat filled. So much for not crying over the man. "I love him, Aunt Elise."

"Oh, my dear. I know." Her aunt pulled Dani into her arms, tucking her into the safety that had always been available to Dani. "I don't know if things will work out with Liam, but I do know this. God is the fixer of broken things."

"Then why has everything stayed broken all of these years? Why did He leave me all alone?"

"You've never been alone." Aunt Elise squeezed.

"I know. I didn't mean that. You and Uncle Seb have been wonderful. But . . ."

"Your heart still aches for your family. And now for Liam. I understand." Her aunt pressed a kiss against Dani's hair, and her arms sheltered her from the blowing wind. "But even if your uncle and I weren't here, you wouldn't be alone. God has never walked away from you. People are sinners, and God lets them walk their path. But He does promise to stay with us, even when we feel alone. The Bible says God is close to the brokenhearted and saves the crushed in spirit. He's been waiting for you all this time, Dani, aching to heal you. You've just been turning to other places for that healing instead."

Quiet tears finally fell from Dani's eyes, and she pressed her face into the soft material of her aunt's sweatshirt. But tears weren't always sad, and these mingled grief over the loss of Liam with hope—hope that her aunt was right. That God could mend what had been broken in her. "I want healing. I just don't know where to start."

Aunt Elise pulled back, smoothed a strand of hair behind Dani's ear, and cocked her head. "You're not going to like what I have to say right now."

She probably wouldn't. But if it meant finally healing, getting past this heartache, not just surviving but thriving, then Dani would do it. "W-what?"

"If you truly want to get right with God and ask Him to heal your heart, the first step is forgiveness. Full and complete, like God has forgiven you."

Dani bit her lip, shook her head. "I'm upset that Liam's gone, and so sad, but I don't really hold it against him. I know he's only doing what he thinks is best for his family. How can I fault him for that?"

But the skin around her aunt's eyes creased at the corners as she gave Dani a somber smile. "I wasn't talking about Liam. I think you need to start where all of this hurt began—with your mother."

Fifteen

EVEN IF IT WOULD BE A GOOD DISTRAC-tion, Liam couldn't find it in him to work today. And sure, it was Sunday, but that had never stopped him before.

Liam reached for the remote on the nondescript, black coffee table and flipped the channel on the penthouse's big-screen television until he hit a basketball game. He rubbed his left bicep, which was sore from the workout he'd put it through yesterday at four a.m. in the tiny hotel gym. That's what happened when a guy couldn't sleep.

And his lack of sleep had nothing to do with all the details he and Dad had discussed last week in the office, readying Liam to take over as CEO. Nope, not at all. He'd even met with the board, all of whom approved of the transition of power. Throughout it all, he'd seen an unexpected and new joy in his dad's eyes. Relief, maybe, too. The thing his father had feared was coming true, but instead of being terrible, for Dad it was turning into the best thing.

Of course, Marianne had a lot to do with that. *She makes me feel like a new man. A younger man. And life has all of these possibilities now.*

Liam was happy for him. Of course he was. This was all he'd dreamed about too.

At least, it had been.

Now, though . . .

He mashed the button on the remote to turn up the volume. Maybe the broadcaster's voice would drown out the one in Liam's head telling him he'd made a horrible mistake in leaving Dani behind.

In not trying.

Was she right? Was he a coward?

But he just couldn't handle the idea of failing someone else—someone he loved.

Groaning, Liam set his head against the back of the couch and stared at the stark white ceiling high above him. Then he glanced around the spotless living room, where white walls and meaningless abstract art mocked him.

There was a beep out in the hallway, and the door opened to Liam's left, near the full-size kitchen that had been cleaned by the hotel staff just this morning. Every plain white mug, plate, and piece of silverware had been put back in its proper place, and the counters had been cleared.

This place may be occupied, but it wasn't lived in.

And Liam was sick of it.

Dad and Marianne walked into the kitchen carrying

a few bags of takeout. Marianne wore her sparkling pink glasses with a chain around her neck, a scarf, and her black coat, which Dad helped her out of with all the care he'd always shown to Liam's mom.

Liam breathed out slowly. *This* was his why—giving Dad the chance to have a life after so many years of taking care of him alone.

He joined them in the kitchen, pasting on a fake smile. "What are you two up to this evening?" Leaning in, Liam gave Marianne a quick kiss on the cheek.

Marianne smiled and patted his shoulder. "Joining our favorite boy for dinner."

"Unless we're interrupting your plans," Dad said, digging into the plastic restaurant bags and pulling out a few containers. "In which case, feel free to go out and do whatever you youngsters do for fun."

"Chaz, don't call him a youngster." Laughing, Marianne swatted Dad's arm and nudged him aside so she could plate the food. "You make me feel old."

"You are old, woman." Dad winked. "But still beautiful."

Liam folded his arms over his chest, a real smile taking over his face now. "You sure you wouldn't rather eat alone? The two of you seem quite content to have a date night."

"Stop it now. You know you are always welcome here." Marianne's cheeks turned pink as she opened the first container, which held a salad with tomatoes, red onions, croutons, olives, and banana peppers. She plated some of it and picked the croutons out then placed a roasted chicken breast from the other container on the plate.

When she handed it to Dad, he scoffed. "The croutons are the best part."

"And they'll spike your blood sugar, you ninny." Marianne glanced at Liam. "You want some, or did you have plans after all?"

"No plans here. But I'm not very hungry."

Dad was already digging in, right there at the counter. But at Liam's declaration, he paused. "Since when?"

Liam shrugged. "I ate a late lunch." It was mostly true, if a container of yogurt and a few nuts equaled lunch.

Waving his fork at Liam, Dad shook his head. "I don't buy it. You've been quiet all week, and at first, I took it as extreme focus with the big changes coming up. But then Marianne pointed out that you haven't seemed like yourself ever since you came home, and I have to agree, especially if you're not eating." His father set his fork down and rounded the counter, placing his hand on Liam's shoulder. "What's going on, son?"

Marianne suddenly snapped her fingers. "Chaz, I forgot to get dessert. I'm going to run to the bodega on the corner, all right? Be right back." Then before either of them could protest, she grabbed her bag and scurried out.

"That woman." Dad's mouth hitched upward to one corner. Then he studied Liam, sighed. "Are you having trouble with the idea of me moving on from your mom? I know we talked about it, but the reality might be different."

"What? No, Dad."

"Is it Marianne then? I thought you considered her like a second mother, but maybe—"

"I love her. I love her for you. That's not it." Liam headed back to the couch and plopped down. After being on Dani's couch, this one felt so stiff, ungiving. "Grab your dinner. I don't want it to get cold."

"I'm not going to eat without her anyway." His father joined him. "Tell me what's on your mind, son."

"I can't." Because if his dad knew, he might not retire. And that wouldn't solve anything.

The buttons on Dad's shirt strained against his stomach as he shifted to face Liam. "Okay, then. Let me tell you what Marianne thinks is wrong. I was positive it was about me and her, but maybe she's right instead." Dad rubbed the corner of his droopy eyelid. "She thinks you don't really want to be CEO."

Liam's chest tightened, and it grew more difficult to breathe. "Why does she think that?"

"I notice you're not denying it." Dad's mouth drew flat. "Son, I thought this was what you wanted. You've been on me to retire for years now. And I know you were all gung-ho about the project with Travis—which I am still planning to approve in quarter three, once we have the funds—but I thought that the main impetus behind that was you wanting to be here in town. Settle down. Get a place of your own like you've been talking about. But if I was wrong, if you don't want to be CEO, I—"

"No, I do, Dad. I see how happy you are, how much healthier you're going to be once this transition takes place. Think of all the stress I'm saving you." He scratched behind his ear. "You've had a rough go of it, and you deserve to relax. To finally be happy."

"Liam, I may have had some knocks in my day, but I've lived a very happy life."

"But Mom. My sister."

Dad pressed his fist against his knee, knocking a few times. "Yes, that was the worst time in our lives. But I've tried to make up for that. Tried to be what you needed anyway."

"You have been. You've been a great dad. A great boss."

"I know I haven't been perfect. Marianne's also pointed out that perhaps I've taught you some of my workaholic tendencies."

Liam had to laugh at that. "She's a very perceptive woman."

"Hmm, don't tell her that or she'll never let me live it down." Then Dad sobered. "Son, back to what you said earlier. It's never been your job to save me. You know that, right? I'm the parent. It's my job to protect you, not the other way around."

"But Mom said . . ." No. He didn't want to burden Dad with that.

"What did she say?"

His dad's eyes looked so earnest, as if desperate to know more about her last moments. By the time he'd gotten back into town from his business trip, it had been too late. Mom and the baby had been gone. And Liam had deprived his father of knowing what had really happened because he'd been ashamed.

Now, though, he poured out the story. Every moment. Every bit of guilt. Even what Mom had said right before they'd loaded her into the ambulance.

Dad was quiet for a while, leaning forward on his knees, staring at the carpet. Then, finally, "Thank you for telling me, son."

"I'm sorry I didn't tell you sooner." Liam wiped away a tear.

"You don't have anything to be sorry for." At Liam's protest, Dad held up a hand. "You were a young boy, but your mother was always in awe of what a big helper you were. And you were so excited to have a sister. You promised to help with her, even do middle-of-the-night diaper changes." His father chuckled. "I think you would have too. You've always been a good boy, someone who wants to help. But somewhere along the way, you took too much on yourself."

Dani had said something similar, hadn't she? "Maybe. But if I didn't, then who would have?"

"We're a lot alike, you know. Both of us afraid to give up control. Afraid to fail the people depending on us," Dad said. "Did you know I started going back to church with Marianne the last few weeks? Before we even started dating. She saw how depressed I was with you gone and at the prospect of this hotel deal sinking the company."

Liam lifted his eyebrows. "Yeah? That's great, Dad. And you've found comfort there?"

"I have. The sermon this last week was about remembering that God cares about the birds of the air, how He feeds them. And if He cares that much about birds, how much more does He care about us and all the people we love?"

The truth hit Liam in the sternum, and he lifted his

hand to rub at his chest. "But that doesn't mean we can just abandon our responsibilities."

"No, but it means we don't have to take on something that was never meant to be ours in the first place. God will take care of us. He will take care of our people. We must do our best, but in the end, He's in charge anyway. And His plans are good. But it's up to us to trust Him and take that leap of faith, even when it seems risky to us."

Liam sat back against the couch cushion. Wow. When he thought about that—about surrendering control and all of his worry to someone infinitely more capable than him—it was like a weight coming off his shoulders. He could breathe again. "But what does that mean in terms of the company?"

"That depends on you, son. Do you want to be CEO? Don't think about me or the employees or any of that. What do you want?"

"Honestly?"

"Of course. Because while there are times when we have to follow God's calling and it might make us uncomfortable, He gave us certain talents and abilities. He gave us passion for certain work. And if you're not finding that passion in being a CEO—something I did love—then I will find someone else who will care for this company and its employees like I did."

"Wait. What?" Liam blinked. "If I turn it down, you won't go right back to being CEO?"

"I might do it part time until we find the right candidate, but Travis and Jimmy both have shown great leadership and potential. I think either of them would be willing to step up in the interim, maybe see if it's a good fit. Especially given their desire to be in Los Angeles more, what with their families and all." Dad frowned. "I never meant for you to feel trapped by this, Liam. I want you to find your God-given purpose. To follow the paths where He's leading you. If you're willing to take the risk."

"Taking risks has never been my strong suit. In business or in life. Love." He blinked. Coughed. "Someone recently told me that what happened with Tiffany a few years ago was me running away. That it was cowardly. I didn't think so. I guess I thought I was saving us both inevitable heartache when things didn't work out. But maybe this person was right."

"When someone experiences loss at a young age like you did with your mom, it's not unusual for them to learn that love can be a risk. That loving—and losing—hurts more than anything else." Dad patted Liam's shoulder. "But never taking the risk might be the greatest risk of all. Think of how dull life would be without love. How aimless. You reminded me of that, Liam. That God has all sorts of good things He wants for our lives. But if we're even too scared to try, well, I think that would be the most tragic thing of all. Even more tragic than losing someone we love."

Oh man. Liam inhaled a trembling breath. "What if it's too late? What if I already lost someone because I wasn't willing to try?"

Dad's eyebrows rose. "Ah, so Marianne was right about that too. There's a young lady. Perhaps that niece of Seb's you mentioned?"

Liam nodded. "But I royally screwed up, Dad."

"The good thing about screwing up is it gives the rest of us the chance to practice forgiveness." Dad gave Liam's shoulder another pat then stood and headed to the door, which he opened.

Marianne was standing in the hallway, looking sheepish. "I was trying to wait until y'all were done."

"We're done. Come on in, and let's hear Liam tell us all about this woman you say he's crazy about."

"Glad to know you will admit when I'm right." With a wink and a bow, Marianne strode inside to the kitchen, where she removed some sugar-free candies from the plastic bag in her hands. "Sounds like we also need to discuss what you can do to make it up to this woman. Dani, is it?"

"What are these?" Dad picked up the bag and examined them. "You trying to kill me with the fake stuff?"

They started bickering, and Liam slid into a chair at the dining room table, a smile easing onto his face. Dad was going to be okay, and not just because Marianne was here to help take care of him.

God was going to do it too. It wasn't all up to Liam. God was working everything out—if Liam would only take the leap.

"Okay, Lord," he muttered under his breath. "I hurt Dani a lot. Walked away from her just like everyone else in her life. Now I need your help to get her to talk to me again. Think we can manage that?"

"Of course He can manage that." Marianne approached with a plate of food she placed in front of Liam. Did the woman have supersonic hearing? "With God, all things are possible."

A week ago, this is the last place she'd expected to be.

Not that it was all that strange for Dani to be sitting on a bench in Blueberry Hill Park on an early Monday evening. From here, she could see the schoolhouse overlooking the park, its windows lit and welcoming, prepared for locals to arrive in the next half hour for the town hall meeting where the Grand Hotel project and plan for the development going forward would be officially announced.

But she would never have guessed a week ago that she'd be here with two coffees, waiting for Mom to show up.

All week long, her conversation with Aunt Elise had banged around inside her head. She'd tried to ignore her aunt's suggestion that forgiveness was the only way forward. Had even protested it at first.

Of course, she had said she'd do anything.

But *that*? "How can I possibly forgive the person who started all of this?" she'd asked.

"In God's strength, that's how." Aunt Elise had locked elbows with Dani, patted her arm, and resumed their stroll as if Dani hadn't just had an emotional breakdown. "And remember. You aren't doing it for her—though I know she will greatly benefit from it. You're doing it for yourself. There's nothing worse than bitterness to break a heart into pieces. And besides all of that, it's what God requires of us."

"Some might say He requires too much."

"He sent his son to die for you, Dani. The least you can do is die to your own self-perceived right to hold a grudge against your mom. Especially when that grudge is killing you on the inside. He just wants you to be free."

Free. What would that feel like? Dani had tried to shake the thought off all week long, busying herself with work. But then she'd think of Liam and her desire to have her family together again. And she'd realized that even if she somehow managed to get everyone back here, there was a lot of forgiveness that was going to have to take place.

And it had to start somewhere. Might as well be with her.

A lone figure trudged up the park pathway, her shoulders hunched against a breeze that only served to bolster Dani—to remind her that she was not alone. Her Heavenly Father was here, in her heart, all around her, in the people of this town. Whatever happened right now with her mother or tonight at the meeting or even beyond that, with the hotel and the revival of the island, Dani would never be alone again.

She placed the coffees on the bench and stood. Waved at her mother, who was now only a few feet away. It had been eight years or so since Dani had seen her in person, and though Becky Jonathon was still beautiful and poised, there was an emotional heaviness surrounding her that hadn't been apparent to Dani before. Maybe because she hadn't wanted to see it. Or maybe the choices Mom had made had finally caught up with her.

With a deep breath, Dani finally spoke. "Hi, Mom."

"Hi, pumpkin."

The term of endearment swaddled Dani's heart and squeezed. Neither woman moved, though something in Becky's expression told Dani she wanted to wrap her daughter up and never let go. But she'd lost that right.

Still, what right did Dani have to hold it against her if she was truly sorry?

Then again, maybe she wasn't sorry. Maybe she didn't know how she'd wounded Dani. And there was a difference between forgiving and forgetting. Dani had had another long talk with Aunt Elise about that last night, and her aunt had explained that godly boundaries were a good thing. That if she bared her heart to her mother and her mother stomped on it, or didn't accept responsibility for her actions, Dani could still forgive her without allowing her to continue to trample her feelings.

Still, Dani prayed for strength to say what she'd come here to say—and to hear what she longed to hear in return.

But if it didn't happen, she'd be okay.

Dani coughed, turned, picked up the coffees, and handed one to Mom. "I hope you still like it black."

"I do." Mom took it between her gloved hands, inhaled the scent of the still-warm brew. "Mmm." Then she took a sip and sighed. "Nobody makes coffee like Jill. I've missed it."

"Then why didn't you come back for it?" The words were out before Dani knew it—and tinged with more hurt than she'd intended.

Mom studied Dani, frowning. "I was ashamed of leaving it in the first place. Knew I didn't deserve to have it in my life anymore. It was too good for me."

Uncle Seb had been right. But despite her fears, Mom was here. And for now, that was enough.

Dani chewed on the inside of her cheek. "Maybe it felt all the more abandoned because you didn't even try. Maybe it felt like you didn't care about it anymore. That you were happier with your mainland coffee." It was ridiculous to continue speaking of things metaphorically, but it was easier than saying the truth.

"Oh, honey." Mom took a step closer, then hesitated. Clearly, she didn't want to overstep or scare Dani away. "I was such a fool to think that anything but Jonathon Island coffee would satisfy."

Dani's throat went dry, and she hugged her own coffee to her chest. "It's really good coffee." Then she started to laugh, because how silly was this conversation? Silly, but healing too.

In a flash, her mom set her own cup back down on the bench and moved toward Dani, her arms open. Waiting. "It's amazing coffee. And I'm so sorry it took me so long to tell it—to tell you—how much I love it. How much I love you."

"Mom," Dani breathed, rushing into her mom's arms, releasing tears she'd held in for so long.

"I'm so sorry, Dani girl. Can you ever forgive me?" Mom finally pulled away and brushed the tears from under her daughter's eyes. Her own glistened too. "I know I ruined our family. I threw it all away because . . . well, I can't even tell you why, and it doesn't matter."

"It does matter. And someday, maybe someday soon,

I'd like to dissect all of that. We have a lot of conversations to have, a lot to catch up on. Some of them will be hard."

Mom nodded. "As they should be. But if you are willing to have them, I will be here for as much time as you have to give me."

"I'm willing. And yes, I forgive you." The words rushed out like a healing flood, bringing with it a peace like Dani had never known. "But as for time, I don't have much more to give you tonight. I'm just glad you were able to meet."

Mom bit her lip, nodded. "Of course. Where are you rushing off to? A date?" She smiled.

"Ha. If you consider a town hall meeting a date, sure."

"Town hall meeting? Is this about the hotel project? Seb told me something about rebuilding it. I'm surprised you got your father to agree." Mom looked like she wanted to say more—to ask more. Maybe about Dad? But she didn't.

"Me too." Dani picked up her drink again, and Mom followed suit. They started walking down the path up the ridge toward the school. "But he did, and I worked with a developer in California who helped me put together some amazing plans." The new lead—a Rob somebody—was supposed to have arrived earlier today, but the admin assistant at Stone Development had called to say there had been a slight change of plans and that the site manager wouldn't make it until later. Possibly not until tomorrow.

Which was fine. She wasn't eager to meet Liam's replacement anyway.

Mom looped her arm through Dani's, and it felt so nostalgic, so familiar, Dani nearly started to cry again.

"Seb told me all about your promotion and what a great job you're doing to revitalize the town. I'm so proud of you, Dani."

"Thanks, Mom."

They approached the school, where several families were in the process of parking their golf carts and walking in. Dani turned to her mother. "You're welcome to come in, but I know you haven't wanted to see certain people, so please don't feel obligated."

Mom squinted her eyes, as if that would allow her to see into the school and know whether the residents who'd made her feel unwelcome on the island were in attendance. Most likely, they were. But then she straightened and shook her head. "I wouldn't miss my girl's big reveal for the world. If you're sure you don't mind me being there."

Just the fact Mom was willing to face the firing squad for her meant a lot. And if she was willing to give Jonathon Island another try, maybe it wasn't as impossible as Dani had thought to get the rest of her family back here too.

Tonight, though, was about sharing their plans with the town. Hopefully everyone would be on board. But if it meant restoring the town's glory, bringing the economy back up so residents didn't have to choose between staying and surviving financially, then Dani couldn't think of anyone who would be against that.

Together, she and Mom strode through the front doors of the brick building, turning left to enter the multipurpose room that served as cafeteria, the school gym, and a place for town assemblies with its small stage at one end. Folding chairs had been set up in two rows, and about half of them were already occupied. Uncle Seb and the town council waited near the stage, and when Seb saw Dani and her mom together, his smile rivaled the Cheshire Cat's. He stepped away from Patrick Kelley and strode toward them.

Mom stopped at the back of the chairs, squeezing Dani's arm before dropping it. "Go get 'em, my girl. I'll be cheering you on from here."

"All right, if you're sure you'll be okay."

"I'll be great." Mom lowered herself into a chair, her hands a bit shaky. It must be really hard for her to be back here.

But she was here.

And now that their reunion was out of the way, Dani could focus on the presentation. She'd been nervous enough at the last presentation, and she'd done that one with Liam—and it had only been the council watching. Now, most of the town was here, and the din of their chatter bounced off the linoleum floor and reverberated from the rafters.

Uncle Seb reached her. "There you are, Dani." He glanced down at his sister, squeezed her shoulder. "Good to see you, Bec."

Mom smiled bravely. "It's good to be seen."

"You'll come by for dessert after the meeting, won't you?"

"Sure."

"Good." He pointed at Dani. "You too?"

"If my stomach doesn't collapse before then." She placed a hand over the organ in question. "I'm so nervous."

"You'll be fine. Just give the same speech you did with Liam, and you'll win everyone over with your charm."

But that was the thing. "Liam isn't here." Her eyes scanned the room, stopping on a group of people gathered at a refreshment table in the corner. "And it doesn't look like the Stone Development rep made it either."

"That's actually what I came over here to tell you. He did make it, and he's backstage, ready to go on with you."

"Seriously?" That was almost worse. She and Liam had practiced their pitch several times before getting it right. Now she had mere minutes to fill in this stranger. "I'd better get back there."

"Break a leg." Uncle Seb gave her a hug. "I'll be introducing you after we begin and cover a few more items of business." He checked his watch. "Speaking of beginning, I'd better get us started."

"Right." Dani hustled through the crowd toward the entrance to the tiny backstage area. People called for her, but she just waved. Hopefully they'd forgive her rudeness, but she really needed as much time as possible to prep her new partner for the presentation.

She opened the door, bracing herself.

"Liam?"

His back was to her, but when the light from the hallway flooded the dimly lit backstage, he pivoted to face her.

And he'd turned into an islander.

He wore jeans, a cable knit sweater, boots. Like he *belonged* here. Worse, even from here, she could smell his cologne, see how his once-gelled hair was now windswept and casual.

His gaze ran over her, and now he swallowed. "Hi, Dani."

She couldn't breathe. "What are you doing here?"

He didn't even flinch at her question. "I'm here to finish what we started."

"Oh." For some reason, the answer didn't sit well. Probably because he wasn't just a job to her. But if he was going to be all business, then she would force herself to be as well. Still, she had to know. "But what about your dad? The CEO position?"

"Turns out, he didn't need me to be something I'm not. He was more than happy to find someone else to replace him."

"That still doesn't tell me why you're here. I thought you were going to deliver the Bertram pitch? Did it not go well?"

"It did, but that project has been postponed indefinitely, since Jimmy has agreed to step up as interim CEO for the time being." He took a step toward her. "And all of that allows me to do the job I was originally assigned."

So that was why he was here then. He felt obligated to keep his word. Nothing more. "Well, since you're familiar with the pitch, I guess we don't need to practice it. Though I did add a minor change to the plans—"

"Dani. Stop. Please." Liam strode over, stopping just shy of where she stood. They were mere inches apart, and even in the darkened space, she saw the sparks of light in his eyes. "When I said I was here to finish what we started, I wasn't talking about the hotel."

Oh. Her heart bumped against her chest, her hopes.

"You weren't?" Aw. And now her voice croaked out, too much of her heart in it.

"Well, I was. I'm here to do the presentation with you. To rebuild the Grand with you, if you still want me to." Then he reached for her hand. "But I'm also here to beg you for another chance. For us. To see if you can ever forgive me for leaving you, for not being willing to try."

Oh, this man. "I do forgive you, Liam," she said quietly.

"You were right. I was a coward."

"I shouldn't have said that."

"But I needed to hear it." He exhaled. "I was a coward. I ran away when I should have trusted that things would work out. I was scared to admit it, but this life is exactly what I've always wanted." He threaded their fingers together, one by one. "*You* are exactly what I've always wanted. And you are worth any risk, Dani Sullivan."

"Liam . . ."

"I love you, Dani." Liam leaned closer, pressing a sweet kiss to her lips that left Dani sighing.

She placed her arms around his neck, hugging him close. "I love you too, city boy."

He laughed. "Not a city boy for long. What do you think about helping me find a house here on the island?"

"Really? You're going to stay?"

"I don't plan to leave ever again unless you're with me."

She shivered at the implication in his words. "Good." Then she tugged his head down and kissed him again, this time deeper and fuller, giving him her whole heart—the one that God had made whole.

A throat cleared behind them, and they broke apart to

find Seb with his head peeking behind the curtain. "Hey, lovebirds. It's showtime. You ready?"

Liam gripped Dani's hand in his and pressed a kiss to it. "So ready."

"Me too." Dani grinned. "Let's bring Jonathon Island back to life."

Epilogue

THEY'D BROKEN GROUND ON THE Grand yesterday, and Liam had been privileged to be holding Dani's hand through it all.

But that wasn't the most exciting thing to happen this week.

This was.

"Here you go." Cody Hart held out the keys to Liam with a smile. "I tried fixing everything up for you as requested, but if you find any rattling radiators, be sure to let me know."

Liam laughed. "Thanks, man. I'm sure it's perfect." He swallowed hard against the lump in his throat. Beside him, Dani squeezed his hand, eyes shining.

Cody stuck his hands in his back pockets. "Mia said she's sorry she couldn't be here to give you the keys herself." Though she hadn't worked as a realtor in years, Mia still had her license and had helped Liam find the small bungalow for sale a few blocks from downtown—and right up the road from her on Lilac Lane—within a few days. The couple who'd owned it had moved out several years ago and was very motivated to find a buyer ASAP.

It was only a thousand square feet. Two tiny bedrooms. One bath. A galley kitchen and a single living area.

And yet, it was so much better than a hotel penthouse.

"I hope everything's okay with her." The keys felt heavy—significant—in Liam's palm.

"Nothing big, but Finn's got a fever."

"Oh no," Dani said. "Poor boy. And poor mama. On Mother's Day weekend too. I'll have to stop by later and see if there's anything I can do."

"I'm headed over now to check in. I'll let her know to text you if she needs anything."

"Thanks, Cody!" Dani called as their friend walked down the sidewalk. Then she turned to Liam again. "You ready to go inside?"

He blew out a breath and pivoted to take in the sight before him. From the small porch to the white-trimmed windows, the angled wooden roof to the robin's-egg blue clapboard siding, everything about it felt as quaint as the rest of the island. The previous owners had left spring flowers in a long planter under the front living room window, and bright colors bloomed there.

Welcoming him home.

"It's beautiful, Liam." Dani tugged on his hand. "Come on. Let's go inside."

He let her drag him through the honest-to-goodness white picket fence and down the brick path that traversed the small, grassy yard until they reached the porch. Taking the steps two at a time, they were at the front door before he knew it.

Dani pointed at the brown door. "I think we should paint that yellow."

"Because yellow is definitely a *me* color." He laughed at the fake pout she put on. The last few weeks together—working alongside each other, dining together at Martha's, watching the Travel Channel and planning their first trip abroad—had only solidified what he knew deep in his gut.

This was the woman he wanted to make his wife.

Not yet though. He didn't want to scare her with the force of his affections. But he'd meant what he said. He wasn't moving away from Jonathon Island unless Dani Sullivan was with him.

"Well, it's a *me* color, and I'm going to be over here enough." She stole the keys from him.

He slid a hand around her waist and pulled her close. "You think so, huh?" Who was he kidding? If all went according to his desires, she'd share it with him someday. "What I *think* is that you're definitely a ball of sunshine, so yellow it is."

"And you're going to give me free rein on the inside too, right?"

"I don't know if I should do that. You might try to pretty up my bachelor pad."

"Oh, are you a bachelor? Guess I should go then." She turned to leave, but he hooked her around the waist again.

"You're not going anywhere."

"Good, because I'm rather partial to my spot by your side."

"Ditto."

One of his hands cupped her cheek as she angled her mouth up to meet his and placed one palm flat against his chest.

Could she feel the way his heart beat for her?

Kissing her slowly, Liam backed her up against the door and feathered kisses along her cheek, her jaw, her ear. He wanted this, with Dani, forever. Little moments and big.

Was this his life? And he'd almost missed it.

Finally, he pulled away and smiled at the hazy look in Dani's eyes, like she was waking out of a dream. Leaning down, he kissed her nose. "You ready to see inside?"

"You know I've seen it before, right? I used to babysit for the Rogers family, who lived here when I was a teenager. Before they sold it to the Matthesons."

He chuckled. "Guess it'll be a while before I can rattle off people's names and island history like that, huh?"

"Good thing you have a great teacher." Dani winked and dangled the keys for him to take back. "Now show me your new home!"

"All right, all right, Miss Impatient." He slid the key into the knob. "Ready?"

"I am. Are you?" Her voice was soft now. She knew what this meant to him.

"I think so." He nodded. "Yes." Then turning the knob, he pushed on the door. It creaked open, and together, they stepped through the doorway. The place looked brand new—freshly painted walls, all the nail holes patched up where previous owners had hung picture frames. The crown molding, which on Liam's first walk-through had been crumbling in places, was now pristine.

Liam whistled. "Cody did a great job getting this place all ready for me."

For him. This was his. He wasn't even renting.

He'd put down roots.

"I still can't believe he wouldn't let me pay for his time. Just the cost of the repairs."

"That may have been my idea." Dani walked into the kitchen and ran her fingers against the smooth, white countertop, which used to be laminate but now was granite.

"Your idea? But why?"

"This house was in a similar state of disrepair as the homes around here that we plan to offer to new business owners for a dollar. You know, Phase Two of our revitalization plan. I thought it would be good to know how much it would cost to fix up the other available houses for new business owners."

"That was very business savvy of you."

"I'm learning." She offered a small smile. "Although I am feeling a bit overwhelmed and out of my depth. It's going to be a fairly massive undertaking to get all of the homes and business fronts ready, plus sift through applicants, vet them, and assign them to spaces. I think I'm going to need some help since I'll be busy with planning the tourism season and working with vendors to get a few festivals up and running."

"And checking up on me and my progress, right?"

"Of course. Gotta make sure you're sticking to our plans."

Speaking of those plans, he still couldn't believe she'd altered them slightly, even before she knew he was coming back. When he'd seen the addition of a Donna's Delights ice cream parlor in the bottom level of the Grand Sullivan Hotel, well, he hadn't thought it was possible, but his love for her had grown right then and there.

"Oh, Dani. If only you knew." He winked at her. "I have so many plans for us."

Her eyes flashed, something flirtatious in them. "Is that a fact?"

"It is." Liam walked up behind her and slid his arms around her, tucking her back against him. Closing his eyes, he breathed in her vanilla scent, daring to picture what future moments in this very kitchen might look like. All the meals they might prepare. The kisses they might share. The slow dances they might take. He pressed a kiss to her temple. "And every one of them is good."

"If they're with you, then I have no doubt." Dani turned in his arms and placed her hands on his biceps. "What do you say we make this into a real home? I've got so many ideas on how to decorate."

"It already is a real home."

She cocked her head. "Right now it's the shell of a real home."

"No." He leaned his forehead against hers. "You're here with me. That's all I need."

"Liam Stone. Are you saying that I'm your home?" Dani

sniffed. "Because if so, that's the sweetest thing anyone has ever said to me."

"That's exactly what I'm saying, Dani. You and God—you're my safe places. Whether I have four consistent walls surrounding me or not, I know exactly where I belong."

And leaning in, he kissed her, making the first memory of what he hoped would be many, right here.

Thank You

Thank you so much for reading *Meet Me at The Grand*. We hope you enjoyed the story. If you did, would you be willing to do us a favor and leave a review? It doesn't have to be long—just a few words to help other readers know what they're getting. (But no spoilers! We don't want to wreck the fun!) Thank you again for reading!

We'd love to hear from you- not only about this story, but about any characters or stories you'd like to read in the future. Contact us at www.sunrisepublishing.com/contact.

Jonathon Island

Mia Jonathon Franklin has been living a nightmare for the last two years—ever since her husband and high school sweetheart died in a fishing boat accident, leaving her to care for her two young kids on her own. She's managed to stay afloat, but her husband's paltry life insurance money is gone—and if she can't find a way to support her family, she may lose the cozy cottage she and Troy had meant to grow old in.

So when Mia is offered a chance to buy her own house for a dollar if she can find business owners to move to Jonathon Island, it seems like the answer to her prayers. That is until she learns the ridiculous quota required to complete the deal. She's in over her head...until her late husband's best friend offers to lend a hand.

Cody Hart has been haunted by survivor's guilt since the boating accident that claimed his best friend's life. Torn between his own dreams of reopening his family's fishing business and his desire to help Mia, the woman he has loved since their youth, he steps up to help. She needs him and he's not going to let her down...or let his heart cause her more pain.

As Mia and Cody work together to breathe new life into the island's Main Street, their shared history and undeniable connection threatens to reignite long-buried feelings. Can they overcome the obstacles that stand in their way and find the courage to embrace a second chance at love, or will the weight of their pasts and the uncertainties of the future keep them from the happiness they both deserve?

One

UNDER THE BEAUTY OF THE SUN BANKing to the west in a brilliant May sky, Mia Franklin could almost, almost believe her life wasn't about to fall apart. She grimaced and pushed harder on the pedals of her bike, the colorful two-child trailer attachment bouncing empty behind her.

In between the shops dotting Main Street on Jonathon Island, Mia caught glimpses of Lake Huron sparkling in the sun. If only each sparkle were a diamond, then her problems would be solved. She knew better though. Knew just how deadly that deceptive lake could be.

Patrick Kelley waved at her from the doorway of his bar and grill. "Hi, Mia." The fifty-something's wiry mustache curved up as he smiled. "Got Finn and Maggie back there? I just got a shipment of peanuts in the shell, and I know how much they like them."

"Nope, sorry." She slowed to a stop in front of Kelley's. "I dropped them off at Mom and Dad's."

"Come by anytime. I'll give them a bag. My treat." He waved again before disappearing back into his building.

Sometimes her life felt like an art piece. She pictured a museum curator explaining to a tour group, "Observe this portrait of Mia Jonathon Franklin. Widowed two years ago at twenty-two, mother of two children . . ."

Everyone on this island had their own way of showing their pity for her plight.

Too bad pity didn't pay the bills.

Her phone alarm buzzed; five minutes until her meeting at the bank.

A chilly breeze floated in off the water and between the buildings as she biked her way down the cobblestone street, ending up at a graying clapboard structure.

Her belly rumbled as she pushed her way into the bank. Crammed into the handbag slung over her shoulder were three months' worth of overdue notice letters sent to her from Great Lakes National Bank. Three months where she'd needed to choose between paying the mortgage or clothing her growing kids. Three months of keeping the heat on. Three months of avoiding Mr. Michaelson on Sundays at church.

She hated that she even needed to make these choices. She shifted the bag on her shoulder, the strap rubbing her through her jacket. Dark paneling lined the walls of the bank's interior.

"Mia, come on back." Mr. Michaelson poked his head out of the office bearing his name.

Gray-haired, tall, and slim, he hadn't changed much in the almost fifteen years she'd known him. His thin lips didn't curve into his normal, cheerful smile. Kyle, her sister's husband, worked for this bank too. For a fleeting moment, Mia wished she'd scheduled this meeting with him at his branch in Port Joseph, but ferrying there and back would add so much extra time away from her kids. Not to mention the expense of the ferry ticket.

She hung her jacket on a coat hook in the corner and then settled into a chair in front of Mr. Michaelson's desk. The cold plastic seat sent another shiver through her. The clean desk, organized within an inch of its life, contrasted sharply with the ratty, thrifted crossbody bag she set on it. Across from her, Mr. Michaelson tented his fingers.

"Look, Mia, let me just cut to the chase here. The board is pressuring me to foreclose on your loan."

Mia sucked in a breath. It was one thing to know what was coming. Another thing altogether to have it said aloud. Her stomach clenched. "Please. You can't do that." She sat on the edge of her chair. Reaching into her bag, her fingers closed around a tattered envelope. Her last lifeline. She handed it to him. "Here, it's not much, but I've been saving some back from my tips." After Troy's life insurance dipped into a four-digit number from the six it had started at, she'd taken a few shifts at Martha's on Main. They hadn't been able to give her regular hours, just some shift work when others had to be off island.

Mr. Michaelson flipped through the meager notes in the envelope. "This isn't even enough to cover half a month."

"You know how slow things have been around here since the pandemic." Of course, things had never really recovered after the Grand Sullivan Hotel fire ten years ago. Mia's heart squeezed as an image of that once majestic hotel flashed in her mind. They'd just recently broken ground on the project, and her cousin and best friend, Dani, had high hopes for a revitalized economy. But until then . . . "Martha has barely been able to give any of us hours. There's just not enough tourists to support the work. Plus, it's been so hard since my husband died. Now, the life insurance is running out—" She cut herself off, hating the whine that started to creep into her tone. She would not whine. Beg if she had to—she had her kids to think about after all—but never whine. This was her lot in life. She'd chosen it. She would live with it.

Mr. Michaelson nodded. "I'm so sorry again for your loss. I really liked Troy. He was on the track team with my son." He fiddled with the envelope in front of him. "I certainly don't want to be turning a widow out of her home. Especially one with little kids."

She pictured Finn and Maggie's sweet faces. Four-year-old Finn's serious look, with his blond curls and brown eyes so like his father's. And Maggie, two years younger, born just after Troy died, pixie-like with her darker blonde hair and blue eyes. She would do anything for them. Even beg.

"Just give me a few more weeks. Now that tourism season has started . . ." But what hope did she have, really?

Please, God. Let something come up. She thought back to the email she'd received from a friend in Traverse City offering her a job. She shoved the thought away. Last resort only. She wouldn't tear her children from their home until it was her only option.

"Maybe you could ask your dad for help," Mr. Michaelson said.

She stood abruptly; the chair rocked on its legs. "No. That is out of the question." She hadn't asked him for help since she'd arrived home, pregnant and unmarried at nineteen years old, determined to show him that she and Troy could make it as teenagers with a child.

Even after marrying Troy, buying a house, and having two beautiful children, she couldn't shake the disappointment that seemed to linger from him.

Mr. Michaelson held up a hand, palm forward. "Okay. Just a suggestion." He rubbed his hand through his thinning hair. "Fine. I'll give you one more month. I'll hold off the board until . . ." He flipped a few pages on his desk calendar, "June 15th. Let's plan to meet again then and see where you're at."

A wave of relief washed over her. "Thank you so much," she said and turned to grab her jacket. Behind her, she heard the scratching of a pen across paper. She kept her back to the banker for a moment, blinking back tears.

After composing herself, she shoved her arms into her jacket then turned back to the desk. "Your kindness means the world to me." She picked up her purse and slung it onto her shoulder.

He shook her hand and she hurried out of the building. She put her purse into the bike trailer, then flung a leg over her bicycle and rode slowly down Main Street. So many of the storefronts closed and shuttered. Abandoned by their owners, the deterioration beginning to show. Some of the buildings had cracked windows, siding sagged, one even had plywood where plate glass used to be. Martha's on Main was still open though, as was Good Day Coffee and Kelley's Bar & Grill. The Kelley siblings—Frank, Patrick, and Jill—had pretty much a monopoly on the restaurants in town.

After dodging a few tourists, she paused outside a small storefront. Gray clapboard siding rose to a peak at the top of the structure. Large windowpanes let in the light. Closed now, the store once held Sampson's, a small art studio and gift shop. If she squinted, she could almost picture her teenage self at the till, ringing up a customer and dreaming of the day she owned her own gallery.

A cold wet sensation in her hand startled her, and she looked down to see a scruffy Jack Russell terrier nuzzling her palm. "Hello, Jack."

The dog lived on the streets of Jonathon Island. He belonged to no one and to everyone. Everyone fed him, and some gave him a place to stay overnight when he deigned to let them. Sometimes Mia thought he should run for mayor—the dog would definitely win.

She scratched behind his ears. "Do you have any idea how to raise enough money to pay a mortgage?" The dog gave a soft roo-roo and then trotted off. "Some help you are."

Her phone buzzed with a text from her mom's number.

Mom

Can you bring a loaf of bread? I forgot to pick one up.

Mia

Sure. Be there soon.

Better quit daydreaming and get back to Finn and Maggie. She pedaled through town and turned into the neighboring street until she came to her own. Hanging a right, she headed halfway down, then turned into the front yard of her little house on Lilac Lane.

The small two-bedroom, one-and-a-half-floor Craftsman sat nested between two much larger houses. The white siding was flaking off near the bottom of the walls. And one shutter hung askew alongside the living room window. These imperfections didn't stop the rush of tenderness deep in her core every time she spotted the home she and Troy had worked so hard on.

They'd gotten plenty done on the inside, including updating the bedrooms and bathroom, but other than painting the front door, they hadn't managed to spruce up the outside before the boating accident.

And now she might lose it.

She shoved the thought into a far corner of her brain—it was getting crowded back there—as she ran past the lilac at the front door and then inside to grab a loaf of French bread from the kitchen at the back of the house. In the kitchen sink, dishes from the morning's breakfast sat waiting for her to scrub the dried-on scrambled eggs. She ignored the urge to move the laundry into the dryer.

Being late for supper wasn't an option. Back outside, she tucked the bread next to her purse and took off again.

A few miles of hard biking gave her time to bury the past hour deep into her heart before the weekly family dinner with her parents.

Her parents' grand house with its sweeping porch and turrets came into view at the northern tip of the island. Jonathon Island had been named for her great-great something grandfather, Jacob Jonathon, who had established the first settlement in the early 1800s.

Kicking down the bike's kickstand, she parked on the lawn. Along the front porch, Adirondack chairs waited for lounging guests. Near each support beam hung the baskets of flowers she and her siblings had chipped in on for Mother's Day a few days before—a Mother's Day she had spent at home with Finn because he had a fever.

She reached into her bag for a Kleenex and her hand brushed a ragged piece of paper. What the . . . ? She pulled out her tattered envelope still stuffed full of cash. Across the front in a slanted script, Mr. Michaelson had written "for the children." She pressed a hand to her mouth for a heartbeat then straightened her shoulders and walked up to the porch.

Following her nose, tickled with the scent of her mother's signature spaghetti sauce, she headed straight for the kitchen.

Finn chased Maggie around the butcher block center island, and her dad, Liam, and Dani were talking over in the far right corner. At the stove her mom stirred a pot, and her big sister, Evie, was pulling plates out of the green-paneled cabinets on the other side of the kitchen.

Mia crossed the room and kissed her mother on the cheek. Her mom's gray-streaked, dark, bobbed hair brushed her cheek, and the scent of her gardenia perfume wafted over Mia.

"Hi, honey." Her mom didn't look up from the pot. "We're almost ready here. Can you take care of the bread?"

"No problem." Mia took a place at the island, slicing the bread and giving it a generous coating of butter before adding some garlic salt, wrapping the whole thing in foil and slipping it into the oven.

Dani crossed the kitchen and gave Mia a hug. "Good to see you, cuz." She pulled back a bit. "What's wrong?" A crease formed between Dani's green eyes.

Mia pasted on a smile. "What do you mean? I'm fine."

Dani raised one eyebrow. "I'm not buying it. We'll talk later." Her cousin moved to the silverware drawer and scooped up a handful of forks before heading to the dining room.

I'll give you one more month. The banker's words swirled through her head. She closed her eyes and took a deep breath, releasing it with a burst when someone ran into the back of her legs.

Her eyes flew open. Finn blinked up at her. "Finn!"

"Sorry, Mommy." He moved around her and dashed three steps before her dad swooped him up into his arms.

"He's just full of energy today." Her dad, every piece of his salt and pepper hair neatly in place, leaned over to pat her on the shoulder, but the timer for the bread began chiming and she whirled away. Behind her she heard her dad sigh and then set Finn on the floor. "Almost time to eat?" His deep voice cut through the chaos.

She nodded and then pulled the bread out of the oven and turned. Finn scampered away, chasing Maggie again.

Nora, her fifteen-year-old sister, slouched into the room, dressed in her standard uniform of leggings and a hoodie. Her dark hair hung loose around her face. "When are we going to eat?"

Evie's three kids joined Finn and Maggie in squealing around the middle of the kitchen.

"Hi, Nora." Her mom turned from the stove and bussed her cheek. "Done with schoolwork? Can you take these kids to the table? We're almost ready." Her mom pulled the pan of spaghetti sauce off the stove. Hopefully she missed the eye roll from Nora before the teen began obeying her mother.

The kitchen fell to near silence after Nora played Pied Piper to the kids.

Soon, they'd all moved to the dining room table.

After saying grace, they began dishing up. Mia tended to her kids' plates while Evie helped fill five-year-old Cora's plate. Eight-year-old twins Chloe and Chase didn't need any help. At the end of the table, Dani and Mia's dad continued deep in conversation.

"Where's Kyle?" Mia asked as she cut Maggie's noodles into small pieces. The toddler shoved the pasta into her mouth almost as fast as Mia cut it. "Slow down, baby. You're going to get sick."

"He had something come up at work, so he told us to

come over without him." Evie reached for a slice of bread. In her L.L.Bean top and her dark hair just brushing her shoulders, she looked like a cookie cutter version of their mom. Minus a few gray hairs, of course. "Mom, have you heard from Bash lately?" Their older brother, a lawyer, lived in New York City. He didn't come home nearly as often as her mother liked, but that was the price he paid for being successful.

"He called on Wednesday just to check in," Elise said. "He said to tell everyone hello."

"We should find out if the town council is fully on board with your plan by the end of the day tomorrow." Her dad's voice boomed over the table.

Mia forked a bite of spaghetti into her mouth and glanced at Dani. Her best friend and cousin lit up at her dad's words.

"What plan?" Evie asked.

Mia missed Dani's reply because Maggie chose that moment to lift her plate off the table.

"All done," the toddler said. Then she tipped the last of her spaghetti into her lap.

The table erupted into chaos. Evie's kids took this as permission to resume their game of chase with Finn, her dad chose to continue his conversation with Dani, only louder, and her mom jumped up right away to catch the pasta before it all went onto her dining room rug.

"Kids, if you're done eating come back and clear your plates!" Evie called.

Mia swooped her daughter out of the seat and took her to the bathroom. Even the cool blues of the room's walls failed to calm her as she wiped Maggie off. Her daughter's eyes lit with a sparkle, and her mouth turned up in a crooked grin.

"I messy."

Mia's chest loosened. Maggie looked so much like Troy. Her dark blonde curls flopped over her forehead, nearly covering her blue eyes. "Yes. You messy. You can't dump your plate when you're finished eating. We've talked about this."

"Okay, Mommy." Her daughter pushed her lip out in a fake pout. Mia laughed and kissed the top of her head. Fatigue tugged at every one of her muscles.

"Let's go get Finn. Time to head home." Hand in hand, they walked back to the dining room. Most of the others had finished eating, and her mom was stacking the dirty plates.

After corralling Finn and herding him and Maggie outside, she paused in the doorway.

Her mom tucked a Tupperware into her hands. "Some leftovers for later. You didn't get much before cleaning up Maggie."

"Thanks, Mom. Thanks for watching them today too."

"I always like having them, you know that." Her mom reached out and squeezed her shoulder. "How did it go at the bank?"

Overhead, dark clouds piled up in the sky. "They're giving me a little time to catch up on my mortgage. So, you can pray that I find something steadier for work." Just like she'd been praying for the past several months.

Maybe she should start to listen to that voice in her heart that had started to whisper that God had abandoned her.

"I wish Troy had planned better." Her mom pursed her lips.

A churning started in her stomach. The little spaghetti she'd managed to eat rolled over. "He was twenty-two years old, Mom. We thought we had plenty of time for things like mortgages. At least he had life insurance."

Her mom sighed. "You're right, of course. Let me know if you need help covering your next payment. Dad and I can write you a check."

Not gonna happen. "Not necessary." She began backing off the porch. "Please don't say anything to Dad. At least not yet."

"Okay, but—"

"I gotta go, Mom." The clouds covered what was left of the late evening sunshine.

A storm was coming. The kind that this time might just take what was left of everything she loved.

And she had less than a month to stop it.

There was nothing better than putting in a full day of honest work. It was one of the reasons Cody Hart used to love fishing so much. Check that. *Still* loved fishing. Even if he hadn't been truly out on the water since his best friend, Troy, had died along with Troy's dad, Steve.

He wiped oil off his hand with a shop rag he found lying on his workbench. Silence echoed in the pole shed that doubled as his home and shop. Situated next to the waters of Lake Huron on a small cove, the building had once housed his dad's fishing business. After the accident that had sunk their boat and shuttered the business, his dad reluctantly allowed him to take over the building, at least until he sold the business. His dad kept most of their old equipment in a shed on the mainland where it had been closer to the places they'd sold their catch. Now Cody lived in the small office, which he'd converted to a bedroom and a small bathroom. Out on the large shop floor, he worked on restoring a commercial fishing boat.

Living in a shop made him feel a kinship with Dirk Pitt, hero of those old Clive Cussler books. Except instead of a shed full of classic cars, he had a beached whale of a fishing boat.

He clenched and unclenched his fist a few times to ease the ache in his fingers. Some days, he operated more like a surgeon than an ex-fisherman. The pieces he worked with could be minuscule. He contemplated the patient in front of him. Along the ten-foot length of the metal workbench spanning one wall of the shop, a John Deere inboard engine lay in pieces waiting for him to reassemble it and reinstall it into his boat.

If he could find the parts he needed.

A wave of cool air washed over him as the shop door opened and closed. For a split second, he thought he would see Troy come around the boat currently occupying the majority of the shop room floor. But, of course, he would not see Troy again. Not on this side of eternity.

"Hey, Cody. How's it going?" Liam Stone—recent transplant to the island and current rebuilder of the Grand

Hotel—appeared. "Whoa. Looks like quite a project you have there."

"Yeah, when I bought this boat, I didn't know it would take so much work to get it back into shape or that parts would be nearly impossible to find." He had been confident he could rebuild the engine in his own shop and save himself some cash. He shouldn't have been surprised that it didn't turn out that way. Bad things always seemed to happen to him. "I waited weeks for a new overhaul kit. Then another two months for the fuel pump."

Two years had passed since he'd stood at Troy's grave and vowed to reopen the fishing business. He'd almost gotten the funds together for the extra gear and the boat parts. If he didn't get back on the water soon, he'd lose all credibility with the restaurants Hart Fishing Company used to sell to. He couldn't keep stringing them along. If he didn't open during this fishing season, he would never open at all.

"I think I diagnosed the problem though," Cody said. He pointed at the piston sleeve. "It's cracked along there."

Liam came closer. "Even I can see that. Will you replace it?"

"I'll have to see if I can find the part on eBay. It's not something they have down at any old hardware store. I don't think they'd have it at the marine store over in Port Joseph either."

"Might be easier to just replace the engine." Liam shoved his hands into his pockets. The guy might wear jeans and T-shirts instead of a full-on suit now, but his expertly tapered brown hair and the high quality of his clothing still spoke of his former executive lifestyle.

Cody had only known the builder for a few months, but he'd come to respect him as someone who knew what he wanted and went after it. "They cost between ten and twenty thousand." He shifted a few of the parts on the long workbench. Keeping them organized meant less of a headache later when he put the whole thing back together again.

"Probably not easier, then." Liam's wry grin matched his own.

"If I can't find the part, I might be screwed." Cody reached up to rub his hair, but remembered his grease-covered fingers just in time. "I'll have to order a custom-made part and that can take weeks."

"Remind me again why you're doing this?" Liam turned and looked at the boat high and dry in the middle of the shop. "I mean, I'm not against hard work, but this seems over the top. Will this thing even float?"

Cody looked at the boat too, all thirty-one feet of her. A Radon commercial class with diesel engine—currently on his operating table—outfitted for trap or long line fishing. The paint was peeling off the hull in several places, and the deck needed a serious scrub down. Inside, the single bunk needed a new mattress, but the cockpit and cabin were clean and had been updated just before he bought it. "She needs a lot of work, but her bones are solid. And I need her if I hope to reopen my dad's fishing business."

"Why reopen? It seems to me you're making a good living as the island's favorite handyman. And there's definitely enough of that kind of work around here to keep you busy."

The trouble was, he couldn't say exactly what it was that gave him this drive to move forward with the fishing business plan. "I guess it's just that Troy and I had dreamed about taking over the company for so long. I can't imagine doing anything else." He paused. Swallowed. "Plus, being out on the water used to fill me up like nothing else. So, yeah, I could keep being a handyman, but I don't love it."

"I get that." Liam ran a hand over the hull of the boat. "So, being a handyman pays the bills, but you're looking for more."

"Yep. I've been putting aside as much as I can spare each paycheck to buy Dad's business and equipment. The money's one issue. The boat's another. But the biggest is getting my dad to transfer his fishing license to me."

"Why wouldn't he? You'd think he'd be glad for the retirement funds."

"You'd think. But my dad's one of the stubborn ones. He's decided that the Hart Fishing Company is dead in the water—took the accident as a sign of sorts—and won't even discuss it." He shrugged a shoulder. "I'm hoping that waving the actual money in his face when the time comes will change his mind though."

"Wow. Why's he being so stubborn about it? You'd think he'd be proud his son was taking over for him." Liam knocked a knuckle against the boat. The *thunk* echoed through the high-ceilinged space.

Cody lifted a shoulder. "Honestly? I think he blames me for the accident."

"No way. From what I've heard it was just that—an accident. A storm. Right?"

"Slightly more to it than that. I don't know. Maybe Dad's right. Maybe it was my fault." Cody braced his hands on the workbench. "But either way, the only way to really move on with my life . . . to honor Troy's memory . . . is to make sure our dream of owning the company comes to life."

"I think that's really great, man. But why can't you go out and get a license if your dad won't sell you his? And a loan for equipment?"

"I already tried that. No one wants to take a chance on a twenty-four-year-old whose last boat sank. And commercial fishing licenses are hard to come by in Michigan. There's a wait list." He shook his head. "I'm going to keep hacking away at this dream a little while longer. I don't want to see another thing I love die."

Liam was quiet a moment. "I get that," he said. Then, "Listen, I mentioned to Dani that I was stopping by and she said she'd meet me here. She's got something to talk to you about."

Dani Sullivan, Liam's girlfriend, worked as the head of tourism on Jonathon Island.

Great. "What does she want? She's not going to hassle me about taking tourists charter fishing again, is she?" She'd mentioned it once before, wondering aloud if it could be a big draw. No thanks. Too much risk. Besides, he wasn't sure how soon this boat would be up and running.

Liam cracked a smile. "No idea. Something about

sprucing up some houses and some buildings in town, I think."

Sprucing up sounded much better than taking drunk, seasick frat boys out to catch fish all summer. "You never said what you came for. Did you just come here to hassle me?"

"I hassle because I love you, you know that." Liam had only been on the island a few months. He'd come to help Dani plan the renovations on the Grand Hotel. Already the islanders had accepted him as one of their own.

"Doesn't answer my question."

Liam crossed his arms. "I was debating whether to do this . . . I need your advice on something. I wondered if you would help me pick out a gift for Dani."

Cody stared at him. "I'm sorry. Did you just say you want me to help you pick out a gift for your girlfriend? You can't be serious." He spread his hands wide. "I'm not exactly the person to ask for romance advice."

"Oh, come on. You're probably a secret romantic."

"As evidenced by the girls lined up, knocking down my door." Above their heads, the shop fan turned on, its huge blades stirring up the oily scent of the building.

"The right girl is out there for you. I know it."

A flash of a smile, brown curls, green eyes. She'd been out there since he'd first met her in elementary school. He shrugged it away. *That* girl was off limits.

"You'll be glad to know there is no romance involved anyway. I just wanted to buy Dani and myself a pair of fishing rods. I thought fishing could be a fun activity for us."

Cody pictured Dani and Liam out on the water, Liam

getting sprayed by fish guts. "You seriously want to do that? Aren't you supposed to be a city kid?"

Liam uncrossed his arms. "Yeah, well, I'm trying to do better. This is a first step."

"I don't know, man, fishing rods are kind of romantic." The newest Bass Pro Shop catalog featured a few that had made his heart skip a beat. Shoot. He really needed to get out more.

Liam laughed. "Maybe for you. What do you say, can you help me find a good starter rod and some tackle?"

"Sure, it's no problem. I'll text you a few links."

"Hello!" Dani's voice echoed through the cavernous shop.

"We're on the other side of the boat," Cody called back.

A moment later and Dani came into view. Cody had known the willowy blonde all their lives. She walked to Liam's side, and he put his arm around her. She smiled up at him, and Cody glanced away, a pinch forming under his breastbone.

"I've got to get going," Liam said. He dropped a kiss on the top of Dani's head. "See you both later."

"I need your help with something." Dani clasped her hands.

A laugh burst out of him. "No warm-up? Just straight to the punch? I already told you I don't want to take out any tourists on charters."

She held up a hand to stop him. "No. It's nothing like that. You know about the revitalization project, right?"

"I was at the town hall meeting, yeah." Cody pulled a stool out from under the bench and placed it in front of

Dani before grabbing one for himself. "We may as well sit, and you can explain. Want a Coke?"

She shook her head and sat. "Okay, so you know that step one of our plan is to rebuild and reopen the hotel so we have a place for guests and seasonal workers to stay, right?"

Cody nodded. The work on the hotel had already begun. Everyone in town knew about that. He crossed his arms and leaned against the workbench, the metal cool through his T-shirt. A tang of engine oil hung in the air.

"Step two is all about opening the businesses themselves. You know how we have all these open storefronts on Main Street?" Dani's gestures grew more expansive as she warmed to her topic. "Uncle Seb owns those, obviously, but as part of our revitalization plan, he's willing to majorly lower the rent for the first several years to attract new owners."

"Sounds reasonable." Cody cocked his head. "But is that really enough to get people here?"

She shifted on her stool, leaned forward. "Not on its own, no. Recently I saw a Travel Channel documentary about a tiny town in Italy. After the pandemic, this town had all of these empty homes and offered to sell them for the equivalent of a dollar just to get people there."

Oh. Wow. He sat up straight. "So, you're going to do the same thing?"

"Basically. So many of the older homes behind Main Street were left abandoned over the last decade. People moved away and couldn't pay their mortgages, so the town pretty much claimed ownership."

"Right." So many families had left over the years. Jonathon Island was still amazing, but to think about what it used to be . . . the comparison ached. "And those are the ones you're going to offer for a dollar?"

"Yes, but not just to anyone. To business owners who apply—and are vetted and approved by the town council. We have fourteen available storefronts and at least that many empty homes. Here's hoping we have a lot of applicants." Dani chewed her bottom lip. "That's the part I'm most worried about." She stared up at the vaulted ceiling for a moment.

In the silence, Cody heard the ticking of the clock mounted on the far wall. Overhead, the fluorescent lights buzzed. Finally, he cleared his throat. "So, what exactly are you wanting me to do?"

Dani's smile flashed again as she looked at him. "I want to hire you to make sure the buildings and houses are move-in ready. We want people to be able to see how charming Jonathon Island really is." She named the amount she'd been authorized to pay him. "Uncle Seb is chipping in a lot of the money, since he owns the buildings, but the town promised to put some up too. We'd like you to start right away."

His shoulders relaxed and a grin spread across his face. "I think I can help with that." He mentally reviewed the list of handyman projects he had going—not too many right now. He'd cleared his calendar when he'd bought the boat, hoping to be back on the water soon. Even this small salary would go a long way toward the parts he needed. And it would be more regular work than the odd jobs he'd been taking around town. "Just tell me which places we're talking about."

Dani hopped off her stool. "Thank you. Come by my office tomorrow and I can get you the list and a bunch of master keys."

He could make that work. "I planned to check Mia's lawnmower in the morning. It shouldn't take long, so I can be there by ten or so."

A strange look passed over Dani's face. She opened her mouth then clapped it shut.

"What?" He pushed off his stool. Dani started walking for the door, and he went with her.

"It's just that I think—never mind." She waved a hand in the air. They rounded the boat. Straight ahead, a line of light shone through the gap in the bottom of the door leading out of the shed.

"At the risk of repeating myself, what?" He reached for the doorknob and twisted it open. The warmth of the May sunlight streaming in chased away the chill always present in the metal building.

Dani gave a little shrug. "I know it's not the same without your third musketeer, you and Mia and Troy were always inseparable, but I don't think Troy would want you hiding away."

"I'm not hiding away." He gazed out toward the boardwalk running past his place, not really seeing it. "I'm keeping my head down. Working toward getting this business back."

"I'm probably way out of line here, but maybe it's time to ask her out."

He whipped his gaze to her. "Ask who out?"

She speared him with a look. "I think you know who I'm talking about."

Of course he did. But... "We're just friends." The words felt wrong in his mouth, but honestly, it didn't matter how he felt about Mia. It mattered how she felt about *him*.

And the fact that Troy would always be between them. "Not gonna happen."

Dani lifted a shoulder and let it fall. "Okay, maybe I imagined it. But Mia could use someone like you in her corner."

His heart squeezed. "I'm in her corner. I'll always be in her corner. As a *friend*."

"My mistake." She waved as she walked into the sunlight. "See you tomorrow, Cody."

After Dani left, Cody plugged in the sander fitted with a heavy grit paper and began attacking the peeling paint along the boat's midsection. The rhythmic motions soothed his nerves. Dani knew Mia best. If she thought he was good enough for Mia then ... Maybe ... No. He couldn't go there.

He popped his earbuds in, donned a pair of safety glasses, and tugged a mask over his nose and mouth. In his ears, the rap artist Flame sang about joy in Christ. Maybe if he listened long enough, some of the truth would sink into his heart.

He soon fell into a rhythm, the sander in his hand swishing across the surface of the boat until he could make out the fiberglass hull underneath. He needed to take off a layer of paint and all of the barnacles and other accumulated biofouling before he could hit the whole thing with a blast of primer. If everything went well, he could be putting the second coat of marine paint on by the end of the week.

After two feet more of the hull gleamed in the harsh light of the shop, he stepped back to admire his progress. Between all the interruptions, he'd finished four measly feet this afternoon. So much for his personal timeline. So much for this part of the project getting done anytime soon.

His smart watch buzzed with a text from his mom.

Mom

Can you stop by the house? Dad needs a hand clearing that branch that fell during the storm last week.

He unplugged the sander, gave the boat a hard stare, then pushed the safety glasses up onto his forehead.

This boat had waited a long time for this paint to be stripped. It wouldn't hurt for it to wait another day.

Now that he had some guaranteed income, it wouldn't be long before he'd be back on the water for good.

And maybe, just maybe, keep his last promise to Troy.

Acknowledgments

Thank you, sweet reader, for joining me on this journey to Jonathon Island, a wonderful place that I wish was real (and honestly, it's real in my mind!). I hope you enjoyed Liam and Dani's story and found hope and peace within its pages.

When Susie told me her idea for this series and asked me to write the first book, I was both honored and terrified! I wanted to do her idea justice. But when I started writing, the fear went away and I fell into this beautiful place where neighbors are friends, and where history, family, and loyalty are paramount.

The people of Jonathon Island are not perfect—far from it. But I think that's why I love them so much. I can learn and love right alongside them. And that's a beautiful thing. I hope you feel the same way. Because we've got many more amazing stories coming your way!

Like any story, this one would not have happened without the help of a LOT of people.

Susan May Warren, obviously my first thank you is to you. Thanks for involving me in this project—and Sunrise at large—and for feeding me all the delicious charcuterie while you, me, and Sarah brainstormed this series on your gorgeous deck. (I guess I should thank Andrew for that too—and for those steaks! Yum!)

My editors, in addition to Susie—Kristyn Fortner, Charity

Henico, and Liz Tolsma. Thank you for catching my errors and helping this story shine.

The amazing Sunrise team—Rel, Essie, Tari, Katie, and Sarah. You guys make the world keep spinning, and bring so much joy with your hard work and dedication. I'm eternally grateful.

Lisa Jordan—Thank you for partnering with me to bring Jonathon Island to life. The authors working with you are so incredibly blessed, as am I, my friend!

My fellow JI authors—Thanks for banding together with us to bring this little island to life. It's been so much fun, and I can't wait to read the stories percolating in your brains!

Lindsey Jesionowski—Thanks for all the texts telling me I could do this. You have no idea how much they meant.

Mike, Elliott, and Teddy—Your continued support and inspiration are everything. I love you guys—up, down, around, and back again.

My readers—Thank you for sticking with me and giving each new story a try. Your reviews, messages, and virtual hugs encourage me daily.

And my God—No story is truly complete without your inspiration. Even when I think THIS is the story that's not going to get written, you swoop in and save the day and prove that, indeed, nothing is impossible with You.

Lindsay Harrel is a lifelong book nerd who lives in Arizona with her husband and kids. She's held a variety of professional jobs over the years, and now juggles school volunteering with being an author and editor. When she's not writing or keeping up with her children, Lindsay enjoys making a fool of herself at Zumba, curling up with anything by Jane Austen, and savoring sour candy one piece at a time.

Connect with her at www.LindsayHarrel.com.

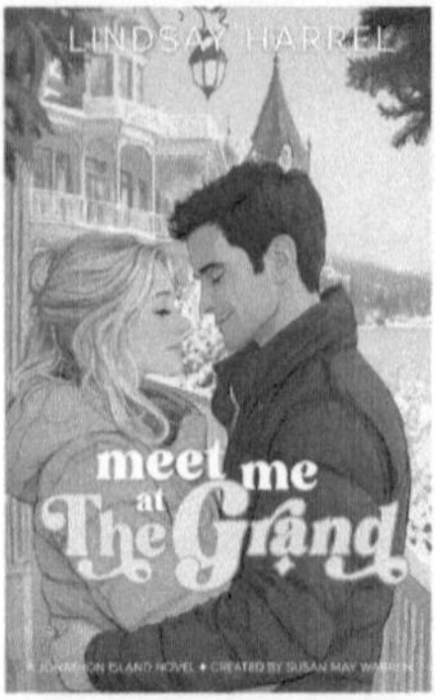

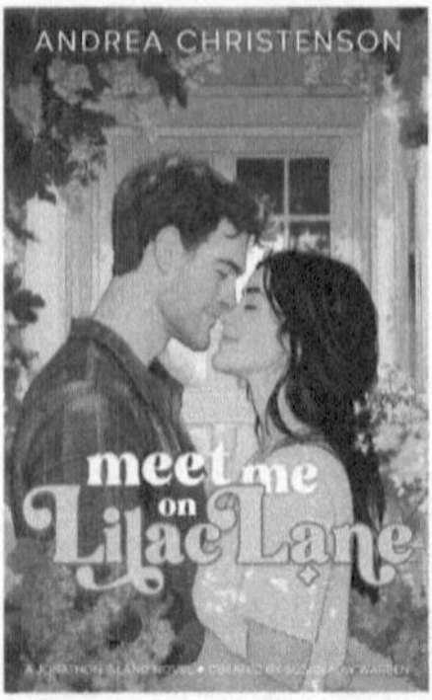

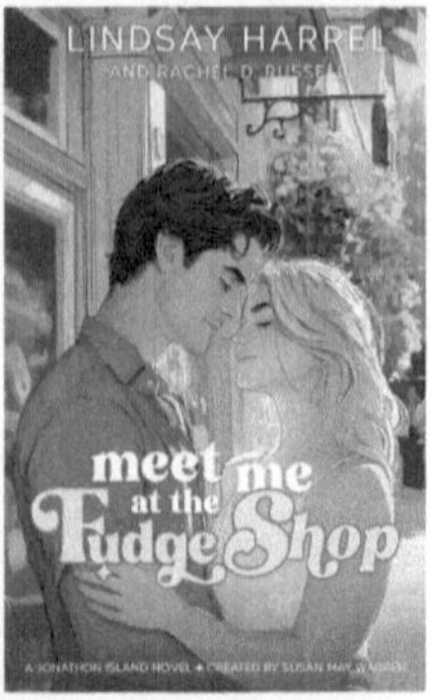

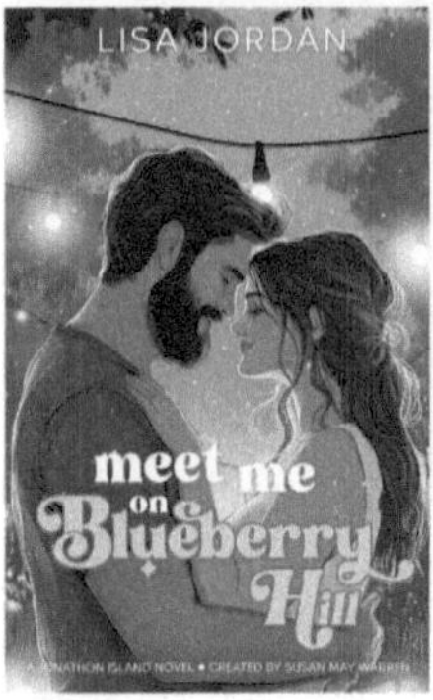

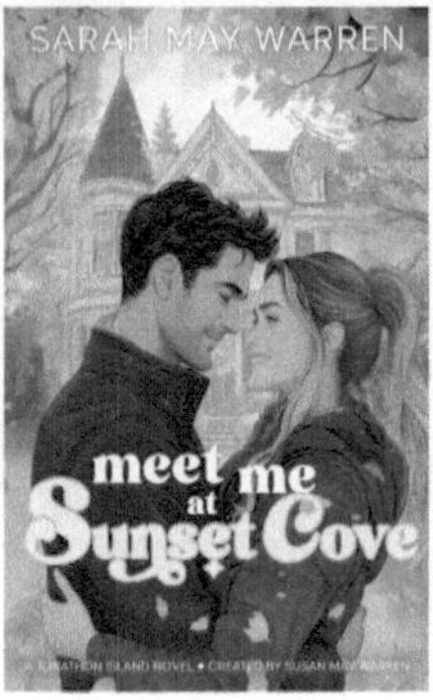

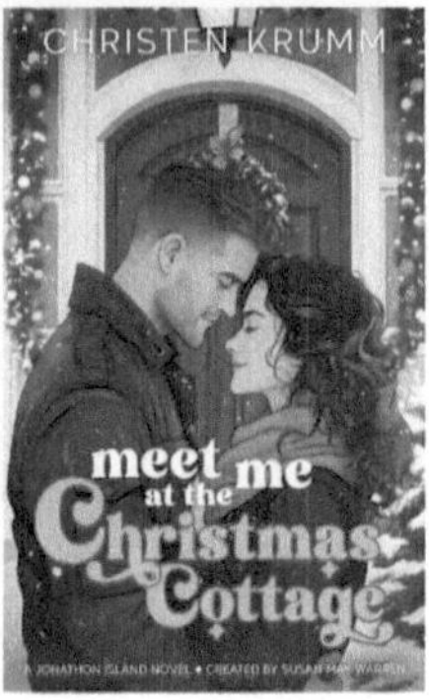

Jonathon Island

Where faith, family, and romance meet small-town, beachside charm. Whether you spend a weekend at The Grand, take a stroll down Lilac Lane, or cozy up in the Christmas Cottage, you'll fall in love with this heart-warming contemporary romance series, full of second chances and unforgettable love stories!

Check out the full series at sunrisepublishing.com.

Sunrise PUBLISHING

We solve the problem of what we read next.

Available on Amazon

FOLLOW THE CLUES.
FIND THE INHERITANCE.
FALL IN LOVE?

"A must-read for those who cherish a good mystery and the power of love to heal the deepest divides. Beautifully written!"

—SUSAN MAY WARREN

USA Today bestselling author

We solve the problem of what we read next.   Available on Amazon

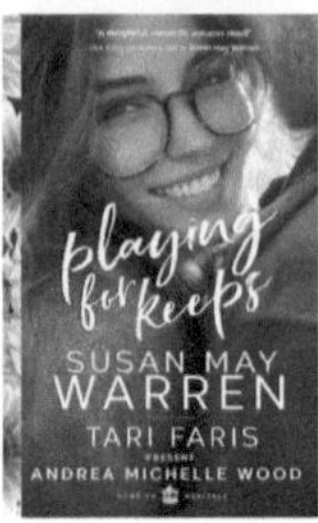
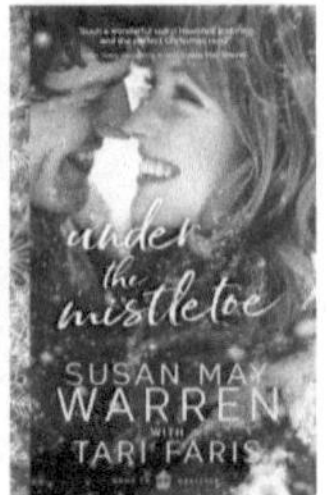

Home to Heritage

SUSAN MAY WARREN and **TARI FARIS**

with **Mandy Boerma** and **Andrea Michelle Wood**

We solve the problem of what we read next.

Available on Amazon

YOU MAY ALSO LIKE...

When a blizzard strikes Deep Haven and Megan is overrun with catastrophes, it takes a former Ranger to step in and help. But the more he comes to her rescue, the sooner she'll move out... Come home to Deep Haven in this magical tale about the one who got away... and came back.

Still the One **by Susan May Warren and Rachel D. Russell**

Working together to keep Fox Bakery from going under, Robin and Sammy find that something more than friendship is simmering between them. But will Robin follow her old dreams back to the glamor of Paris, or will she discover how sweet it is to be loved in Deep Haven?

How Sweet It Is **by Andrea Christenson**

Wounded and on the run, Jamie and Logan must fight for their lives in a deadly game of cat-and-mouse. But the biggest risk of all is the sparks between them... and the terrible cost of a second chance at love. Burning Hearts is an edge-of-your-seat journey of peril, faith, and finding the courage to love one last time.

Burning Hearts **by Lisa Phillips**

We solve the problem of what we read next.   Available on Amazon

9 781963 372793